Anna Hoghton is really rather special – as you'll know if you read her Venetian-set debut, *The Mask of Aribella*. In this novel, she mixes Celtic mythology-inspired peril with real-life drama as a brother and sister face up to the Wild Hunt, a terrifying host of dark creatures who feed on grief. Luckily, they have a touch of supernatural help! But their fantastical journey across Ireland will teach them something about loss, too. After all, myths and legends are there to help us with all the hard stuff about being human.

BARRY CUNNINGHAM
Publisher
Chicken House

ORLA AND THE WILD HUNT

ANNA HOGHTON

Chicken House

2 Palmer Street, Frome, Somerset BA11 1DS
www.chickenhousebooks.com

Chicken House/Scholastic Ireland, 89E Lagan Road, Dublin Industrial Estate, Glasnevin, Dublin D11 HP5F, Republic of Ireland

Cover and interior design by Helen Crawford-White
Typeset by Dorchester Typesetting Group Ltd
Printed and bound in Great Britain by CPI Group (UK) Ltd, Croydon, CR0 4YY

FSC
www.fsc.org
MIX
Paper from responsible sources
FSC® C171272

1 3 5 7 9 10 8 6 4 2

British Library Cataloguing in Publication data available.

PB ISBN 978-1-912626-11-3
eISBN 978-1-913696-83-2

For my Granny Ireland, who still inspires me every day
And for Bo, who we will love and miss for ever

'Tis better to have loved and lost
than never to have loved at all.

Alfred, Lord Tennyson

Also by Anna Hoghton

The Mask of Aribella

From the Author

This story has been inspired, in part, by my own Granny Ireland's tales. I've brazenly plucked and blended creatures from Irish mythology with other favourite myths and legends from my childhood, as well as taken liberties with my own artistic interpretations.

I hope readers enjoy and forgive these embellishments and modifications. After all, myths have long been living, breathing things, shared and shaped from person to person, evolving with each iteration. In the end, what matters isn't the accuracy of the details, but how these stories connect us; to our grandparents and theirs, and theirs before them.

The Wild Hunt rides in the dead of night,
Spreading terror, misery and fright,

They'll feast on your despair and pain,
Whatever you do, don't say their name.

For speak it three times and you will call,
Clouds black as coal, a hideous squall —

Birds, horses, beasts — who'll break your soul apart,
Sorrow hunters who once had mortal hearts.

CHAPTER 1
Too Good to be True

Orla had already lost Apollo.

When they'd landed at Belfast International Airport, Orla had nipped to the loo, and by the time she'd returned Apollo was nowhere to be seen. She eventually spotted her ten-year-old brother's blue hair in the confectionery section of WHSmith.

'Why do you have to run off like that?' she growled, shoving him towards the exit doors of the arrivals terminal.

'I didn't *run off*! I was only gonna get a Mars bar. I'm starving,' retorted Apollo, pulling away so hard that several people wheeling suitcases had to dramatically change course to avoid colliding with him. They eyed Apollo and Orla disapprovingly, clearly wondering where their parent or guardian was. Orla bristled and felt even more cross with Dad for not coming.

Instead of being here with his children, Dad was on his way to France to drink cocktails in the sunshine with his new fiancée, Penelope Toogood, and her *too good* sons, Charles and William. He'd barely even entertained the idea of coming to Ireland instead. They'd all only been to visit Gran once since Mum died. *Once.* In two whole years. Dad always made some excuse about work or school or flight prices, but Orla knew it was really because he'd found the last visit to Gran's too hard. Gran's house was inextricably tied to Mum, and Dad seemed to be doing his best to erase Mum's entire existence from his life. He was such a coward.

Orla had always enjoyed going to Gran's. Gran was a champion of life – warm and kind and exactly how a grandma should be. Orla had loved their last visit for exactly the same reason Dad seemed to have found it difficult. Everything had felt so strange and different since Mum had died, except for Gran's house, which had felt the same as always: a time warp, with photos of Mum everywhere. Dad might be content sailing off into the sunset with the Toogoods as if everything was hunky-dory, but Orla wasn't going to play along. It was bad enough that they all had to live together in a new house – she couldn't bear to go on holiday with them too.

Orla had nagged and nagged until Dad had finally been forced to give in and say she could go to Ireland.

It had been a surprise to everyone when Apollo had insisted that he wanted to go with her. Orla knew Apollo adored Gran and missed her a lot, but she'd thought he would have liked to go on the expensive beach holiday. While Orla could barely stand to be in the same room as the Toogoods, Apollo annoyingly got on with them all fairly well. He got on with everyone.

As they bustled out the exit of the terminal building, the strong Irish wind sent Orla's blonde hair dancing around her face. She shivered. It was always colder and wetter here in Ireland than in Bristol, even in summer. With all that rain, it was no wonder everywhere was so lush. She could see the low-lying hills around the airport, green as gumdrops.

The Emerald Isle.

That's what Mum had always called it.

Orla felt the same warm fizz of anticipation in her belly that she always had when she arrived here, though she knew the week ahead would contain nothing but gardening, games of Scrabble and reading books. There was just something comforting about being back in Ireland. She'd never have admitted it to anyone, but deep down she hoped that this trip and seeing Gran would help fill the big empty space she'd been carrying around inside her since Mum had died.

Orla's stomach twisted as she remembered Gran's first response to her suggestion of coming. She'd expected Gran to be delighted, but instead it had felt almost as if Gran was trying to put them off. Maybe Gran just wanted Orla and Apollo to get on with their new stepbrothers and not to offend Penelope, but it had still felt like a snub. In the end, though, Gran had said she couldn't wait to see them . . .

Where was she? When they'd done this flight with Mum in the past, Gran had always been there waiting for them by the doors. Orla fiddled with her crescent moon earrings nervously, making sure they were still firmly in place. They were Mum's and she never took them off. She jumped as a car horn beeped twice, jolting her from her thoughts.

Gran!

Her heart lifted. Without checking if Apollo was following, Orla shrugged her backpack further up her shoulders and hurried past the taxi bay, heading towards the short-stay car park.

'Orla, wait!' Apollo called.

Orla ignored him, searching the cars for a battered red Fiat. For a moment, she couldn't spot it but then – there it was! And there was Gran! Waving wildly through the windscreen, looking as tiny and birdlike as ever hunched behind the steering wheel.

When she smiled, Orla felt the knot inside her chest loosen.

She and Apollo raced up to the car and pulled open the doors. 'Hi, Gran!' they called in unison.

Gran was dressed in her trademark tartan trousers and a baggy red jumper. *Just like old times*, Orla thought happily.

'Why, hello, my darlings,' Gran replied, as they slid into the seats. 'Ach, I love the blue hair you've got on yer, Apollo. Very fierce!'

Apollo's hair had, up until recently, been brown like Dad's. However, on his tenth birthday, he'd dyed it a luminous shade of neon blue.

Apollo grinned. 'Thanks, Gran! It's great to see you.'

'Grand to see youse too, so it is. My two favourite grandchildren!'

Apollo laughed. 'We're your *only* grandchildren, Gran!'

'And what difference does that make, now? You're still my favourites.' Gran beamed. 'Was the flight all right? Big journey for youse both on yer own. Sure you'll be needing a wee lie down later, won't ye? Ach, it's just grand to see youse, so it is, just grand!'

Gran handed around the packet of Polos she always had in her car. They both took one and crunched on them. The minty taste, Gran's soft accent, and the lavender scent of the air freshener were all so familiar to Orla that she found herself relaxing for the first time in months. For once, the world didn't feel like it had been flipped upside down and inside out.

Everything was going to be all right.

Gran's house looked the same as it always did, like it was about to come tumbling down, with a front garden that was wild with flowers and plants.

Grabbing their backpacks, they followed Gran up the drive and along the overgrown front path, through the towering foxtail lilies and past the twisted rose bushes. The front door's faded red paint was wrinkled and peeled like the cover of an old book.

Orla happily breathed in the heady scent of the lilac wisteria that hugged the front of the house and almost covered the windows completely. Everything was as she remembered. Everything except—

Orla was so surprised to see a gleaming brass lock on the front door that she only just avoided putting her foot in the saucer of milk on the doorstep, which Gran said she left out for fairies but Orla knew was really for stray cats, foxes and other wildlife.

'Since when did you have a lock, Gran?' she asked. 'I thought you said no one in the village ever bothered locking anything!'

'Ach, well, the world is changing,' Gran replied, rummaging in her pockets furtively and pulling out a jangling set of keys. Was it Orla's imagination or was Gran deliberately avoiding making eye contact? 'Been a few break-ins around here over the last few months, and it's better to be safe than sorry now, isn't it?' she added, unlocking the door.

Orla's eyes narrowed. 'You always said you didn't have anything *worth* stealing.'

'*Orla!*' Apollo hissed. 'If Gran wants to lock her door, so what?'

It was *different*, that was what. It wasn't just the lock itself. Gran seemed unsettled, like she was hiding something, just when Orla needed her to be strong and solid and the same.

'Well, I do have something worth stealing now – I've got youse here, don't I? My most precious treasures.' Gran smiled and ruffled Apollo's blue hair affectionately – but her expression quickly became serious again. 'I mean it about the break-ins though. Things have been a little . . . odd around here lately. Best be careful, all right? So no going out after dark by yerselves or anything silly like that, and keep the windows and doors locked.'

Orla's eyes got even narrower. She didn't want things to be odd. She opened her mouth to ask more questions but Apollo gave her a sharp kick in the back of her calf. 'Ow!' she exclaimed.

'I'll fix youse up something to eat now, shall I?' asked Gran, already ahead of them inside the house. 'You must be hungry after that early flight?'

'Yes, please!' said Apollo enthusiastically. 'I'm

starving. Orla wouldn't even let me buy a Mars bar at the airport.'

Orla tried to give him a kick back but Apollo dodged.

'I'll get a fry on. Will just be a wee minute. Why don't you go put those bags of yours in your room, pets? Would one of you mind getting the camp bed down from the attic, and the other fetching some sheets and towels from the hot press . . . or "airing cupboard" as youse lot call it?'

'Yes, no problem, Gran,' said Apollo, being a suck-up like always.

As Orla stepped into the hall, her breath caught. Hanging above the hall table was the framed photograph of Mum that had always been there. It had been taken on her graduation day from Trinity College. She was wearing a green dress under her gown and her dark blonde hair fell long and loose around her shoulders. Her eyes were the same shade of green as Orla's, her cheeks were rosy and she was smiling brightly.

The photo gave Orla a stomach-swooping feeling, like when you think there's an extra step up in the dark but there isn't and instead your foot sinks through thin air. Dad didn't have any pictures of Mum around their new house, and although Orla kept lots in an album under her bed and had looked at those photos every night in the first few months after Mum had died, she hadn't done so recently. A part of her wondered if she was afraid to look at them. *No, of course that wasn't it*, she told herself. She'd just been busy . . . Now, though, seeing this photo and experiencing the unsettling feeling it gave her, she began to wonder if there was another reason. Maybe she wasn't so different to Dad after all.

All the rooms in Gran's cottage were on the ground floor, with the exception of the attic. To the left of the entrance hall, a narrow corridor led away to Gran's bedroom, the spare room and the bathroom. To the right, three other doors led to the kitchen, into which Gran had disappeared, the tiny living room, which they'd always called the Den, and a study. The door of the study was open. Orla avoided looking at the dusty old piano. The closed lid made her think of the lid of a coffin.

She noticed Apollo hurrying along the corridor, trying to beat her to the spare room. Annoyed, Orla raced after him. Apollo reached the room first and immediately swung his backpack on to the bed. Orla knew that this meant Apollo thought he'd be entitled to sleep in it and that she'd be the one who'd have to heave the camp bed down from the attic.

No way. That wasn't how it was going to go down.

Orla hurled Apollo's backpack off the bed. It hit the

wall with a thud and the zip, which had already been partially open, came all the way loose, spewing Apollo's clothes everywhere.

'Orla!' Apollo yelled, as a cuddly toy bunny flew out and on to the floor by her feet.

Orla stared down at it in surprise. 'You brought Rabbit? Apollo, you're ten! You told me you'd thrown that out.'

Apollo went bright red. 'I did – I – er, it must have got in there by accident . . .'

'Yeah, right! You're such a baby, Apollo.'

Apollo went even redder. 'Don't call me that!' he yelled and launched himself at her. They tumbled on to the floor.

Orla pummelled him with her fists. One of Apollo's hands was in her hair, pulling painfully. The other pinched her arm. Orla winced and tried to shove him off, hitting harder. It felt good to release some of the tension that had been building inside her since she'd seen the lock on Gran's door. Her fist collided with Apollo's jaw and he let out a low moan.

'All right, truce, truce!' Apollo held his hands up. Orla gave him one last punch in the arm before pulling away. She stopped short when she saw the window.

'She's put bolts on the windows too!' she gasped incredulously.

'Yeah, because of the break-ins. Gran already explained that.' Apollo rubbed his jaw. Orla wondered if he was regretting coming. It was his own fault if he was.

'Didn't you get the feeling Gran wasn't telling the truth about that?'

Apollo's nose wrinkled. 'Why would she lie to us? What else could the locks be for?' He suddenly paled and let out a whimper. 'I wonder if it's for the Wild Hunt . . .'

Orla scoffed. According to Gran's folk tales, the Wild Hunt were monsters who could transform from a black cloud into birds, horses and humanlike forms. They stole mortals from the streets at night, or from their bedrooms if the windows were unlocked. They always left behind a single black feather as their calling card . . .

The tales were nonsense, of course, but Orla still shivered. Something about Gran's house and the Tangled Woods just down the road made magic seem more possible here. It was because her memories of this place were all entwined with Gran's stories, she told herself.

'You don't really still believe in all that rubbish, do you, Apollo?'

'It's up to me what I believe,' Apollo retorted

crossly. 'Just like it's up to Gran if she wants to install locks. You sounded like you were *interrogating* her about it just now. You know you don't always have to be so horrible to *everyone*, Orla.'

Orla scowled. She hadn't been horrible. She'd just been confused. Apollo was such a boring peacekeeper. He'd rather say nothing than risk offending someone. Except with Orla, of course.

'And *you* don't always have to be such a baby!' she spat back.

Apollo glared at her. For a moment, another fight threatened but, in the end, Apollo relented. He dragged the camp bed down from the attic, wiping the cobwebs off it. Begrudgingly, Orla fetched the sheets and towels.

She put her bag on to the bed and, on impulse, checked her phone, though hardly anyone texted her these days because she'd stopped replying ages ago. It had just felt so false, pretending like everything was fine when it really, really wasn't.

There was one new message from Ellen, her oldest friend, who was the only one who hadn't given up on Orla completely. It had been Ellen's birthday party last night. She'd sent a photo with '*Wasn't the same without you xoxo*' written underneath. They were all there: Sarah, Aisha, Kiran, Emma and Shantelle. Smiling with their arms wrapped around one another.

Despite herself, Orla felt a twinge of envy. This was quickly followed by annoyance. She knew Ellen was trying to include her, but if anything the photo made Orla feel worse. She felt so different from them all nowadays.

'You OK?' Apollo asked quietly.

Heat rose in her cheeks as she looked up to see him watching her. 'Fine, why?' she snapped.

'You just look . . . funny.' It was Apollo's turn to flush.

'You're the one who looks funny with that ridiculous hair!'

Apollo flinched, then went off to the kitchen in a huff.

Orla took one last look at the photo before deleting the message.

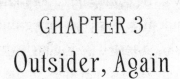

CHAPTER 3
Outsider, Again

Orla sloped down the hall, which was already full of delicious aromas. Outside the kitchen, she paused and peered through the doorway. Apollo was sitting at the table. Gran was hunched over the stove clattering pans as the pair of them chatted and laughed together.

Orla lingered outside, feeling awkward and left out.

'Look, Gran!' Apollo exclaimed, pointing at the kitchen window where a royal-blue butterfly fluttered against the glass. Even on the dull grey day, the edges of the insect's wings glittered as if they'd been dipped in molten gold. They'd seen butterflies like this a lot at Gran's when they were younger. Whatever the species was, it seemed to like her garden. Orla had never seen such beautiful butterflies in England.

'It's one of the fairy king's spies!' Apollo added excitedly.

Out in the hallway, Orla rolled her eyes. Gran used to say that the fairy king Oberon sent these butterflies to keep an eye on things in the mortal realm. Apollo was likely just pretending to still believe in the stories so that he could stay close to Gran. Orla found herself feeling far away from both of them, resentful of their easy closeness and of the way Apollo could still take joy in things like silly stories. For her, all the joy had been sucked out of the world two years ago, and any brief moments of happiness she did have made her feel instantly guilty.

'So it is, Apollo,' said Gran, ruffling his hair.

Apollo froze as if he were playing musical statues. It was a game they used to play with Gran; every time you saw a fairy spy you stopped moving so that it wouldn't be able to see you. It was a silly game.

Gran pretended to become a statue too. This made Apollo laugh and he stopped being still.

'Do you think I'll see the fairy people sometime?'

'Maybe,' Gran said, putting an arm around his shoulder. 'But, to tell the truth, it's best not to. The Good Folk, like all magical beings, are tricksome creatures. I'd rather you stayed away. You're too important.'

Apollo smiled up at her and Orla felt another stab of envy. This trip had been *her* idea. She should have known Apollo would hijack it.

Orla's gaze drifted down to the hall table. Perched

amid Gran's typical assortment of knitting needles, garden trowels, odd gloves and unopened junk mail was, of all things, a newspaper.

A newspaper wouldn't have been strange to see in most houses, but Gran never paid any attention to the news. She always said she was far more concerned with what she could see was going on in her garden and local area than with what a few corrupt politicians were arguing about that week.

First the locks, now the newspaper . . .

These would both be small things if it were someone else, but with Gran any change was a big one. Gran had had the same routines for as long as Orla could remember.

The newspaper was two weeks old. *WOMAN GOES MISSING*, read the headline. Gran had underlined sections of the article below in red pen. *Beloved mother, Mary Hart, aged 42 . . . disappeared from her bedroom last Thursday night . . . The window was found wide open . . .*

'You all right there, pet?'

Orla stiffened. Gran had popped her head out of the kitchen.

'Fine,' Orla replied quickly. She didn't want to prove Apollo right by *interrogating* Gran about the news-paper straight away, so instead she looked up at the photo of Mum. Mum smiled back, frozen in time.

Gran looked up at it too, misinterpreting Orla's unease. 'You're more like her every day, you know? Both so beautiful and clever . . . She'd be very proud of you.'

Orla shifted uncomfortably.

'You must miss her a lot . . . I miss her too. You can talk to me about her, you know.'

There was a lump in Orla's throat. She looked down at the hall table to avoid meeting Gran's eye.

Gran moved over to it. 'Oh, this table is such a mess!' she exclaimed and quickly tidied it, tucking the newspaper away out of sight. 'Now, come along and have some food,' she added, bustling Orla through into the sunshine-yellow kitchen where various pots and pans were sizzling away on the old stove.

Apollo didn't look round when Orla entered.

On the wall, the home phone started to ring. Gran picked it up. 'Oh, Malcolm! Hello! I was just thinking of calling. Oh, to be sure . . . All safe and sound. No trouble at all . . . Do say hello to Penny from me . . . Oh, she prefers Penelope, does she? Well, fair enough . . . We will . . . Ach, we're all set, don't you worry . . .' Gran turned around and smiled at Orla and Apollo brightly. 'Want to say hi?'

Orla shook her head and Gran's smile slipped.

'I will,' said Apollo quickly, taking the phone. 'Hi, Dad, mm . . . yeah, it was fine . . . mm . . . yes, she's fine . . . we will. OK . . . Love you too. Bye.' He passed the phone back to Gran.

Gran offered it to Orla once more, but she pretended not to see. Gran pursed her lips and put the phone back to her ear. 'All right, then . . . Don't you worry. You enjoy your holiday . . . I will. Thanks a million. There we go now . . . Bye now.' She hung up. 'Didn't want to speak to yer dad, Orla?'

Orla shrugged. She didn't want to hear about the wonderful time Dad was having with his new family. He should be here in Ireland. She'd wanted him to *want* to come. To be with them.

Gran sighed. 'Wet the tea now, will you Orla? Apollo, if you fooster around in those tins, you might just find something sweet.'

'Tiffin?' Apollo asked excitedly.

'Maybe . . .' said Gran, giving him a wink.

Apollo let out a whoop. 'Yes! Your tiffin is the best, Gran. Chocolatey and raisin-y with just the right amount of crunch. It's better than Marks and Spencer's and that's saying something.'

'Ach, you're too kind.' Gran's eyes sparkled.

Again, Orla felt left out. They were so easy with each other. And here she was, like a dark cloud. It wasn't fair; Apollo had lost Mum too. As had Dad, and Gran. So why was she, Orla, so much sadder and more broken than everyone else?

CHAPTER 4
Eyes in the Bushes

Orla hoped she'd feel better as the day went on but she didn't. If anything, watching Apollo and Gran together made her feel more isolated than ever.

When Gran suggested a game of Scrabble in the Den, Orla tried to refuse. But Gran insisted, so she reluctantly joined in, hoping the familiarity of the game might at least take her mind off the way she was feeling.

The Den was the tiniest room in the house and a squeeze for all three of them now Orla and Apollo were bigger. They'd have arguably been more comfortable in the kitchen but the Den felt more cosy and Gran-like. It was full of odd bits and bobs, and groaning bookshelves stacked with decaying volumes – mostly encyclopaedias, dictionaries and reference books on things like mushrooms and constellations. All manner of curios were hidden between the pages of these books, such as pressed flowers, Gran's old library cards, black-and-white photographs, old love letters from Grandpa and even a lock of human hair, which Orla hoped belonged to someone in the family.

Gran didn't have a television, so entertainment had always been limited to the old-fashioned kind that came in a cardboard box. Orla and Apollo used to happily play endless games of Scrabble.

This game, however, did not go at all smoothly.

Apollo was winning and it was annoying. As the game went on, Orla found herself becoming increasingly desperate to beat him, but Apollo continued to rack up more points and was soon far ahead.

'Well done, Apollo!' Gran exclaimed as he made the word QUIXOTIC.

'Thanks, Gran,' Apollo beamed.

Orla ground her teeth. 'FUGH is not a word,' she pointed out when Apollo tried to lay this on his next turn.

'Are you sure?' asked Apollo. 'Let's check the dictionary.'

'It's not! What does it mean?'

'I'm not sure, let's just check—'

'It's NOT A WORD!' Orla slammed her hands on the coffee table so hard that the Scrabble tiles rattled.

Apollo glared at her warningly.

'I'll check it,' Gran said, riffling through one of her battered old dictionaries. 'Ach! Well, so it is. "FUGH: an exclamation of disgust".'

Orla muttered her own exclamation of disgust. 'But he didn't know that! So he shouldn't get the points.'

'Oh, come on, Orla.' Gran tutted. 'Let your little brother have it.'

'No! That's not fair!'

It wasn't. None of it was. It wasn't fair that this trip had been *her* idea, yet here was Apollo stealing all Gran's love and attention, like he stole everyone's. It wasn't fair that Dad would prefer to go on holidays with stupid Penelope and her boys rather than them. It wasn't fair that Mum had died.

Her frustration bubbled over into the rage that had become so familiar these past two years.

'We shouldn't treat him like a baby,' she spat, 'Apollo's already enough of one as it is.'

Apollo flushed. 'Stop being horrid, Orla!'

'You're the one who's horrid! Why did you have to come and ruin everything?' Orla shoved the board over. Tiles flew everywhere. Gran looked horrified and Apollo started to cry.

Orla stared at the mess and hot shame washed over her. She ran out of the Den, slamming the door and racing down the hall. When she reached the spare room, she threw herself down on her bed, pressed her face into the pillow and let her hot, heavy tears fall.

Things didn't feel better here at all. Instead, they felt worse than ever.

Later, Gran came and coaxed Orla back to join them with one of her warm apple pies fresh out of the oven. Orla couldn't resist the sweet cinnamon smell. She sat at the kitchen table and hung her head, waiting for Gran to give her a talking-to. That's what she'd usually have done: told Orla to apologize, hug and make up.

But Gran regarded her sadly. 'You should be kinder to him, you know. You need each other more than you realize.'

'I don't need anything from *him*,' Orla muttered.

Gran looked like she wanted to say more, but she just sighed.

With Scrabble quite literally off the table, Apollo and Gran spent the rest of the afternoon braving the drizzle to do some gardening.

Orla watched them through the rain-flecked glass of the spare room window. She remembered spending days in Gran's garden with Mum, hacking back weeds together and them all daring each other to get closer to the wasps' nest next to the unused shed. The memories stung. Orla pushed them from her mind and went back to pretending to read.

*

The following morning, Gran suggested Orla have a go on the piano. 'The old thing's dying to be played,' she said, 'especially by someone with your musical talent.'

Orla had been expecting this suggestion to come at some point but she still tensed. 'I don't play any more,' she muttered.

'Yes, your dad said. That's a real shame. You were so good. What was it your music teacher used to say? A natural, even from a young age. That you put your whole heart and soul into the music and really *felt* it.'

Orla shrugged. That was exactly the problem with music: it made her feel too much. It had been her and Mum's special thing. They used to play that piano together for hours, sharing the stool. If she closed her eyes, Orla could still recall the feeling of Mum's hair brushing her shoulder as their fingers overlapped on the keys.

Sometimes Mum would sing too, throwing her head back and smiling. All the worry lines on her face would smooth and she'd suddenly look as young as she did in the graduation photo hanging over the hall table. Gran would join in the singing too, taking the lower harmony. Their voices would meld as they sang Irish folk songs about capricious fairies, know-it-all giants and bloodthirsty merrows. Orla and Apollo had gradually picked up the words to some of these songs and used to sing along to the ones they knew.

Whenever Mum had been feeling her worst, music had seemed able to revive her and there was a time when Orla had thought that maybe, if she just played well enough, she could use music to make Mum better again. It was why she'd practised so hard, playing until her fingers were sore and she'd got the chords perfect. But when the song ended and the last note faded, Mum's strength would fade with it.

Gran's voice jolted Orla back to the present. 'Go on, just play one wee tune for your old gran,' she pressed.

'I already said no!' Orla snapped.

She regretted her tone. Gran turned away quickly, but not before Orla saw her eyes were glistening and felt wretched for it.

'I'm sorry for upsetting you, pet,' Gran said later, after they'd had lunch. 'Why don't you come and do some knitting with us in the Den?'

Orla wished she could smile and say yes; that she could spend the afternoon knitting and laughing with them. But instead she hugged herself tightly and didn't reply. She spent the rest of the day alone in her room instead.

As dusk fell, Orla's restlessness got the better of

her. Hearing Apollo and Gran in the Den, she sneaked past their door and went out into the garden for some fresh air.

She stood in the lengthening shadow of the house and breathed deeply. Why had she been stupid enough to think that coming to Gran's would make her feel any different?

There was a rustle in the bushes. Something moving . . . The hairs on the back of Orla's neck rose. What was it? A cat? A fox? She moved closer. A pair of orange eyes stared back at her from the bushes. A *very large* pair of eyes. Orla jolted backwards in alarm and the eyes vanished. She blinked.

'Orla, come in now,' Gran called brusquely from the house. 'What did I say about not being out by yerself in the evenings?'

Orla turned to see Gran hurrying across from the back door, tense and agitated. But why? In the past, she'd let them go where they wanted at any time of day and said children needed more freedom to make their own mistakes and have adventures. What had changed? Orla was only in the garden.

She looked back at the empty bushes. Had she imagined the orange eyes?

'Come on in. Now.' Gran's voice was firm.

Bewildered, Orla followed her inside.

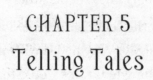

CHAPTER 5
Telling Tales

After tea, Gran insisted Orla join them in the Den. Not wanting to upset Gran by being rude again, Orla did. Apollo tried to catch her eye as she sat down in a battered armchair but Orla ignored him.

On the radio, music played softly and Gran hummed along. Orla pretended not to notice. She didn't want to give Gran any more ideas about her playing the piano again.

She took a reference book about trees down from the shelf, intending to pretend to read it so she wouldn't have to talk. As she did, she knocked down a book called *Irish Folktales, Myths and Legends*. It landed open on the carpet, showing a two-page spread illustrated with the most hideous monsters. There were inky black feathers around the border and a swirled title read: *The Wild Hunt or Sluagh*.

The Wild Hunt were depicted in all their alleged guises: as a black cloud, as fearsome ravens, as skeletal horses and, finally, in their haggard and monstrous mortal forms. In this last form the creatures had sagging skin, gangly limbs and leathery wings that were folded on their backs, so it looked like they were wearing tattered cloaks. Orla shuddered. She'd always hated these drawings.

She remembered from Gran's songs that you had to be careful not to say the Wild Hunt's real name (*Sluagh*) aloud, because if you said it three times, you'd call them. She remembered the words of the song as she read:

> *The Wild Hunt rides in the dead of night,*
> *Spreading terror, misery and fright,*
>
> *They'll feast on your despair and pain,*
> *Whatever you do, don't say their name.*
>
> *For speak it three times and you will call,*
> *Clouds black as coal, a hideous squall –*
>
> *Birds, horses, beasts – who'll break your soul apart,*
> *Sorrow hunters who once had mortal hearts.*

Orla's eyes flitted across the page.

. . . *After three nights of being the Wild Hunt's captives, mortal victims lose their minds. After three months their hearts lose all their love and the victims become Wild Hunt themselves.*

Orla stopped reading. She'd noticed a piece of paper lying on the carpet next to the book that must have slipped out of the pages. On it was a hand-drawn map of Ireland. The map was covered in tiny red crosses, each with two capital letters written next to them.

'What's this?' Orla asked, picking it up.

'Oh, never you mind that,' Gran said, taking the map and quickly sliding it back inside the pages of *Irish Folktales, Myths and Legends*. She seemed flustered, like she had been when Orla had asked about the lock on the door.

Orla opened her mouth to ask more questions, but Apollo must have seen her intention because he quickly interrupted. 'Will you tell us one of your stories, Gran?'

Orla rolled her eyes. 'You're too old for stories.'

Apollo blushed a deep beetroot and Orla was glad. She knew she should try to be less horrible but, at the same time, part of her enjoyed making her brother feel even a fraction as miserable as she did.

Gran's eyebrows raised. 'No one ever gets too old for stories, do they now?'

Apollo smiled and Orla scowled.

'Anyway, they're not *just* stories, are they, Gran?' said Apollo. 'There's truth in them. Everyone who lives around here knows that.'

Gran's eyes sparkled. 'Which story would you like, Apollo?'

'The one about the giants and the magic fish, please!'

Orla groaned. 'You must know that one by heart by now.'

Apollo ignored her and leant his head on Gran's knee.

'Very well.' Gran stroked his blue hair. A faraway look came into her eyes. Her voice deepened and became soft as velvet.

'In the River Boyne,' Gran began, 'there was once an enormous magical fish called the Salmon of Knowledge. It was said that its silver scales shone like a rainbow whatever the weather, and that the first to taste its flesh would become wiser than any being that had ever lived. Many of the cleverest and most foolish creatures of this earth tried to catch the salmon but none succeeded.'

As usual, Orla felt herself being pulled in by Gran's words despite herself. Her mind filled with images.

A fish with a thousand silver scales, covered in rainbows.

People trying to catch the fish.

The fish darting out of reach.

Again and again.

'That was until two giants came along, one by the name of Fionn, the other Ben,' Gran continued. 'Not

37

many folks know that Fionn and Ben are brothers, and all sorts of tales have been told of them since, but brothers they are, with Ben residing in Scotland and Fionn here in Ireland . . .'

'Fionn lives in the Tangled Woods, doesn't he?' piped in Apollo.

'So he does.' Gran smiled, before resuming her storytelling voice. 'So that the brother-giants could visit each other, they built a bridge together that crossed the sea, for neither could swim. Ben was the smaller giant and was often jealous of how much stronger Fionn was. So when Ben visited Fionn in Ireland, he was determined to get the Salmon of Knowledge from the River Boyne and be the wisest giant that ever lived instead. He went fishing every day for a hundred years. Fionn did not understand his brother's obsession with the salmon but helped him anyway, enjoying the time they were spending together.'

In her mind's eye, Orla watched two giants, one bigger than the other, fishing in a sparkling river.

'Then one day, by some miracle, Ben caught the fish! He was delighted but also tired after his struggle to reel it in, for the salmon was surprisingly strong. "Cook it, Fionn," he says. "But don't eat it now, not even a wee mouthful."

'Fionn would never deliberately defy his brother.

So he built a fire and cooked that salmon carefully. But while he was turning it over, the hot skin burnt his thumb. Fionn put his thumb into his mouth to numb the pain and accidentally tasted the salmon.

'He brought the fish to Ben but Ben immediately noticed the change in his brother. A new wisdom gleamed in Fionn's eye, like a thousand rainbows reflected on silver scales. "Have you eaten any of my salmon?" Ben says. "No!" says Fionn. But then he remembered how he had burnt his thumb and put it to his mouth. Stricken with guilt and shame, he confessed.

'"You eejit," says Ben. He knew that Fionn must have the wisdom of the salmon in him now, and was so full of begrudgery that he wouldn't listen when Fionn tried to explain that it had been an accident. Fionn was upset that Ben didn't believe him. They fought for years. In the end, Fionn was so angry at his brother for not believing him that he smashed their bridge to smithereens. Now Fionn remains in Ireland always, and Ben in Scotland. They haven't seen each other for centuries and wouldn't be able to now even if they wanted to, for neither can rebuild the bridge alone.'

Gran gave Orla a meaningful look. Orla looked down and played with the yellow scrunchie on her wrist, feeling uncomfortable.

'All the wisdom and knowledge in the world is often too much for Fionn,' Gran continued, 'who never wanted it in the first place. So he hides in the Tangled Woods, with his head in the clouds, trying to forget all that he knows and trying to forget his brother, who he misses very much . . . It is a very sad story really,' Gran finished, shaking her head.

'It is,' Apollo agreed forlornly. 'But for some reason I like it, even though it makes me feel sad. I'm not sure why.'

Orla wanted to point out that this was just a story and not worth crying over. There were real things to be upset about.

The music programme on the radio that had been playing softly in the background ended and a news report started.

'*Breaking news,*' said the announcer. '*A ten-year-old boy from Ballymapooley has been reported missing. Liam Armstrong disappeared from his bed last night. He's the third person from the County Tyrone area to go missing within the past three months and the first child. His family are extremely worried . . .*'

Usually, Gran would have turned off the news as soon as it started but this time she didn't. Instead, she sat up in her chair, listening intently. '*Ballymapooley?* That's not all that far from here . . .' she muttered.

Apollo glanced over curiously. While Orla was glad

he finally seemed to be acknowledging that Gran was acting weird, she was alarmed by how pale Gran looked.

Noticing their stares, Gran shook herself as if remembering where she was and hurriedly switched off the radio. 'Best be getting to bed,' she said.

Orla looked at the clock and frowned. It was only eight. They usually stayed up until at least nine during the holidays and it was still so light outside.

'But, Gran, it's early!' Apollo protested.

'Well, I think we could all do with an early night, don't you?' Gran tried to smile but it did not meet her eyes. The report of the missing boy had clearly rattled her.

Apollo begged for one more story but, to their surprise, Gran put her foot down. Reluctantly, Orla and Apollo sloped off to the bathroom to brush their teeth.

When Orla went to the spare room, she caught Gran checking the lock on their window. 'Best to be secure now,' she said in a too-bright voice that rang false. 'Don't you be opening this for any reason. Sleep tight now.' She hurried out of the room.

Orla stared after her. She climbed into bed with her head spinning, unable to make any sense of Gran's behaviour at all.

*

Later that night, Orla woke and heard Gran moving about in the hallway, then the front door opened and closed softly. What was Gran doing?

She waited, her ears straining for Gran's return. But as the minutes stretched, Orla started to worry . . .

She considered getting up to check where Gran was, but she must have fallen back to sleep because the next thing she knew she was dreaming of black birds circling above the house, getting closer and closer. As they did, their squawks became screams.

Mum's screams. *Help me, Orla. Help me. Why won't you help me?*

Orla often heard Mum calling for help in her dreams. As always, she desperately wanted to go to wherever Mum was and save her, but she couldn't move. It was as if her limbs had turned to stone. All the windows in the house suddenly shot open and the birds rushed in, scattering black feathers everywhere.

When Orla woke, she was drenched in cold sweat.

CHAPTER 6
The Stray

The next morning, Gran kept yawning and seemed anxious.

'Where did you go out to last night, Gran?' Orla asked.

Gran started. 'Go out? I didn't go out.' She turned to fuss over the stove.

Orla regarded her back stonily. 'I heard you.'

'Ach, you must've been dreaming!'

Orla's eyes narrowed. Gran was lying again, just like she'd lied about the reason for the locks, and Orla wanted to know why.

In the afternoon, Gran left them in the Den saying she was off to fetch some biscuits. When half an hour passed and she still hadn't come back from the kitchen, Orla grew suspicious.

'She's probably making them from scratch or something,' Apollo said, but he followed Orla down the hall.

They poked their heads around the kitchen door. Gran wasn't there.

'Gran?' Orla called.

The back door was open.

'She's gardening!' said Apollo, sounding relieved.

They went out into the garden, right up to the back fence where the shed and the wasps' nest were. There was still no sign of her anywhere.

Orla heard a banging noise.

'*Shh!*' she said, halting.

'Why?' asked Apollo.

'I said *shh!* I heard something . . . in the shed.'

'Gran's in the shed?'

'Just be quiet, will you?'

They waited, holding their breath.

Sounds of a tussle were coming from inside the shed. Bangs and scuffles, and an odd growling that made the hairs on the back of Orla's neck stand up.

Apollo's eyes widened. They exchanged bewildered looks and crept closer.

The shed door was ajar.

Had Gran gone inside to fetch something and fallen over? Was that her groaning they'd just heard? But it hadn't *sounded* like groaning. It had sounded like growling . . .

Was Gran trapped inside with some wild animal?

Then came an unfamiliar voice. Or at least Orla *thought* it was a voice, though she wasn't totally sure. It sounded like it was saying something about *going*?

'Did you hear that?' she whispered.

'Hear what?' Apollo hissed. 'The growling?'

'No, that voice . . . Gran?' she called nervously, pushing the shed door open.

They both peered into the gloom inside. Something in the darkness flew at them. For a split second, there was a flurry of black fur and more terrifying growling. Orla and Apollo both shrieked as they lurched backwards.

Then Gran appeared in the doorway in her tartan trousers. For someone so small, she did an impressive job of shielding whatever was behind her from view.

'Gran!' Apollo exclaimed with relief.

'Ach, hello, my dears. Looking for me, were youse? Go on inside, now. I'll just be a wee minute.'

Behind her, there was a metallic clanking and more growling.

'What's that?' Apollo asked fearfully.

'Oh, just a stray cat . . . a large one. Found the wee dote in the garden, injured.'

Apollo's expression changed completely. 'Oh, poor thing! Can I see it?' he pleaded, pushing forwards.

'No.' The sharpness in Gran's voice surprised them

both. 'I mean, it's best you don't. Very mean and manky, this one. A biter, carrying goodness knows what diseases. Rabies, probably. I'm going to call the vet to come and get it, but in the meantime I'll be keeping it in here and keeping youse two safely away from it!'

Orla glanced sideways at Apollo and saw her own confusion reflected in his eyes. Since when had Gran been so overly cautious?

The clanking got louder. As did the growling.

Did cats make noises like that? Why did it sound like it was chained up?

And Orla could have sworn she'd heard a voice . . .

Gran ushered them both backwards and closed the door firmly behind her. 'Now, promise me you won't be coming near this shed until I say it's OK.'

Apollo still looked perplexed, but nodded slowly. 'If you want us to stay away, Gran, then we promise. Don't we, Orla?'

Orla shrugged. Gran took this as a yes.

'Grand!' The tension in her face eased and, when she smiled, it was like clouds clearing. 'C'mere now, inside we go. Suppose you'll be wanting some lunch, won't ye?'

Orla and Apollo blinked. They'd had lunch. Three hours ago.

'Gran, we already ate. It's four in the afternoon!' said Apollo.

'Oh, so it is,' Gran muttered, shaking her head. 'It was chocolate biscuits you were after. I remember now. Come on, then.'

Orla frowned. First Gran had lied about sneaking out last night and now this . . .

She was definitely hiding something.

The question was – what?

CHAPTER 7
Connecting the Dots

All that evening and the following morning, Gran was distracted. She didn't encourage them to play games, or help Apollo knit, or tell them any more stories – no matter how much Apollo begged. Every so often she disappeared into the garden with an opened tin of tuna or water in a bowl, so they knew she must be visiting the animal in the shed. But she still wouldn't let them anywhere near it or answer their questions with more than one-word replies.

Orla was determined to find out what she was up to. After Mum died and Dad started dating Penelope, Gran had been the only person Orla thought she could still count on. Now it felt like she was losing Gran too. Orla wasn't going to let that happen. At least, not without knowing why.

That afternoon she found something else that was curious. While Gran and Apollo were in the Den, Orla went to the kitchen to make a cup of tea. As the ancient red kettle started to boil, she discovered, to her annoyance, that Apollo had drunk all the milk in the fridge. She went to the cupboard where Gran stored the long-life milk and there, sitting on top of the cartons, was a yellow folder.

What was that doing in here?

Orla pulled the folder out and flipped it open. She knew she shouldn't look inside without permission – it could be stuff that she wasn't meant to see. But all she found were newspaper clippings. One was the underlined story of the missing woman called Mary Hart that had been on the hall table the day they'd arrived.

It soon became obvious that *all* the stories in the folder were of people going missing across Ireland in the past year. There were at least a dozen. Each person's name, as well as the date and location of their disappearance, had been underlined in red pen.

Orla stared at the contents of the folder, utterly bewildered.

Why was Gran collecting news stories about missing people?

The red pen marks reminded Orla of something else she'd seen recently . . .

She looked again at the underlined names, her heart beating faster. The map she'd found in that book of folk tales with initials marked all over it! Orla was willing to bet that all the missing people's initials and the locations of their disappearances matched Gran's map.

For a moment, the thrill of her discovery zinged through her. But her elation quickly faded. For, despite solving one puzzle, she was more perplexed than ever. Were these disappearances the reason Gran was acting so funny about locks, and Orla and Apollo going out by themselves? Did she think they could go missing too?

Stuffing the clippings back in the folder, she hurriedly returned it to the cupboard.

And there was another mystery. Her gaze travelled towards the shed. Gran was definitely lying about what she was keeping in there. Was there some link between the missing people and whatever it was?

She moved towards the back door.

'What are you doing?' Apollo's voice made her jump.

'Nothing,' she said quickly, whirling around.

'You're going to go snooping around the shed, aren't you?'

'Of course not. I just feel like doing some gardening for Gran.'

'As if!' Apollo darted past her and blocked the back door.

'Get out of the way, moron!'

'No. We promised we wouldn't go near, Orla.'

Orla sighed, exasperated. 'Gran's lying to us, Apollo. You and I both know that whatever was making those noises wasn't a stray cat. I don't have to keep promises when she's being a liar.'

'Don't call her that.' Apollo bit his lip. 'If Gran says it's a stray cat, then I believe her.'

'If it *is* just a cat, then don't you think it's weird she won't let us see it?'

Apollo shook his head. 'She said it was dangerous.'

'Gran also said she'd call the vet yesterday, so why haven't they shown up? I haven't seen her on the phone to anyone, have you? I'm sure the ISPCA wouldn't be too happy with an injured cat being shut in a garden shed for so long. What if it needs to see the vet urgently and dies without treatment? Can you live with that, Apollo?'

Apollo glanced at the shed nervously. 'Gran will have made sure it gets what it needs,' he replied firmly.

Orla decided to try a different tack. 'If you really think it's a stray cat, then you're even more dumb than I thought.'

'Shut up!' Apollo clenched his hands into fists. She almost had him.

Orla knew exactly what to say next, though she felt guilty for it. But it was his own fault for getting in her way. 'Did I ever tell you how stupid and babyish your blue hair looks? You look like an alien, Apollo. *Everyone* says so.'

It worked. Apollo lunged at Orla, who dodged out of his way and then, once the path was clear, sprinted out of the house, across the garden, through the bushes, to the shed—

She stopped in her tracks.

A fat brass padlock hung on the latch.

Unbelievable!

She heard Apollo running up behind her and whirled around defiantly. 'See! This proves it.'

'What?'

'That padlock! Why would she lock the shed if she's not hiding something? Would *you* padlock a sick stray cat inside a shed?'

Apollo stared at the padlock, blinking fast as if doubting his own eyes. 'Maybe she let it go already . . .' he mumbled, but he didn't sound convinced.

'Where is everyone?' Gran's voice came from inside the house and made them both start.

'Just doing some weeding!' Orla called quickly, leaping away from the shed and wrenching up some plants that she hoped *were* weeds.

Apollo also moved hastily away, glaring at Orla.

Gran popped her head out of the back door. 'Well, who knew I had *two* green-fingered grandchildren!' Her eyes flicked to the padlocked shed. 'Although, Orla, in future it'd be grand if you could leave my petunias alone. I rather like them.'

Orla let go of the petunias hurriedly.

Gran's eyes narrowed as she took in their flushed cheeks. 'Not been trying to peek inside the shed, have you?'

'No!' Orla said hurriedly. 'I mean, Apollo *tried* to but I stopped him.'

'*What?*' Apollo spluttered. 'That's not true, you—'

'I'm joking!' Orla interrupted quickly. 'Neither of us went anywhere near the shed, Gran. We just wanted some air . . . and to help with the weeding. Right, Apollo?'

Apollo glared at her. '*Right,*' he replied through gritted teeth.

Gran looked at them carefully. 'Well, good. Who'll be after a wee cup of tea?'

'Me!' Orla said quickly. As she ran inside the house, she felt Apollo's glare continue to bore into her like a laser beam. Orla ignored him, already trying to figure out how she could come back to investigate the shed without him getting in the way.

CHAPTER 8
Bumps in the Night

To Orla's immense annoyance, Apollo wouldn't let her out of his sight for the rest of the day. He even followed her to the toilet, making it impossible for Orla to do any further snooping. Her only option was to wait until he was asleep.

That night, she climbed into bed while Apollo was in the bathroom so that he wouldn't see that under her duvet she was still fully dressed in her hoodie and jeans. She shut her eyes as someone came into the room. By the way the person sat down softly on the end of Orla's bed, she could tell it was Gran.

Orla pulled the duvet up higher under her chin and squeezed her eyes shut more tightly, though Gran was unlikely to believe she'd nodded off already. The overhead light was still on.

Orla could sense Gran wanted to say something. She kept clearing her throat then stopping herself. Orla wished she'd get on with it and go. She didn't want

Gran to notice that she was still fully dressed.

Gran took a deep breath. 'I know things have been really hard since we lost your mum. Her death was a tragedy for us all and so hard to bear at your age. But I want you to know that you are allowed to let yourself feel happy sometimes too, Orla. You're not betraying her or leaving her behind. She'd want you to enjoy your life. You understand that, don't you?'

Orla kept very quiet. She hadn't been expecting this, at least not right now. She was too focused on the shed to respond and didn't know how to react.

'I know you're angry and that is very normal,' Gran continued, 'but try not to take it out on your poor brother. He loves you so much and he just wants to be your friend.'

Orla glowered. *Of course, they'd been talking behind her back.*

'Same with yer dad. You need to talk to people, Orla. Let them in! It helps, honestly it does. Don't just let everything keep tormenting you inside all the time, it will drive yer mad. I know it's really hard but we all love you and we're here for you. Like I said before, you can always talk to me about her. I'd *like* to talk about her with you, you just have to let us in.'

Orla bit her lip. Part of her longed to sit up and hug Gran and tell her all about the pain she'd been carrying inside for so long; to let Gran soothe and comfort her. To let Gran take all the sadness and hurt away. But Gran couldn't do that, could she? No one could and another part of Orla was still too angry. Gran didn't get it. None of them felt as bad as she did.

'Why would I want to open up to someone who doesn't tell me the truth?' she snapped coldly, opening her eyes narrowly.

Gran looked pained. 'There are things it's best I keep to myself, Orla, to protect you. You've had enough to worry about—'

'I'm so sick of everyone saying they're doing things to protect me! Mum used to say it when it turned out she'd lied to us about how ill she really was. Then Dad said it when I found out he was sneaking around with Penelope after she died. Now you're saying it too! But none of you have protected me from anything at all!'

'Orla . . .' Gran's voice cracked. She tried to stroke Orla's hair.

'Leave me alone!' Orla yelled, jerking away.

'If that's what you want, pet,' Gran whispered and left the room.

It's not what I want, Orla wanted to shout after her. *Please stay. Hug me. Tell me everything will be OK. Tell me you forgive me for being so awful. Tell me that you're not lying and that I can trust you after all, and that I'm not as alone as I feel.*

She heard a noise at the door and looked up, hoping Gran had come back. But it was Apollo, back from the bathroom. From his wide and judgemental eyes, she could tell he'd heard the whole thing. Orla rolled over and pulled the covers over her head.

'You've become really selfish, Orla,' he hissed.

For once, Orla did not insult him back. *Maybe he was right.*

She lay still in the darkness for a long time after Apollo had switched off the light.

Maybe she shouldn't go nosing around the shed tonight. What if Gran caught her and it made things worse? It probably *was* just a stray cat . . . wasn't it?

But why the padlock?

And what about that voice?

Orla couldn't let it go. She had to know.

After a while, Apollo started to snore softly in the darkness.

She was about to get up when she heard shuffling sounds out in the hallway again.

Orla got up silently and cracked open the door. A familiar hunched figure was creeping out of sight.

Gran *was* sneaking out again!

Orla heard the front door open and close and the soft jangle of keys. Hurrying down the hall, she shoved on her trainers and tried to open the front door but it had been locked from the outside.

She raced back along the hall to Gran's room. Gran's bed was made and unslept in. Orla crossed to the window and looked out.

The full moon illuminated Gran striding purposefully down the road, her thin yellow torch beam shining ahead of her.

Orla stared in bewildered astonishment.

Gran was heading into the Tangled Woods.

CHAPTER 9
Into the Woods

Orla unbolted Gran's window and slid it open, shivering as the cold night air rushed in. She clambered out and hurried down the driveway, following Gran into the woods, trying to catch up.

But Gran was too far ahead and, no matter how quickly Orla ran, she couldn't see any sign of her.

Orla began to wonder if she'd taken a wrong turn. The deeper she went into the woods, the more the path narrowed, and the tree branches became so tangled above her that the moonlight barely broke through at all. Prickles of fear crept up her neck and she started to imagine strange creatures watching her in the darkness.

Be rational, she told herself firmly. But there were rational things to be afraid of too. The newspaper stories of the missing people flashed through her mind, and Orla imagined her own name in one of those headlines: *Orla Smith, 13, missing . . .*

Oh, what *was* Gran doing sneaking off into the

woods in the middle of the night? And what on earth had possessed Orla to try to follow?

She decided to head back. Orla pulled her phone out of her pocket and switched on the torch, relieved to have it with her. A small circle of light spooled on to the forest floor, illuminating the dark undergrowth.

Criss-crossed roots and dead leaves.

No sign of the path.

Orla's stomach dropped. She must have lost it.

She whirled around, peering through the dense trees. They seemed to stretch for miles in every direction. Which way was home? Orla tried the maps function on her phone but she had no signal or GPS and the screen just showed her as a tiny blue dot in the middle of a swathe of empty grey.

Worse still, her phone battery was only on five per cent. Orla cursed herself for not charging it earlier.

She picked a direction, hoping it was right, and forged on desperately, too afraid to stand still. She tripped over tree roots and got horribly scratched by brambles. Her hair kept getting caught on branches so she tied it out of her face with her yellow scrunchie, all the time trying to ignore the horrible sinking feeling that she was moving further in the wrong direction.

One of Gran's folk songs came unwelcome into her head.

Child, never walk in the woods alone,
For if you stray to where the hawthorn grows,
There you'll find a ring of stones,
Where the fairy folk have their fun,
Oh, if you do, run, child, run, child, run . . .

Orla flinched at every sound. The rustle of the wind. Twigs breaking under her own feet. An owl hooting.

There were stranger noises too. Horrid scuffling in the undergrowth. Distant howls. And an eerie whispering that she prayed was just the wind through the trees. Panic clawed at her. She was sure now that she was being watched by *something*.

Orla gripped her phone tightly. Her hands were shaking. Then the screen went black and Orla was plunged into pitch darkness.

She stumbled forwards and crashed into a tree. Panting hard, she paused, clutching the ridged trunk. The noises grew louder and closer.

Amongst them, she heard a new sound.

Soft and rhythmic.

Music.

Orla started.

Was she imagining it?

No, she was *sure* she could hear singing in the distance. She could smell something comforting and familiar too now. Burning wood. That meant fire. And *people*.

Somewhere close by.

Orla's body sagged with momentary relief. People would be able to tell her how to get out of the Tangled Woods and back to Gran's house. But this feeling was quickly replaced by more uncertainty. Who would be having a fire deep in the woods at this time of night? Whoever it was probably wouldn't want to be disturbed . . .

Still, finding them was her best chance of getting home.

She crept cautiously in the direction of the music. As it got louder, she spotted the orange flicker of a fire ahead of her through the trees and her footsteps quickened. She could hear both instruments and singing now. Orla recognized the tune. It was one of the folk songs Gran and Mum used to sing!

'*Oh, some call us the Good Folk,*
Some call us the fae,
Leave us out a bowl of milk,
And good luck will come your way . . .'

Peeking through the trees, Orla saw a clearing, in the centre of which was a squat, white-flowered hawthorn. Its twisted grey trunk was lit up by the fire burning below it.

Around the edge of the clearing there was a ring of large, ancient-looking stones. Dancing inside the stones were men and women. As they danced, they sang and played instruments. Some of these instruments Orla recognized – flutes, fiddles, tin whistles and accordions – but others she had never seen before. The players danced so rhythmically that it was as if their bodies were part of the music itself. The effect was hypnotic and Orla found her feet tapping along.

The dancers all had long hair and loose-fitting clothes, some of which looked like they were made from leaves. Bells tinkled on their bare toes. Their shimmering capes were designed like butterfly wings and swirled around them as they danced, flinging glitter in the air, so that the clearing was full of a sparkling golden haze. They looked just like the drawings of the Good Folk in Gran's book. Even down to the butterfly wings! Their skin glittered too with some special make-up and all their faces were beautiful, with high cheekbones, gleaming eyes and sharp jawlines. Was this some kind of summer festival performance? But why would there be a festival in the middle of the night in the woods by Gran's sleepy village?

'. . . *Never dare you cross us,*
Lest you want to lose your luck,
Oh, we can cause you quite a fuss,
Turn the world you know to muck . . .'

The song continued to build into a frenzy as the dancers spun faster and faster, the bells on their toes ringing louder.

There was movement above. Orla looked up and suppressed a gasp as she realized that the branches tenting over the clearing were quivering with royal-blue butterflies with golden-tipped wings.

Hundreds of them.

Orla took a step backwards, unable to understand what she was seeing. She felt like she was dreaming but the smarting scratches on her arms and legs told her otherwise.

Suddenly Orla realized what was different about the song. In Gran's version the pronouns had been 'them' and 'they'. These singers used 'us' and 'we' . . . Did that mean—

The song reached a giddy crescendo. Shimmering tambourines were raised towards the stars as the dancers whooped and cheered. They bowed to one another before flopping on to the ground in exhaustion, among cushions, rugs and scattered goblets. Their beautiful faces turned in unison towards one side of the clearing, and Orla saw then an enormous wooden throne.

Lounging in it was a man wearing a crown of antlers. Butterflies fluttered around him and rested on his arms and thighs. His every finger sparkled with rings and he wore a frilled shirt, over which hung a bejewelled breastplate. Trailing behind him was a cape that, like the others, looked like an enormous pair of butterfly wings. His long, dark hair tumbled softly around his face, but his eyes were sharp and menacing.

Seated to his left in a low wooden chair, looking entirely at home, her wrinkled face shining in the firelight, was Gran.

CHAPTER 10
Gran's Strange Friends

The shock was like being punched in the stomach. Orla's mind reeled. *Gran got lost and these people welcomed her to join them . . .* But that still didn't make sense. For one thing, Gran looked totally at ease, as if this night-time gathering was something she did often.

The crowned man turned to Gran. 'Did you enjoy the show, Ms Elizabeth?'

Gran nodded. 'Indeed, King Oberon. Wonderful, everyone.'

King Oberon? That was the name of the fairy king!

Gran smiled at the seated congregation, who let out more whoops and beat their hands on the ground until it sounded like an earthquake. Orla stared at their shimmering capes that looked so much like butterfly wings. The material was iridescent, almost see-through. They looked so . . . *real.*

King Oberon smiled. 'We're glad you enjoyed it, Ms Elizabeth. It's not often we move our midsummer festivities from the Fairy Kingdom to the mortal realm.'

From the Fairy Kingdom? Orla felt like she was going to faint.

'As I said, I am honoured, Your Grace,' replied Gran.

'Well, you are our treasured friend, Ms Elizabeth, and my butterflies told me that you have been so eager to see us.'

Gran bowed her head humbly. 'I thank you, Your Grace. Forgive me, but the boy has been missing for two nights now. If he's with them a third . . .'

Orla's ears pricked. Did Gran mean the missing boy in the news? Who did she mean by 'them'?

'Hush, Ms Elizabeth, you do worry yourself. It's time for you to tell one of your amusing tales about mortals. It's been so long since you've told us a story.'

'Yes, tell us a story!' the others cooed.

Orla shifted and a branch snapped under her trainer. At once, the faces of the congregation turned to stare into the darkness where she was hidden. Their expressions were no longer joyous and playful.

'Who goes there?' King Oberon boomed.

Gran was right there! If she was safe with these people, surely Orla would be too . . . But for some reason, Orla didn't feel like this was true. She felt a flash of terror.

King Oberon flicked his hand and, to Orla's astonishment, the butterflies on his arms and legs rose into the air and flew through the trees towards her.

Instinct kicked in and Orla stumbled backwards, tripping over ferns and tree roots. She had no idea where she was headed. She'd never outrun the butterflies. In the stories, you didn't have to outrun them, though, you just had to stop moving . . .

Orla halted dead, staying as still as she could.

Her heart was pounding and she didn't dare breathe.

Out of the corner of her eye, she noticed glints of gold and fluttering shapes moving against the dark branches over her head. Orla's chest tightened, but a moment later the butterflies circled back to King Oberon.

She only let out a shaky breath as she heard the king say, 'Now it's time for stories!'

'Yes, yes!' the other fairies chimed.

Silently Orla crept closer, positioning herself so that she could spy on the gathering again. She knew she should probably seize her chance to run, but curiosity got the better of her and Gran was still here.

The fairies swigged from their goblets. They looked beautiful and childlike once more. For some reason, this changeability made them terrifying. They were exactly how Gran had always described: beautiful but cruel and fickle.

When one laid their head on Gran's lap, Orla bristled. But Gran stroked the fairy's hair affectionately.

'Why don't you tell us stories of Kathleen any more?' one called.

Orla stiffened. Kathleen was Mum's name.

'I told you, she passed away,' Gran said quietly, sadness etched on her face.

'Well, what about stories of the wee ones?' said another. 'Your grandchildren. That's what you call them, isn't it?'

'Oh, don't tell us about them. The butterflies said they seem very dreary!' said the first fairy.

'And boring,' said another.

'And ugly,' said one more.

Giggling followed.

Orla flushed, but Gran smiled and some of the sadness on her face melted away. 'Oh, they're none of those things. Actually, they're the most extraordinary people in the world, at least to me.'

For a moment, the icy fist unclenched its fingers from around Orla's heart and a warm feeling rose inside her. Even after Orla had been so awful, Gran was still her biggest fan.

'Anyway, I don't have time for stories tonight,' Gran continued. 'As I keep trying to tell you, there are urgent matters that need your attention.'

A groan went up. The crowd drummed their feet and bared sharp teeth. Again, Orla's breath caught and she feared for Gran's safety, but Gran did not flinch. She was clearly used to these creatures.

'Ms Elizabeth, we've come to the mortal realm for two nights now,' objected King Oberon. 'In the midst of our midsummer revels. The least you could do to thank us is not bother us with silly mortal concerns and provide some entertaining stories!'

'While I am immensely honoured, as I said, I'm here to discuss the problem of the Wild Hunt, which must not be put off any longer. This is for the sake of mortals and fairies alike.'

Orla's stomach dropped. *The Wild Hunt?* She thought of the ghastly drawings in Gran's book and a shiver ran down her spine. If the fairies existed, did that mean the Wild Hunt did too? It was a horrifying thought.

'Forgive me for speaking so directly, Your Grace,' Gran continued hurriedly, 'and please do not feel I am ungrateful for your hospitality, nor that I do not understand how important a time of festivity this is for you. However, the Wild Hunt have grown too strong and something must be done! They've already taken many victims including a child, and more lives are in danger. If the Wild Hunt grow too strong, even your fairies won't be able to stop them.'

There was a moment of silence before the fairies broke into jeers of outrage.

'Of course we can beat the Wild Hunt!' one shouted.

'The Wild Hunt is not our problem!' cried another.

Others cheered in agreement and banged goblets on the ground.

King Oberon held up his ring-encrusted hand for silence. Orla waited, her heart in her mouth.

'As I said last night and all the other times before that when you have come to us with cases of missing mortals, we don't get involved in the Wild Hunt's affairs any more, Ms Elizabeth,' said King Oberon coolly. 'Our ancient rivalry was solved with the peace treaty long ago. So long as they do not encroach on fairy territory, we leave them to theirs—'

'But they are getting stronger!' Gran interrupted. 'Stronger than ever before. Especially since midsummer – the Wild Hunt will soon be stronger even than you fairies . . .'

'We are stronger than the Wild Hunt and always will be,' King Oberon interrupted angrily.

'You *were*. But the Wild Hunt's leader Balor has grown a powerful army without you keeping him in check.'

The king's eyes flashed dangerously. 'You must not forget who you are speaking to.'

Gran bowed her head. 'Forgive me. I do not mean to insult you, Your Grace. I'm troubled by what is happening.'

'Why do you care, Ms Elizabeth? These missing mortals are not your kin.'

'No, but they'll *have* kin – mammies and daddies, sisters and brothers, grandparents who'll be missing them dearly. The Wild Hunt torture the mortals they take by feasting on their sadness until there's nothing of that person left. I can't stand by and let so many lose their loved ones.' The sad look came over Gran's face again. Orla wondered if she was thinking of Mum.

King Oberon studied Gran. 'You should be careful, Ms Elizabeth, and think of yourself. The Wild Hunt will come for you . . . Your sadness is a scent, and you do not want to attract their attention.'

'I've already attracted their attention,' Gran replied bitterly.

King Oberon looked surprised. 'And yet you still came to meet us tonight? You know you are not protected when you are not within the safety of our territory. You are clever to the ways of magical beings, Ms Elizabeth, but you are also vulnerable.'

'I had to come tonight to make you listen. Please, you must stop them,' Gran begged.

King Oberon didn't seem angry any more; instead he seemed amused. He held up his right hand and several of the blue butterflies landed on his fingers.

'Why do mortals do that?' he marvelled, looking at the butterflies. 'You put yourselves in great peril for each other, but you all die anyway in no time at all, like little butterflies. You spend your precious days and nights worrying, when you should be dancing and singing!' He raised his goblet and the crowd cheered.

Gran smiled a small smile. 'Well, maybe we can agree on that.' She had always been a champion of enjoying life. It was one of the many reasons Orla loved her. 'But this is important—'

'Tell me, Ms Elizabeth,' he said, cutting her off, 'why are mortals so sad? The Wild Hunt don't create that in you. They're attracted to it, worsen it, prey on it – but they don't *make* it. It is you mortals that make them stronger with your sadness.'

Gran sighed. 'We're not always sad. We feel all sorts of things. But sadness is a part of being mortal. It shows how much we've loved and it makes us appreciate our gifts. Sometimes we don't know why we feel sad, but other times we know exactly why.'

'When?' King Oberon asked curiously.

'When people we love die. People we miss.'

Orla bit her lip.

'Please, Your Grace,' Gran implored. 'I'm begging you, if only as a gesture of goodwill to our friendship, go and see the Wild Hunt. See how strong and powerful they have become. I guarantee it will make you see that they need to be kept in line.'

'There is a treaty.' King Oberon sounded bored now. 'Besides, this is our last trip out of the Fairy Kingdom until the autumn. Maybe then we'll think about fulfilling your wish.'

'But that will be too late!'

'Enough!' King Oberon commanded sharply. 'I am tired of this conversation. If you will not tell us a story, then it is time for more music! Dance, everyone, dance!'

He flicked his fingers. The crowd cheered and rose to their feet. Gran was lost from Orla's sight in the swirling of bodies and wings as a new melody began to play and glitter spun into the air.

CHAPTER 11
A Late Start

Orla woke in the spare bed at Gran's house. Grey daylight pooled through the open curtains. Over on the camp bed, the duvet was thrown back messily. Apollo was already up.

Orla stared at the ceiling, her head spinning as images from the night came flooding back.

What a wild dream! Gran, the Tangled Woods, the music, the strange gathering, King Oberon, *fairies* . . . it had all felt so *real*. Here lying in Gran's spare bedroom again, however, breathing in the musty smell of the paisley duvet and listening to the clock tick in the hall, she knew it was *impossible*.

Her face and pillow were wet. Had she been crying in her sleep? Could you even do that? Orla pushed the duvet off and gasped. Under the covers, she was still fully dressed in her hoodie, jeans and trainers, which were covered in mud that had smeared the sheets. Orla stared, her eyes widening. She *must* have gone into the woods, then, but why couldn't she remember getting back or what had happened there? Surely the rest of the dream hadn't been real . . .

Orla got up and went to the bathroom where she took a long hot shower to try to clear her head. As she towelled herself dry, she caught sight of scratches running along her arms and legs.

She quickly dressed in clean clothes, burying her dirty ones and the muddied sheets deep in Gran's laundry basket. She tried to tie her hair back, but couldn't find her yellow scrunchie anywhere. Her fingers fluttered anxiously to her earlobes. Thankfully, Mum's crescent moons were still in place.

She hurried down the hall to the kitchen. She needed to speak to Gran immediately.

Gran's walking boots stood by the front door. Like Orla's trainers, they were covered in fresh mud. Her torch was on the hall table too. At least that meant she'd got home safely. Had she brought Orla with her? But wouldn't Orla remember that?

Orla started to feel the first prickles of her anger return. What had Gran been playing at last night? Orla would never have ended up in the woods at all if it wasn't for Gran sneaking around.

No more secrets. Orla wanted answers.

'Morning, sunshine!' Apollo called sarcastically as

Orla stormed into the kitchen, slamming the door open. He was sitting at the table amidst a wreckage of crumbs and knives that were sticky with jam. 'Sleep well, did you?'

'Where's Gran?' she blurted.

'I don't know.'

'What do you mean, you don't know?'

'I mean she's not here.'

'Yes, I can see that!' Orla snapped. Did Apollo always have to be so annoying? She glanced at the microwave clock and started.

The digits read: 14:32.

'That time can't be right,' Orla spluttered.

'It is. I've been trying to wake you for hours!'

She turned to look at him. Apollo's expression was bemused.

'You were completely passed out,' Apollo continued. 'Did you get up and go out early or something? You had all your clothes on . . . I was shouting so loudly that I thought you were having me on, I even poured water on you.'

So that was why her pillow had been wet! Usually, Orla would have pummelled Apollo for less, but she was too startled by what she was hearing. She'd never slept so late before and she was a notoriously light sleeper. Why hadn't Apollo been able to wake her?

Despite the familiar warmth of Gran's kitchen, Orla felt cold. She cast her mind back. The last thing she remembered from last night was the glittering mist. Had she been put under some kind of enchantment? And by whom? None of the fairies (if they hadn't just been a dream) had seen she was there, so far as she recalled. So what had happened?

Apollo was staring at her. 'Why have you gone so pale? You really didn't hear me?'

Orla tried to organize her whirling thoughts. *Gran.* She needed to find her. Now. 'Where's Gran?' she asked again urgently.

'I already said, *I don't know.* I haven't seen her today.'

'You haven't seen her at all? And you've not been worried?'

'Of course I have! But I didn't know what to do, did I? When I woke up, you were passed out and Gran wasn't around – I knocked on her bedroom door, but there was no answer. And, well . . . I didn't think I could go *in* there. What if she wasn't, you know, dressed or something. And we both know she *never* sleeps late anyway. So I was just hoping she'd gone out and would come back soon . . . that she was at the shops or a friend's or something, and she forgot to leave a note. I thought about calling Dad but . . . You don't think anything's happened to her, do you?'

Apollo stopped babbling and made a strangled sound.

Orla didn't reply. She was remembering everything Gran had said about the Wild Hunt, and King Oberon's words about Gran being vulnerable. Gran had said she'd already caught their attention . . .

What if they'd got her, like the other missing people?

Orla couldn't keep all of this to herself any longer. She needed to share it with Apollo. No matter how bonkers it sounded.

'Listen, this is going to sound crazy . . . but last night I followed Gran into the Tangled Woods.'

'What? When?'

'When you were asleep. Just listen, will you? I found her with these . . . people. Only they weren't really people.' She hesitated. 'They were f-fairies.'

'*Fairies?*'

'I know you think I'm winding you up, but I'm not, I swear. They *really* were fairies, and King Oberon was there – I saw him! He was sitting right next to Gran. He had an antler crown and everything! And there were hundreds of those blue butterflies and the fairies – they were just like in Gran's stories . . . with wings and everything. Gran wanted the fairies to help because of the Wild Hunt. Because they've been taking people.'

Apollo was staring at her like she'd gone completely mad.

Orla went to the cupboard where the yellow folder was hidden and pulled it out. She shook the newspaper stories on to the kitchen table and spread them out between Apollo's mess.

'See! That's why she was collecting these.'

Apollo gazed at the clippings, looking bewildered. It was only now that Orla really registered the fact that as many as fourteen people had gone missing in a matter of months.

She shivered as she thought of how reckless both she and Gran had been, going out by themselves last night when the Wild Hunt was at large. She understood now why Gran had been so funny about them going out alone after dark, even in the garden. Her stomach twisted. But what had happened to Gran? She must have made it home. The boots and the torch proved that . . .

'So Gran thinks the Wild Hunt took all these people?' Apollo said slowly, pulling her from her thoughts. Thankfully he was starting to sound as if he believed her.

'Yes! That's why she's installed locks everywhere. It's probably why she tried to put us off coming in the first place,' Orla added, realizing this. Then she realized something else awful.

Locks . . .

Gran's window.

Last night, Orla had unlocked it to climb out. Gran wouldn't have known the window had been unlocked by anyone when she came in later to sleep . . .

What if Gran *had* got home but then—

Orla's heart pounded.

She raced out of the kitchen and down the hall.

'Orla, where are you going?' Apollo shouted after her, but she did not slow down.

As soon as she pushed open Gran's bedroom door and stepped inside, cold air blasted her. She took in the room's disarray in dismay. Gran's pillows were scattered across the floor. Some were torn and white feathers had spilt everywhere. The curtains had been slashed and hung limply off the rail.

But the worst thing of all was that the window gaped open.

And beneath it was a single long, black feather.

Orla felt like the breath had been crushed out of her lungs.

'What the—' Apollo gasped as he came in behind her. 'What happened?'

Orla couldn't respond. All she could do was point at the feather.

Apollo let out a cry. 'The Wild Hunt!'

Her knees felt like they were going to give way. She reached out for the wall to steady herself. They couldn't have lost Gran. Not after Mum . . . Not after the awful way Orla had spoken to her last night.

Guilt and grief washed over her, and she felt she might throw up. She cast her eyes around the room for something – *anything* – that might help them.

But there was only the hideous feather.

Then Orla's gaze caught the glint of something shiny. Gran's keys were splayed on the floor next to the smashed bedside lamp. Orla went over and scooped them up with trembling hands.

One key was labelled: *SHED*.

CHAPTER 12
The Secret in the Shed

Orla hurried across the garden with Apollo traipsing behind.

'Do you think we should, Orla? We promised.'

Orla halted beside the shed door. 'Apollo, this is serious. If Gran has been taken by the Wild Hunt, whatever is in that shed might be a clue that can help us get her back! We have to know.'

'It's just . . . a lot to take in.'

Orla knew what he meant.

'*Shh.* Listen!' Apollo grabbed her arm.

From inside the shed, a voice growled, '*I can hear you there. Let me out!*'

Apollo turned pale. 'Someone's—'

'I *told* you I heard a voice . . . Hey, where are you going?'

Apollo was racing over to Gran's woodblock. He heaved up the ancient axe that no one had been allowed to touch for years, especially not Apollo. He could barely support its weight and wobbled all over the place as he took a few shaky steps towards the shed. Despite all the frightening things Orla had seen in the last twenty-four hours, this was by far the most alarming. Her brother with a butter knife was concerning enough.

'Apollo, put that axe down!'

'Move out of the way, Orla! I'm going to bust it open.'

'You're going to bust *yourself* open. Put it down *now*!'

Apollo didn't listen. Instead he swung the axe haphazardly in the direction of the lock and missed completely. The axe sliced through the empty air, luckily avoiding Orla, but the weight of it made Apollo topple forwards.

'Argh!' he groaned as the axe slammed into the lawn and made a nasty gouge.

Orla sighed, held up the keys and jangled them.

Apollo flushed. 'Well, you could have said,' he huffed.

Orla slid the key marked 'SHED' into the padlock. The key turned easily and the heavy padlock clicked open and hung off the latch. Orla removed it and put it in her pocket. Nervously, she pulled open the shed door and peered into the gloom.

For a moment, everything was very still and quiet. *Too* quiet.

'Can you see anything?' Apollo hissed nervously.

Orla squinted. 'There's a shadow by that garden chair . . . in the far left corner.'

Suddenly there was a loud clang. Something lunged out of the darkness at them, snarling ferociously.

They both screamed and jumped backwards. Orla caught a glimpse of shaggy fur, sharp teeth, claws and a pair of orange eyes that were oddly familiar . . .

She slammed the shed door shut and they collapsed against it, panting hard, as the creature hammered the other side.

'That's a pooka!' Apollo gasped in astonishment. 'I'm sure it is! Remember them from Gran's stories?'

Orla felt dazed. She remembered Gran telling tales of pookas, but she couldn't remember much about them. 'Are you sure?'

'Positive. You could tell by its ears. They were big like a rabbit's.'

Orla hadn't had time to notice its ears, she'd been too focused on the teeth and claws. 'Are pookas good or evil? I mean, bad or evil?' she corrected herself, for no magical creatures from Gran's stories could ever be described as 'good'; even the 'Good Folk' were cruel at times.

'Think they can be both, so far as I remember. But you definitely can't trust them. Especially not one that's been locked in a shed for days.'

'That's reassuring,' Orla muttered through gritted teeth.

Apollo frowned. 'There was something specific about pookas. Something important . . . Argh, I wish I could remember what it was . . .'

'*I said, let me out.*'

Apollo's eyes were wide as saucers. Orla was sure her own must be just as big. The growling continued, as did a clanking sound.

'Do you think it's chained up in there?' Orla hissed.

'Sounds like it.'

Once more, Orla was flummoxed. Chaining up the terrifying pooka seemed entirely at odds with the sweet grandmother they both knew.

Gran.

Orla's throat tightened as she thought of Gran with the monstrous Wild Hunt. *What would they be doing to her?* They were wasting time with this pooka. Whatever it was doing here, this was not the monster that had taken Gran.

Unless . . . what if it knew something?

'Reckon the chains are secure?'

'How am I meant to know?' Apollo replied, shoving the door as the thing pushed the other side so hard that it gave a little.

Orla took a deep breath. 'I want to open the door again and speak to it.'

'Have you lost your mind? Didn't you see its claws?'

'We've got to ask it if it knows anything about where Gran's gone. It's got to know more than we do about where the Wild Hunt take people and how to get her back.'

Apollo looked a bit sick but he nodded. 'All right. It does sound like it's chained up – though it can clearly reach the door. But providing we stand far back, we should be OK, right?'

'Right.'

Neither of them moved. They exchanged nervous looks.

'Let me just grab the axe again, in case. Can you hold the door on your own for a moment?'

The thing thrashed harder as Apollo moved away. Orla sunk her heels into the grass and gritted her teeth. 'Hurry, Apollo!'

'All right. Count of three. One – two – three! Ahhhh!'

Orla leapt away from the door as a hollering Apollo came careering towards her, the blade of the axe flashing. The door slammed back on its hinges. Apollo raced forwards and promptly tripped over Orla as she tried unsuccessfully to get out of the way in time. He lost his balance. The axe crashed uselessly to the ground again, this time only narrowly avoiding Apollo's toes.

They looked up fearfully at the shed's doorway where a terrifying creature now loomed, a creature unlike any Orla had ever seen before.

At least, not in real life.

CHAPTER 13
The Pooka

The pooka was restrained by chains attached to cuffs around its back legs and looped through a ring on the shed wall. As the grey daylight hit its black fur, it hissed and cowered backwards into the shadows, but enough of it was illuminated for Orla and Apollo to get a good impression.

It had huge ears like a rabbit's, a monkeyish face, those orb-like orange eyes and a mouth full of sharp teeth that it was now baring ghoulishly at them.

Orla and Apollo scrambled to their feet.

'Wow!' Apollo breathed.

'Wish I could say the same,' the pooka sneered.

Orla blenched. Even though she'd heard its voice several times now, actually *seeing* the pooka speak was another matter.

'Apollo, get back!' she called, as with a clang of metal the pooka lunged for Apollo.

Apollo shrieked and jumped back. Thankfully, the

pooka's chains wouldn't allow it to reach more than a few inches beyond the doorway.

It groaned and slumped down on to the shed floor, sitting cross-legged. 'There goes my plan to use the blue-haired boy as a bargaining chip.'

Apollo stared at the pooka. 'Look at the way it's sitting. It's so . . . weird.'

'*Charming*. You're rather weird yourself,' the pooka replied.

Apollo shook his head in wonder. 'Is this really happening?'

'Unfortunately for all of us, it is,' said the pooka.

Orla searched for the right question to pull out of the hundreds running through her head. 'Why are you in our gran's shed?'

'Oh, so you're the grandchildren, are you?' The pooka looked them up and down unkindly. 'I'm a guest of hers. A friend.'

A friend? Surely not. Gran being friends with the fairies was one thing. She'd told them stories of being taken by King Oberon in the Tangled Woods when she was little and how she'd gone back to visit the Good Folk often ever since, but Gran had never mentioned being friends with a pooka. Looking at this rude, monstrous creature, Orla found the notion extremely hard to believe. 'If you're her friend then why did she lock you up?' she asked.

'All right, perhaps "friend" is a bit of a stretch. Acquaintance, maybe. Adversary might be more accurate . . . Details.' The pooka rolled its eyes.

Adversary? First the Wild Hunt, now the pooka – how many enemies did Gran have?

Very seriously, Apollo said, 'Did you *eat* our gran?'

Orla shot him a look. They already knew the Wild Hunt had taken Gran.

The pooka's eyes sparkled malevolently. 'Yes, I did. Yummy, yummy. KFG. Kentucky Fried Granny. She was delicious, tasted like old slippers and wellington boots.'

Apollo looked horrified. He took a step towards the axe.

The pooka didn't seem to realize how empty this threat was. 'I'm joking!' it said hurriedly. '*Jeez*. Where is she anyway? She's had me locked in here for a day and a half, and today she didn't bring breakfast or lunch or *anything*. Not even an afternoon snack. I'm so famished even a chewy old granny is starting to sound appetizing. Or perhaps a gangly little boy.' The pooka licked its lips.

For a second, Apollo looked even more afraid but then he shook his head. 'Gran said pookas don't eat mortals.'

'They might do if they've been locked in a shed

starving for days,' the pooka huffed, clearly annoyed it hadn't managed to scare Apollo. 'All in all, it's been terrible hospitality. I'm leaving a crummy review. Not even one star . . . But you didn't answer my question. Surely she didn't *let* you open her shed to see me, so where is she? Haven't misplaced her, have you?' It looked at Orla.

Orla's cheeks burnt and gave her away.

'You *have*. Naughty, naughty. You shouldn't go losing grandmas, it's bad luck.'

'We didn't lose her,' said Apollo indignantly. 'The Wild Hunt took her!'

'Apollo!' Orla groaned. If this pooka was an adversary of Gran's, they didn't want to be telling it *anything*. She didn't like the way its ears pricked up and it suddenly looked a great deal less bored.

'The Wild Hunt got her? Are you sure?'

'We found a black feather in her room.'

'Apollo, stop talking!'

'Well, well. I thought she was too smart to get caught.'

Orla was sure guilt was written all over her face. Gran *was* too smart to get caught. But stupid Orla had messed everything up.

'Do you know how we can get her back?' asked Apollo.

'As if it's going to help us, Apollo!'

'I don't. But I *can* take you to someone who will. Just help me out of these chains . . .'

'Fat chance!' scoffed Orla. 'You're lying!'

'I'm not,' said the pooka, holding its front paws up in an innocent gesture, but its claws were sharp.

Orla shook her head. 'We're not going to release you whatever you say, so don't waste your breath. We're not *idiots*.'

'You could have fooled me . . .' the pooka muttered. 'But you're being idiots if you don't. I really *can* take you to someone who will know how to get your gran back. It's your only chance of saving her.'

'Yeah, yeah. Sure you can. Come on, Apollo, let's lock the shed up again.'

'Wait!' For the first time, the pooka looked panicked. 'You can't just leave me in here to rot!'

'Watch us,' Orla spat, reaching for the door.

'Orla,' Apollo murmured. 'It's right. We can't just lock it in here . . .'

'Quiet, Apollo.'

'I'm telling the truth. The giant is the only one who will know how to get her back.'

Orla stopped dead.

'Did you just say *giant*?' Apollo exclaimed.

'His name's Fionn . . . Don't suppose you've heard of him?'

93

Apollo gasped. 'Fionn – the giant who knows everything?'

The pooka smiled, revealing all its teeth. 'Bingo. Good to know you've heard of him at least. I was beginning to think that sweet old granny of yours had told you nothing. Yes, Fionn knows everything. Doesn't mean that he'll *tell* you everything, mind, but he's your only hope. On your own, you've got no chance. All you've got to do is unlock my chains. I can see you've got the key there on that ring . . . I can't go out in the daylight – sensitive fur – but as soon as night falls I'll take you to him.'

Orla wavered, clutching Gran's keys tightly. She'd been intent on not believing a word this creature said but now its offer was hard to ignore. It was right that they had no chance of rescuing Gran from the Wild Hunt on their own. If Gran's stories about the giant were true, then Fionn probably was their best hope of getting useful information. But even if the giant existed, it didn't mean the pooka was really going to take them to him. It was fairies that couldn't lie, not pookas.

'How can we trust you?' she asked dubiously.

The pooka's smirk stretched. Orla did not like how pleased it seemed by her response. Why did it feel like the pooka had the upper hand, despite it being the one in chains?

'You can't,' it said, still grinning.

Great. That was helpful. Orla needed to think this through. 'Well, seeing as you can't leave until nightfall anyway, we'll take some time to consider your offer.' She slammed the shed door in the creature's face, quickly reattached the padlock and locked it. Her hands were shaking.

'We should do what it says, Orla,' whispered Apollo urgently. 'If anyone can tell us how we can save Gran, it's the giant.'

Orla shook her head. Only a day ago she'd not believed in giants, pookas, fairies or the Wild Hunt. 'These things shouldn't exist.'

'Oh, charming.' The pooka's voice came from inside the shed, making them jump. 'I'm just a figment of your imagination, is that it? Well, I'm a figment that has not been allowed out to use the jacks in twenty-four hours. Mull on that, will you!'

'Yuck,' said Apollo.

Orla thought of Gran, trapped by the Wild Hunt. They'd be feasting on her sadness, draining her of all hope until she lost her mind, then her heart, then turned into one of the monsters herself. If they didn't save her soon, they'd lose her for ever. Like they'd lost Mum.

After three nights of being the Wild Hunt's captives, mortal

95

victims lose their minds, according to Gran's book.

Orla shivered and wished the Wild Hunt was still only a story.

She looked at her brother's earnest expression. He trusted her to decide what to do next. Her stomach twisted. She knew she should tell him that she'd left Gran's window unlocked. But she couldn't face the look in his eyes when he found out this was all her fault. Not yet.

She ushered him back inside the house and out of the pooka's earshot. 'I still don't think we can trust it,' she said.

'Me neither,' Apollo agreed. 'But we don't have any other options. It's not like we can call the police. They've not found any of those other missing people so they won't find Gran. This is magical stuff and we need magical help.'

Orla thought about the fairies last night. They were the only ones the Wild Hunt feared, which was why Gran had sought their help. They'd said they didn't get involved in the Wild Hunt's affairs any more. Still, if they went to them and told them Gran had been taken, would they break their peace treaty to save their friend? Gran always said there was an entrance to the Fairy Kingdom in every wood in Ireland. You just had to find the fairy ring of stones. Supposing they could . . .

No, that wasn't an option. Orla remembered how hostile the fairies had been last night. Orla and Apollo were strangers to them and would surely be killed before they could say or do anything to help Gran. They had to find another way and, if anyone would know it, it would be Fionn.

Still . . . the thought of unchaining the pooka was alarming. It might not eat mortals but it could certainly do them harm.

But no one was going to come ringing on the door to help.

At that exact moment, the doorbell rang.

Apollo and Orla stared at each other.

'*Gran?*' Orla gasped hopefully, though she knew it was extremely unlikely.

She raced ahead of Apollo to the front door.

Of course, it wasn't Gran.

It was a boy.

CHAPTER 14
The Boy on the Doorstep

The boy looked about Orla's age. His dark hair was longish and flicked back, and he was dressed in a plain white T-shirt and jeans. His eyes were a piercing blue – the colour of the sea in sunshine – almost too vivid for the cold Irish day, especially now it had started to drizzle.

For a moment, the boy regarded them incredulously, as if they had knocked on *his* door, not the other way around.

'Er – hello?' Orla said. Who on earth was this?

'Hi!' the boy replied warmly. He did not seem to have noticed her frosty tone and gave her an easy smile as if they'd been friends for years. He reminded Orla of the arrogant boys at school whose lives had been filled with skiing holidays in the Alps, tennis clubs and expensive birthday presents. Boys for whom nothing had ever gone wrong.

She scowled and deliberately laced her voice with

more hostility. 'Who are you? What do you want?'

'*Orla!*' hissed Apollo. 'Sorry, she means how can we help you?'

'That's *not* what I mean.' Whoever this boy was, they didn't have time for distractions. They had to work out what to do about the pooka and finding Gran.

'I'm sorry to bother you,' said the boy in a soft Irish lilt, still smiling widely and not looking sorry in the slightest. 'We've never met, at least not officially, but I've been a friend of your gran's for a long time. I'm here to see her.'

More alleged acquaintances of Gran's they'd never heard of! At least this one didn't have wings or claws, so far as Orla could tell. 'Well, she's not here.'

The boy's face fell. 'Oh no, but I need her help urgently.'

'Well, you'll just have to come back another day.' She tried to close the door but Apollo stopped her.

'Sorry for my sister,' he said. 'We've had a bit of a strange day. Maybe we can help you instead? Would you like to come in out of the wet for a moment? I'm Apollo, by the way.'

Orla glared at her brother. 'What are you doing?' she hissed. It was typical of Apollo to offer to assist a total stranger when they had problems of their own to figure out. *Just small things, like a dangerous talking creature chained up in Gran's shed. Oh, and Gran's kidnapping by the most evil creatures in folklore.* He should know better than to invite someone they didn't know in! Even if the boy was only about their age . . .

'Just hang on one second,' Apollo said apologetically, before half-closing the door so he could whisper to Orla behind it. 'Look, the pooka can't take us to the giant until nightfall. We might as well be nice to Gran's friend. She'd want us to help him if we can. And who knows, he might even be able to help us.'

'*How* exactly?'

Apollo ignored her death stares, pulled the door open and ushered the boy into the hallway. 'Sorry about all that. Please come in. Any friend of Gran is a friend of ours.'

The boy smiled brightly again, as if a door hadn't just almost been shut in his face. Orla didn't like the keen way his eyes darted around Gran's house either.

'So this is what it's like inside,' he said, still beaming. 'It's so . . . profoundly dull and ordinary!'

Orla made a face. Who did this boy think he was? 'You're a friend of Gran's, yet you've never been inside her house?'

'We always met elsewhere,' said the boy, flicking his hair in a way that Orla immediately found immensely irritating. Again, if he'd sensed her venomous tone, he didn't show any sign of it. He stared at the photograph of Mum.

Orla moved in front of it defensively.

'What's your name?' asked Apollo.

'Conor.'

'Nice to meet you, Conor. Orla has an Irish name too. And I—'

'*You're* named after a god, I heard. I like your blue hair.'

'Oh, thanks.' Apollo grinned sheepishly. 'Your hair is cool too.'

Orla groaned. Why did Apollo have to suck up to everyone?

'How come we've never met you before, Conor?' she asked. 'It seems a bit strange that Gran never introduced us.'

'You've not been back to Ireland for a while, have you?' said Conor. 'Where is she anyway?'

'She's out,' Orla replied before Apollo could say anything. The last thing they needed was Conor finding out what was really going on and alerting his parents to the fact that Gran was missing and they were staying in her house unsupervised. What if the local authorities called Dad to come and get them before they had the chance to even try to save Gran?

'Well, when will she be back?'

'She's very busy at the moment. You should try next week,' Orla said, attempting to usher him to the door.

'Next week?' Conor exclaimed. 'But I have to talk to her now.'

'Well, you can't,' Orla said flatly. 'So you might as well be on your way.'

Out of the corner of her eye, Orla noticed Apollo's mouth open. She shook her head at him furiously but it was no good.

'Gran's missing!' he blurted.

'Apollo!'

'Missing?' Conor gasped, his face crumpling.

Apollo seemed bolstered by Conor's reaction. 'This is going to sound crazy . . .'

'Apollo, don't you dare! She's at the shops, that's all—'

'She's not at the shops, she's been taken by the Wild Hunt!'

Orla stared at Conor in panic and forced a hollow laugh. 'As you can tell, my brother's a real joker. The Wild Hunt are just a dumb story he's—'

'I know what the Wild Hunt are.' Conor's expression was grave.

Orla was taken aback.

'See, I *told* you he might be able to help, Orla!

You're from around here, right, Conor?'

Conor nodded.

'So you know the stories? About fairies, giants and pookas?'

A new expression flitted across Conor's face, but the next moment it was gone. 'I do,' he said slowly. 'I also know that they're not *just* stories.'

If Orla had heard someone say this yesterday she would have scoffed. But today, Conor's words sent a chill down her spine.

'You're right! They *are* real and we have proof!' Apollo was full of excitement now.

'Apollo, that's enough!' Even if Conor did believe in the folk tales, so what? It didn't mean he could help them.

Apollo, of course, ignored her. 'There's a pooka in Gran's shed!'

'He's pretending,' Orla said quickly. 'It's another joke. Honestly, he's such a—'

Conor blinked. 'A pooka? In a shed? How'd it get there?'

'Gran trapped it and chained it up, but we don't know why.'

'Show me,' said Conor. Orla did not like the way he commanded instead of asked, as if he'd rarely heard the word *no* before. Well, he'd hear it from her.

'No. We only just locked it back up,' she said, trying to assert some control over the situation and realizing too late that, in doing so, she'd accidentally admitted that the pooka existed.

But Apollo grabbed Conor's arm and pulled him through into the kitchen. Orla had no choice but to follow, still protesting loudly.

Apollo pointed through the kitchen window at the padlocked shed. 'It's in there. Give us the keys, Orla.'

'No,' said Orla, clutching them tightly. How could she get Conor to leave?

'Did it say anything to you?' asked Conor.

Apollo nodded. 'Lots. It was quite rude actually.'

'Did it say anything about the Wild Hunt?'

'It said it could take us to someone who could tell us how to get Gran back from them.'

'Who?'

'Fionn the giant.'

'Ah,' said Conor, nodding as if this made sense. 'If anyone can find the giant it's a pooka. Fionn keeps himself well hidden – even the fairies can't find him. Pookas have a good sense of smell, though . . . Mind you, I don't think the giant likes visitors much.' He shook his head. 'I still don't understand how the Wild Hunt got your gran. She's always so careful.'

Orla gave him a funny look. How would he know

that? She felt betrayed. Had Gran shared more about her life with this stranger than she had her own grandchildren?

Apollo nodded. 'She had locks but they still managed to get in through her bedroom window.'

'And the pooka was chained up in the shed last night?'

'Seems like it, why?'

'I just wondered if it had anything to do with her capture.'

Orla stared at the ground, her cheeks burning. She was sure she was being obvious and knew she ought to tell Apollo the truth about opening Gran's window, but she definitely wasn't going to say anything in front of Conor. 'The pooka was padlocked in,' she said firmly.

'Right. Well then, you should let it take you to the giant.'

'Yes,' said Orla, again finding Conor's bossy tone irritating. 'That's what we decided earlier, but it's not that simple. It *says* it will take us to the giant but for all we know it could take us somewhere else entirely.'

'Quite right. You should never trust a pooka's word,' Conor agreed. 'Only its promises.'

Apollo smacked his forehead. 'That was it! That was what I'd forgotten! *A pooka has to fulfil any promise it makes or else it'll die.* We can use that to make sure it does what it says. Brilliant, Conor!'

Orla frowned. Now Apollo mentioned it, she did vaguely remember this from Gran's stories. But if they were going to be relying on it, she'd like to be sure. 'How exactly does that work?'

'Well, all magical beings live by an honour code, which means they have to keep their word. Pookas, however, are notoriously dishonourable and tricksy. Many of them never used to keep their word, which was why a witch cursed all pooka to keep any promise they make or die.'

Orla stared at him. 'How—' she started to ask.

'Well, blood comes out of their eyes and their throats—'

'I mean, how do you know that?' she interrupted.

Conor shrugged and flicked his hair back in that irritating way of his. 'Everyone I know knows that.'

'See? I told you having a local around would be useful,' Apollo hissed.

Orla sighed. She'd have liked more proof than just Conor's word, but it was worth a shot. She examined Gran's bunch of keys and found a small one, which was likely to unlock the pooka's chains. 'All right, so we'll set the pooka free like it wants,' she said slowly, 'but *only* if it *promises* to help us find Gran?'

'Sounds like a plan!' said Conor, grinning.

Orla didn't share his enthusiasm. It wasn't a *good* plan, by any means, but it was the only one they had.

CHAPTER 15
Making Promises

'Finally!' the pooka exclaimed as the shed door swung open and he squinted into the daylight. 'I hope you've at least brought me something to eat. The welcome here has been *most* unsatisfactory.'

'You're a hostage!' Orla pointed out.

'*Details.* Jeez, how many of you are there?' it added, catching sight of Conor and wrinkling its nose in disgust. 'I didn't think it was possible but this one smells even worse than you two. Yuck!'

Conor took a step backwards. For a moment Orla thought he was scared, but when she looked over her shoulder at him, he gave a nauseatingly bright smile showing off his pearly white teeth. He seemed as relaxed in front of the pooka as he had been when he'd stood on their doorstep and not at all as shocked as they had been to see it talking.

'He's no one,' Orla replied.

'Charming,' said the pooka, grinning ghoulishly.

'I see your good manners extend to all your guests, or is this another sibling?'

'Conor's a friend of Gran's, so he's also a friend of ours,' said Apollo firmly. 'But you're right, we should at least give you some food. I'm sorry, I can't believe we didn't think to before.'

'Maybe because it was threatening to claw out our eyeballs?' Orla suggested.

But to her annoyance, Apollo was already making a beeline back into the house. There was a metallic clang of tins. He returned with an open packet of chocolate biscuits, which he offered to the pooka.

The pooka snatched the packet, tipped its head backwards and poured all the biscuits down its throat, swallowing them in one gulp. 'Delicious. I'll take another.'

'That was the last packet,' said Apollo, regarding the empty wrapper mournfully. 'You're meant to eat them one at a time.'

'Shame.' The pooka tossed the wrapper to one side with a sigh. 'Well go on, then. Out with it. I don't imagine you've come here just to give me biscuits. The fact you're still hanging around like bad smells means you've come for a reason. Honestly, by the way, have none of you ever heard of deodorant? The pong coming off you is otherworldly.'

'I had a bath yesterday,' Apollo said, sniffing his armpits.

'Ignore it, Apollo,' Orla muttered. 'It's trying to get under our skin.'

'Believe me, I've no interest in getting anywhere *near* your skins, except maybe to use them as rugs for my current living quarters, which could do with a little sprucing up.' The pooka leered, baring its sharp teeth again.

Orla tried to hide the shiver that ran down her spine. Whatever Apollo had said about pookas not eating mortals, she wasn't keen to test it.

'On second thoughts, you can keep your skins. They look a little thin and furless for my taste. How do they possibly keep you warm? No wonder you have to wear those ridiculous rags . . . Look, as nice as my stay here has been, by which I mean it hasn't been remotely nice at all, I think it's high time you let me go. This is by far the worst sleeping arrangement I've ever been subjected to, and I've slept in a bog! Multiple times! Have you ever tried using a spade as a pillow? I wouldn't recommend it. Let's level with one another, you don't want me in your shed as much as I don't want to be in it. It's mutually beneficial for all of us to go our separate ways. So come on, unlock my chains and I'll get out of your hair.' The pooka eyed the bunch of keys in Orla's hands hungrily before descending into a mock bow.

'Should we try what we discussed?' Apollo asked nervously.

The pooka snapped upright immediately. 'What did you discuss?'

Orla nodded. 'It's worth a shot.'

The pooka's voice rose. '*What did you discuss?*'

Orla jangled the keys and the pooka hushed.

'Yes, that's it,' it cooed. 'Look, I'll even turn away. See how cooperative I'm being?'

'We want you to promise us something,' said Orla loudly.

It was like all the air suddenly went out of the pooka's body. It let out a howl and slumped back down into that cross-legged position that looked so unnatural for an animal. 'So you're not *quite* as stupid as you look. The blue hair could have fooled me. And those ridiculous noses of yours. They're so small! Maybe it's so you can't smell your own stench. I don't see how you could bear it otherwise.'

'You're one to talk,' said Orla, sniffing pointedly. 'This shed smells worse than the bathroom after Apollo's used it.'

'Hey!' Apollo blushed.

'Well missy, as I mentioned earlier there are no

toilet facilities in here and a pooka's got to do what a pooka's got to do. Anyway, how did you find out about the promises? There I was thinking your darling granny had failed to tell you anything important.'

'So it is true!' Orla exclaimed.

The pooka glared at her. 'No. What promises? Who mentioned promises? Not me! I don't even know how promises—'

'You just said—'

'Oh, *fine*. Let's hear it! What do you want? A pony? I can get you a pony! Though hair appointments might be a better idea, for that one especially . . . Or some lessons in hospitality.'

'You said you could take us to a giant who could tell us where Gran is,' said Orla.

'I did, *yes*. Thank you *so* much for telling me exactly what I already told you. *So* useful.' The pooka shook its head. 'I take back what I said just now – you definitely are as stupid as you look.'

'So we'll set you free . . .' Orla continued, ignoring its insults.

'Perfect!' The pooka clapped its hands together. 'Well, get on with it then. And I will promise to take you to Fionn.'

But Orla shook her head. 'No,' she said. She glanced back and saw Conor's eyebrows rise.

Next to her, Apollo hissed, 'Orla, what are you doing? I thought we agreed—'

'We will set you free *if* you promise that you'll help us with anything we ask *until* we find Gran,' Orla said loudly.

Apollo understood what she'd done and shot her an approving look. 'Good wording,' he whispered.

She almost smiled.

'Hang on a minute,' spluttered the pooka. 'That wasn't the deal. I said I'd take you to someone who could tell you where she was and how *you* could get her back yourselves, not that I'd help you with whatever idiotic requests you have until you find her! That's a very different contract, much more long-term.'

'That's the deal,' said Orla. 'Or else get used to your spade pillow.'

The pooka glowered. 'Fine,' it growled. 'But on certain terms. You know how it works, right? After three nights the Wild Hunt's mortal victims lose their minds, then their hearts wither, and after three months they transform into Wild Hunt themselves. After your dear granny has lost her mind, there will be no point in you saving her: she will be gone. You could still spend months trying to save her, with me stuck with you, only to bring home an empty shell. It would be pointless. So I propose this: in exchange for my release, I will help you with anything you ask until you find your gran *or* she loses her mind, whichever comes first. Do we have ourselves a deal?'

Orla hesitated, probing the pooka's words for some trick. But reluctantly she saw its reasoning. 'OK, it's a deal.'

'Good. Now unlock my—'

'I didn't hear the magic "p" word.'

It looked her directly in the eye, its gaze full of loathing.

Orla resisted the urge to blink or look away.

'I *promise*. But you have to unlock me right now and I want you to remember that you asked for this. This is by far one of the worst promises I've ever made and I once promised I would marry a leprechaun. *That* did not end well for him and neither will this for you. Mark my words, you'll regret this. But on your nostrils be it.'

CHAPTER 16
A Giant Hunt

Orla had to summon all her nerve to unlock the pooka's chains. She hastily stepped away, half expecting the pooka to bolt, but it remained where it was.

'Don't look so surprised,' it huffed, grooming its fur. 'I already told you I can't leave until nightfall. Anyway, I've promised to help you now, haven't I? We'll head into the Tangled Woods as soon as it gets dark. Bring more chocolate biscuits.'

Orla followed Apollo and Conor back into the kitchen, where Conor immediately draped himself over Gran's usual chair, making himself extremely comfortable. Orla bristled with annoyance.

'Would you like a cup of tea, Conor?' Apollo offered. 'Least we can do after how much you helped us.'

Conor's eyes lit up. 'Oh, tea! Yes, that would be lovely.'

'He didn't help *that* much,' Orla pointed out. 'We would have remembered the promise thing on our own eventually.'

Apollo shot her a reproachful look as he put the kettle on. He opened the top cupboard and managed to find a packet of gingernuts.

Orla did not join the boys at the table, where they sat together hugging their warm cups and crunching on the biscuits. Conor stared around the room at everything and made over-the-top noises of approval as he ate and drank, as if he'd never had tea and biscuits before. Apollo explained the newspaper clippings while Orla lurked alone by the cooker and ate four gingernuts in a row.

It felt awful to be sitting there eating biscuits while Gran was going through who-knew-what terrors.

'Are you going to come with us tonight?' Apollo asked Conor.

'Of course he's not!' Orla said quickly.

'Stop being so unfriendly, Orla. Conor knows more about this stuff than us. *And* he's a local, so he'll know the area well. It'll be useful to have him along,' said Apollo.

Orla didn't want Conor coming along. He made her feel uncomfortable, the way he stared all the time. She just wanted to focus on finding Gran. 'I'm sure Conor has better things to do.'

'Oh no, I've got nothing better to do, I'd love to come,' Conor replied, flicking his hair back and checking his reflection in the door of the microwave.

Orla ground her teeth. 'Not the coolest thing to admit . . .'

'We'd be very grateful for your help,' Apollo insisted. 'We need as much as we can get.' He looked down at his mug and bit his lip. It was the red one that said *World's Best Granny* on it; they'd given it to Gran for Christmas four years ago. 'I hope we get her back. I don't know what we'll do if—' He swallowed. Orla knew how he felt and her heart ached.

'We will get her back,' Conor said, patting Apollo's shoulder.

Apollo smiled at him. Alone by the cooker, Orla glowered.

She jumped when the phone rang.

Apollo raced over and picked it up. 'Dad!' he burst out. 'Hello? Can you hear us?' He put it on speakerphone. Orla immediately wished he hadn't. She didn't want Conor listening. Why didn't he politely leave the room? Any normal person would.

There was a lot of noise in the background. 'Hello?' Dad's voice sounded muffled and faraway. 'Apollo? How are you?'

'We're fine, it's just—'

'Sorry, the reception is awful. I'm just at the beach—'

'*Mal!*' They heard Penelope scream in the background.

Dad started laughing. 'You'll never guess what just happened! A wave got the remains of our picnic— My flip-flops! Can you grab them, Charles?'

Orla grimaced. She felt Conor's eyes on her and deliberately turned away.

'Dad, listen,' said Apollo. 'Gran's gone missing.'

'Your gran's gone fishing? What?! Sorry, the connection's terrible . . . Oh, great work, Charles! William, get those towels!'

'*Dad!* We can't find Gran, we think that she—'

'You can't find the ham? You're not making any sense . . .' The line crackled and Dad started gasping.

'Dad?' Apollo exclaimed in alarm.

It took them a moment to realize he was laughing.

'Sorry, Penelope's trying to push me in. Pen – wait!' The phone cut out.

Apollo hung up slowly.

Orla wondered what Conor made of that conversation and immediately felt more annoyed. It didn't matter what Conor thought.

'Well, that's that, I suppose . . .' said Apollo. He looked down at the newspaper clippings on the kitchen table and, after a pause, said, 'Do you think it will be safe for us to go out to the woods tonight if the Wild Hunt are around?'

Orla knew it was definitely *unsafe*. 'We'll just have to try not to be sad. The Wild Hunt are drawn to sadness. We'll have to stick together too, you're more likely to end up as their victim if you're alone. We won't be alone, though, we'll have each other,' she added offhandedly, meaning it as a statement of fact more than anything, but Apollo got up and gave her a hug. Orla was so surprised that for a moment she stood stiffly before remembering to hug him back.

'That's true,' Conor agreed. 'The Wild Hunt don't usually attack mortals in groups. Besides, the woods are fairy territory.'

Maybe Conor did know his stuff.

'Why don't you go home and grab some supplies, Conor?' Apollo suggested, checking his phone. 'We'll probably all need torches and warm layers. It says that the sun goes down around ten, so meet back here a bit before then?'

'Right, yes. I'll . . . go home and come back then.'

Was it Orla's imagination or did Conor seem disappointed to be leaving?

'You won't tell anyone, will you?' Orla said urgently.

'I pooka-promise,' said Conor, giving her another

irritatingly dazzling smile.

Apollo saw Conor to the front door. Then, without a word, he and Orla went to the Den. Neither of them said it out loud, but the room made them feel closer to Gran. They slumped in the tattered armchairs and Apollo started reading the *Irish Folktales, Myths and Legends* book. Orla went to find some warm jumpers and torches from the cupboard. She also investigated Gran's biscuit tins for provisions and found a fresh tray of home-made tiffin in one, which both lifted her spirits and made her heart ache.

When she returned to the kitchen, she found Apollo had made sandwiches, which he was packing in his own backpack. He held up a penknife that he must have found in one of Gran's drawers.

'What's that for?' she asked.

'Protection.'

'It's better than you trying to pack the axe, I suppose.' Orla feigned nonchalance but her heart was beating fast. Would they need protection? And if they did, would a penknife really be enough?

As dusk fell, Conor reappeared wearing a green jacket and carrying a heavy-looking paper bag. Inside, to their delight, were warm parcels of fish and chips.

'I saw people queuing. Figured they must be good,' he said.

Apollo laughed. Conor looked at him curiously, as if he didn't get the joke, and when Apollo tried to offer him a tenner, he shook his head and wouldn't take it.

Apollo shot Orla a pointed look to say: *See! I told you he was nice.* Begrudgingly, Orla had to admit that this was generous of Conor. It was definitely good to have a proper meal before whatever happened tonight. Eagerly, they unwrapped the warm bundles. The kitchen filled with the mouth-watering aroma of fried golden batter and salty chips. The hot food restored them all a little and, as they ate, Apollo and Conor even laughed and joked with one another.

As night darkened the windows, however, their chatter died away as they started to contemplate what lay ahead. Orla began to feel more and more doubtful about visiting the giant. Would he be friendly? What if he wasn't?

Apollo got up. 'I need a wee.'

'Again?!'

'I'm nervous!' Apollo glanced from her to Conor, who was sucking a chip like it was a lolly. Orla raised her eyebrows. '*Be nice,*' Apollo hissed.

While Apollo was in the loo, Orla looked at her phone to avoid having to make conversation. When she looked back up, she nearly jumped out of her skin. The pooka was sitting cross-legged at the kitchen table, finishing off Apollo's chips.

'Not bad,' it said, smacking its lips.

Orla shot Conor a look. Why hadn't he alerted her? He was still sucking his chips, unperturbed.

'Are you ready?' the pooka asked impatiently.

Orla nodded. 'Apollo's just coming.'

It sniffed. 'You still stink. Not just regular old mortal stench either, I'm catching a faint reek of fairy dust too. One of you roll around in it or something?'

Orla thought back to the gold glitter last night. Had she been bewitched with fairy dust and did that explain why she couldn't remember how she'd got home? The gap in her memory was extremely troubling. But there were bigger mysteries to solve right now.

Giant ones, in fact.

The pooka wrinkled its nose disgustedly. 'Do me a favour and spruce yourself up with some of these.' He held out the remaining vinegar sachets.

'No way!'

'Fine,' the pooka said, slamming down the vinegar. 'But stay downwind or I might puke. Let's get this over with, shall we?'

Although Orla had fully charged her phone, she wanted to bring proper torches but had only managed to find two in Gran's cupboards. She kept hold of one and reluctantly gave the other to Conor who, despite

Apollo's instruction to bring useful supplies, had only turned up with the fish and chips.

Nervously, they set off from the house in the direction of the Tangled Woods. The pooka led the way, moving on all fours. It looked foxlike in the darkness, sticking to the shadows. Apollo, Orla and Conor hurried behind it in silence.

They reached the edge of the trees.

'Course the giant has to be in the creepy woods,' Apollo muttered. 'Couldn't be hiding in a well-lit supermarket or something? An ice cream shop, perhaps?'

As they followed the pooka down the path, Orla shone her torch up at the twisted branches, regarding them warily. The woods looked more frightening tonight than ever . . .

She thought of the black feather and swallowed hard.

Apollo appeared to be having similar thoughts. 'Conor's right, we should be safe in the woods: the Wild Hunt never dared enter fairy territory in Gran's stories.'

'What if it's different now?' Orla wondered aloud.

When wings flapped above, Orla wheeled her torch into the branches, panting hard. Conor did the same and their beams criss-crossed, sending strange shadows dancing everywhere.

'Probably just an owl,' he muttered, but even he seemed jumpy.

After that, they all moved closer together.

'You'd better really be taking us to the giant and not trying to trick us, Pooka,' Orla hissed.

'Would *I* do a thing like that to *you*? My most esteemed and generous hosts . . .'

Orla glowered. It seemed precisely what the pooka would do, despite its promise.

'Have you visited Fionn before?' Apollo asked. Underneath the obvious nervousness in his voice, there was also excitement. Apollo had always loved the stories of Fionn.

'A few times.' The pooka's voice floated out of the darkness. 'I find myself in promise agreements more often than I'd like, thanks to the wide circulation of that unfortunate bit of information you used today. The giant normally knows how I can fulfil these promises.'

'So he'll help us?' Orla pressed hopefully.

'Oh, he'll certainly *help* . . .' the pooka replied. Orla did not like its tone. Why did she have the feeling that the pooka was deliberately leading them into harm's way?

'We won't be waking him up, will we?' Apollo asked nervously. 'Only, I remember that giants sleep for weeks at a time and get very angry when they're woken up . . .'

'Oh, I wouldn't worry,' the pooka said.

Orla was not reassured.

They walked for about twenty minutes. Every now and then, the pooka would pause to sniff the air and either continue in the same direction or divert in another. They had to hold branches back for one another and kept tripping over unseen roots. It was hard to keep track of the pooka in the darkness. While it had been frightening in Gran's shed, it had also looked out of place and even a little funny, seated cross-legged between her tools and garden chairs. But there was no longer anything funny about it now.

Here, the pooka was in its element.

And they were very much not.

'You're the local, Conor, any clue where we are?' she hissed.

'I'm not sure,' he said, surprising her. She'd assumed he was incapable of admitting he didn't know something. 'I've never been this way, but it's probably a good sign,' he added. 'It means the pooka must be taking us to the giant's secret hiding spot.'

Orla looked up at the sky, searching for the moon, but all she could see was blackness. When she pointed the torch ahead again, she could no longer see any sign of the pooka's shadow.

'Where did it go?' she asked nervously.

'I don't know,' said Apollo, 'I lost sight of it.'

'It won't have run off. It promised,' said Conor. 'It can't just leave us.'

'Oh, can't it?' Orla hissed loudly. 'Where is it, then?'

'Shh!' Apollo whispered. 'Listen.'

There was a strange noise coming from the darkness up ahead – a deep rumbling, like a boulder being rolled back and forth. Frequent and *loud*.

'Pooka?' Orla hissed. 'This isn't funny . . .'

'Over here!' the pooka called mockingly.

They moved in the direction of its voice. The rumbling was getting louder . . . She cast her torch around wildly. Conor was doing the same. The beams seemed suddenly weak.

'That sound . . . I-I th-think it's snoring,' Apollo squeaked.

All of a sudden, the rumbling noise cut out.

The ground moved. *Really* moved. Like an earthquake.

'The giant . . .' Apollo squeaked. 'I think we've woken him.'

'You think?!' Orla cried, swallowing a silent scream as she looked up at the column of darkness separating itself from the other shadows above. It grew taller and taller until it loomed over them. Her entire body zinged with fear and amazement.

It was a giant.

An *actual, real-life* giant.

An *actual, real-life* giant they had angered.

'Oh no,' whimpered Apollo. 'Oh no, oh no, oh no . . .'

'Run!' shouted Conor, darting nimbly away into the bushes. He was impressively quick on his feet. Orla and Apollo, on the other hand, were not. They tried to run back in the direction they'd come from but it was thick with undergrowth. Orla could both feel and hear the giant following. Each of its booming footsteps felt like the entire world was collapsing in on itself. She was terrified of them being stepped on and crushed. Where was the pooka? Probably long gone. This must have been its plan all along!

Mark my words. You'll regret this.

She knew they should never have trusted it, promise or not!

Suddenly Apollo was no longer beside her. Orla looked back, panicked. He'd fallen.

'Get up!' she called, running back to him. 'Quickly!'

The ground continued to shake violently. The giant was moving closer, bearing down on them. Apollo screamed as it reached for him with a hand the size of a dustbin lid.

'Apollo!' Orla cried out, as her brother was lifted from the ground. The giant's other hand was already reaching for her.

Enormous fingers closed around her torso and squeezed her tightly. Struggling, Orla caught a flash of the bright moon as she was hoisted above the treetops. Before she knew what was happening, Apollo was pressed into the same hand, the giant holding them like an ice cream cone. Unlike pookas, some giants definitely *did* eat mortals. Apollo was still screaming but Orla felt too paralysed with shock to even do that. The giant lifted them towards its face. Orla braced, preparing for the worst.

CHAPTER 17
Fionn McCool

There was a fizz, then a bright burst of warm, yellow light. The giant had struck an enormous match on a tree trunk and used it to light a lantern the size of a treehouse.

Orla blinked into the sudden brightness and stared into a huge, bearded face.

'Mortals!' the giant spat, spraying them with hot globules of spit. His voice was deep, like a sound from the centre of the earth.

'P-p-please don't eat us!' Apollo whimpered.

'I don't eat mortals, they get stuck in my teeth,' the giant snarled. 'Got no problem killing them, though.' He squeezed tighter. Orla felt like her ribs were going to crack at any moment.

'Wait,' Apollo gasped. 'Mr Fionn, please. I-I-I'm a big fan.'

Orla was astounded. Even when death was imminent, Apollo was still trying to be charming. He had a serious people-pleasing problem.

'Is that right?' Fionn boomed. His hot breath blew their hair backwards. Under a pair of wildly bushy eyebrows, the giant's eyes shone with rainbow colours, just like in Gran's story.

'Y-yes. And I know you already know that already, because you know everything and that's so cool!' Apollo babbled. 'I w-wish I kn-knew half as much as you do, although it must also be t-tough knowing so much all the time. Especially when you didn't even want that knowledge in the first place! If you don't mind me saying, I always thought your brother was mean for not forgiving you for tasting the salmon. It's not like you did it on purpose!'

'O'course I didn't!' roared Fionn.

Riling the giant up did not seem like a good idea. What was Apollo doing?

'No, you didn't. Your brother Ben was being unreasonable!'

'He was!'

'Definitely,' Apollo squeaked hurriedly. 'It m-m-must be hard for you, being without him. Especially kn-knowing everything as you do. Your mind must be very full all the time.'

'Ach, so it is.' Fionn sighed. 'Sometimes knowing so many things fills my mind with non-stop chatter and it's hard to turn it off, but that's why I have my clouds.'

To Orla's surprise and relief, the giant's grip relaxed and she could breathe normally again. She almost wanted to high-five Apollo but didn't think it would be wise. His ability to always seem to know the right thing to say had paid off yet again and for once she wasn't annoyed by it.

'Clouds?' Apollo asked curiously.

'Yes, clouds! I catch the best ones from all over Ireland and bottle 'em – nice, natural clouds. I mix 'em to make the perfect blends with just the right fluffiness so's they can hover over my bed when I go to sleep. Watching them slowly dissolve makes all the thoughts in my mind go quiet and I can finally drift off.'

Now that she wasn't so afraid her lungs were about to burst, Orla was able to take in more of their surroundings. Over the giant's shoulder she could see an enormous wooden house built between the trees. Through the open door she glimpsed a giant-sized bed, stove, table and chair. On the table was an assortment of coloured glass bottles, each as tall as Orla. Most appeared to be empty.

'It must be nice to escape sometimes,' Apollo said kindly. 'I bet it can feel overwhelming, being the only one to know everything you know. Lonely too – without anyone to talk to about it.'

'Sometimes.' The giant sniffed. 'But it's easier being on my own than it was before, when I had all kinds of creatures coming to see me wanting to know all sorts of things. That's why I keep my home a secret.' His eyes narrowed and Orla gulped.

'We won't tell anyone where you live,' she said hurriedly. 'We don't even know where we are.'

'Tha's right, youse didn't come here by yerselves, did yer?'

Orla and Apollo were jerked through the air as the giant leant down and rummaged in the bushes below. There was a squeak of alarm and a yell, then both Conor and the pooka were being lifted up in the giant's other hand. The pooka's long rabbit ears were pressed right back. Conor also looked shaken; the smug smile had been wiped from his face and his hair didn't look anywhere near as perfect.

'Pooka, what were you thinking bringing mortals here?' Fionn boomed.

'They wanted your help, they made me promise. You know that,' the pooka squeaked. 'I was just trying to do what was right.'

'You were trying to get us killed more like!' Orla glared at it. 'I knew not to trust you!'

'Oh, cry me a river. Can you really blame me for wanting to terminate my contract? You can see how annoying they are, Fionn.'

'I rather like the one with the blue hair . . . *You*, however, have been spilling my secrets and leading mortals to my home.' Fionn's eyes flashed and his voice was thunderous. Things seemed about to get ugly again.

'We're so sorry we disturbed you,' said Apollo, trying to smooth things over before the giant's temper heightened further. It reminded Orla of how Apollo sometimes spoke to her. She didn't feel great about the comparison. 'We wouldn't if it wasn't a major emergency,' he continued, 'but we're trying to get our gran back—'

'He already *knows* why you came,' the pooka interrupted irritably. 'Gosh, you lot really are slow. Salmon of Knowledge, *remember*? Fionn knows *everything* – what you had for breakfast, how much you floss – the truth, not what you tell the dentist – when you last washed, which in your case was far too long ago . . .'

'Why should I care?' Fionn boomed. He had a point. In Gran's stories, no magical creature had ever helped mortals without good reason. They'd been stupid to think the giant would give them information out of the kindness of his heart.

Suddenly Fionn screwed up his eyes and his nose wrinkled.

'*Ah—*' he exclaimed. '*Ah— Ah— Ah—*'

Too late, Orla realized what was coming.

'*Ah – CHOO!*' Bright green snot flew from the giant's nostrils and missed them by a hair.

'Gross!' she exclaimed.

Fionn sniffed. 'Whoops! I'm allergic to fairy dust. These woods are full of it.'

Thankfully, he placed them on the ground so that he could remove a giant spotty handkerchief from his pocket and blow his nose. Orla wobbled as she found her feet again.

'Mr Fionn, I'm sorry to bother you with our questions,' said Apollo, wobbling too. 'But do you know . . . I mean, could you tell us . . . is our gran . . . is she all right?'

The pooka, Orla noticed, was trying to make a break for it through the bushes, but Fionn put his foot lazily on its tail, trapping it like a mouse.

'Depends what you mean by all right,' the giant replied with another sniff. 'She's not lost her mind . . . yet . . .'

The heavy feeling in the pit of Orla's stomach worsened. They had two nights left to save Gran. After tonight, they'd only have one. 'Can you tell us how to get her back?'

Fionn folded his handkerchief. 'Of course I *could*.'

Orla waited, hoping the giant would add more, but he didn't. 'Please,' she begged. 'I know what happens to her doesn't matter to you, but it matters to us. A great deal. Please, tell us how we can get her back and we'll get out of your way at once.'

'Oh, you will, will you?' Fionn scoffed. 'Tell ya what, why don't you skedaddle right now and I won't kill yer? How's that for a deal? I'd say that was extremely magnanimous of me, after youse so rudely woke me up! Now I'll be needing to use another cloud to get back to my kip and my supplies are extremely low right now. In fact, this happens to be my very last one.'

He brought a stoppered bottle from his pocket and pulled out the cork with a loud pop. A pearly white cloud bloomed out from the mouth of the bottle, but before it could fully emerge, the pooka leapt into the air at a surprising height, collided with the cloud and sliced it to shreds with its claws. Silvery mist billowed in all directions as the cloud disintegrated.

'Whatcha do that for?' Fionn howled in fury. 'That was a perfect altocumulus and cirrus blend! I'd been saving it.'

Orla cowered. The pooka had really done it now. They needed to get out of here quickly. She grabbed Apollo's hand and started to pull him away. If they were lucky, they might be able to escape while Fionn was distracted by the pooka.

'Can we stop with this charade of asking questions, Fionn? You already know *why* I did it. You already know *everything*!'

Orla expected Fionn to crush the pooka right then and there, but for some reason its words seemed to take the wind out of him. Fionn's shoulders slumped and he gazed at the disappearing cloud vapour forlornly. 'Doesn't mean I don't get to ask things like any other giant,' he muttered. 'It's not my fault that you got yourself into another stupid promise that might kill ya, Pooka. I don't especially care if you die; I've actually got half a mind to kill you meself after you wasted my last cloud.'

'If you did that, then you wouldn't have me to help you catch more of them. You know you can't get the best clouds without my help, Fionn. And seeing as you don't seem like you're going to squash my problem for me – which would have been a lot easier for all parties – I need your knowledge to solve it. And you won't be able to do that if you're asleep,' said the pooka. 'If you don't help, then I won't just stop helping you catch clouds but I'll tell all the creatures of the magical realm how to find where you live, including the fairies. Then they'll come visiting you to ask all sorts of things at all

136

sorts of times, particularly during your naps. Do you think your allergies and your sanity could cope?'

'You wouldn't dare!' Fionn roared.

'Try me. Even if you move to another wood, I'll give them a list of tips on how to find you. Unless, of course, you give us the information they need to get their grandmother back . . . or simply crush them right now – either works for me.'

Orla glared at the pooka but thankfully Fionn shook his head.

'I'm not crushing them. The boy's a fan. It'd be rude. Oh fine, I'll tell them what they want to know. But if I do, you're helping me restock my cloud supply in full. Some good ones have just blown in up north, which you can help me catch.'

'Fine,' the pooka glowered.

'You promise?'

'I promise,' the pooka said bitterly. 'But that's the last promise I'm making. If anyone asks me for any others, I swear I'll scratch out your eyes. You have been warned.'

'Grand. We've got ourselves a deal.' Fionn turned to Orla and Apollo. His suddenly pleasant smile reminded Orla of the way the fairies had so quickly switched from friendly to fearsome and she made a mental note never to trust the giant either, even if he had just agreed to help them.

'It won't be easy. And, as you know, you don't have much time. If you don't get her back by the last moments of tomorrow night, she'll have already lost her mind. After that, she'll eventually become part of the Wild Hunt herself.'

Orla gulped. They already knew this, of course, but somehow the giant putting it into words made it feel worse.

'Your only hope is to persuade the Wild Hunt to release her before that happens.'

'Persuade them? *How?*' Orla asked, dumbfounded.

'By offering them something of value to trade in exchange for her release.'

'*A trade?* But that's ridiculous,' Orla baulked. Remembering she was addressing a very temperamental giant, she added hastily, 'I mean it's just that from the stories, the Wild Hunt aren't reasonable beings you can bargain with.'

'You're right, most of them have no sense of reason left at all. However, their leader does. Balor. He's the one who controls the rest. So it's him you'll have to trade with.'

'But what can we trade?' Apollo asked nervously. 'Surely we have nothing to offer Balor that he can't take himself . . .'

'All beings have a weakness. For mortals, it's the fact

138

that you're often led by yer hearts instead of your heads. For pookas, it's that they have to keep their promises or else suffer a horrible death . . .'

'Thanks for reminding me,' said the pooka bluntly.

'What's Balor's weakness?' interrupted Apollo.

'He can only take mortals that are already vulnerable. Not only do they have to be really sad in their hearts, but they also have to be out alone at night or leave their windows unlocked. Which is why Balor was planning on using the pooka here to open yer gran's window,' Fionn added.

'What? You were working for the Wild Hunt?' Apollo gasped.

Orla felt equally horrified.

'*Great,*' the pooka muttered. 'You're never forthcoming with information, Fionn, yet now you decide to be. As if my current working arrangements needed to get any more unbearable . . .'

With a jolt, Orla remembered the conversation between King Oberon and Gran.

'*The Wild Hunt will come for you . . . Your sadness is a scent, and you do not want to attract their attention.*'

'*I've already attracted their attention.*'

Orla felt like she'd had a bucket of cold water tipped over her. She suddenly knew how she'd recognized the pooka's orange eyes. She'd seen them in the garden the night they'd arrived . . .

'It was you! I saw you in the bushes. You were going to unbolt the windows and let them in, that's why you were lurking around Gran's house. That's why she captured you!' Orla was appalled and outraged. But at the same time shame rolled over her. In the end, the pooka hadn't opened Gran's window, Orla had. *She'd* been the one to do the Wild Hunt's dirty work.

'Thanks a lot, Fionn,' growled the pooka. 'Yes, it was me, all right. But Balor made me promise to help him. Much like the rest of you filthy creatures, I might add.'

'We should have left you in the shed!' Orla spat.

'Look, I don't choose the promises I get stuck with, as well you know. Balor got me the same way you did when I was accidentally in Wild Hunt territory . . . Honestly, this whole promise death thing is a real pain in the ears.'

'Are you still working for Balor and the Wild Hunt now?' Conor asked.

Orla blinked. She'd almost forgotten Conor was here as he'd been so quiet.

'No! The promise was nullified when their darling granny unlocked her own window and saved me the bother.'

More shame rolled over Orla. She glanced up at

Fionn. He knew everything so he must know that she'd been the one to unlock the window. Would he give her away?

'So . . . I guess what Balor wants is to be able to make more people vulnerable to him, so he doesn't have to wait? But how would he do that?' asked Apollo. 'It's not just about opening more windows, is it? People also have to be really sad. Maybe he wants something to make more people sad?'

'Maybe,' said Fionn.

There was a long pause.

For a moment, it seemed like Fionn wasn't going to tell them anything else.

'What does he want? Please tell us,' Apollo begged.

Fionn sniffed. 'You're on the right track. What Balor wants more than anything is a weapon that will give him the power to call up the sadness locked in all mortals' hearts, so he can lure more of them into his army and grow stronger.'

'What kind of weapon?' Apollo asked fearfully.

Whatever it was, Orla already did not like the sound of it.

'A weapon like Dagda's Harp.'

CHAPTER 18
The Trouble with Endings

Orla seemed to be the only one to whom the words meant nothing.

Conor's eyes widened, Apollo gasped and the pooka's ears flattened.

'Oh, come on,' the pooka groaned, 'there's got to be something that's easier to get. What about a nice tambourine instead? I'm going to be stuck with this lot for ever otherwise! Go on, just step on them for me, Fionn, won't you?'

'We can totally get Dagda's Harp,' said Conor, giving Apollo a reassuring pat on the back. 'Don't worry!'

'Ha!' the pooka scoffed. 'I would find your tragic naivety amusing were I not so personally *involved*.' It let out a wail of despair and hid its face behind its claws.

'Who's Dagda?' Orla interrupted, feeling left behind. However, as she said it, she realized the name did feel familiar.

'He's an ancient Irish god, isn't he, Fionn?' said Apollo.

'That's correct, Mr Apollo,' said the giant.

'Dagda was the leader of the Tuatha Dé Danann, who were a tribe of ancient Irish people that possessed supernatural powers,' Apollo added, when Orla continued to look blank.

'Right . . . What does an old god's harp have to do with getting Gran back?'

'Don't you remember the song Mum and Gran used to sing, Orla?'

Orla shook her head. She'd deliberately buried many of those songs deep in the recesses of her mind.

But as Apollo started to sing, the words came back to her:

'Once a great god walked this Emerald Isle,
Four sacred treasures were his –
A mighty spear that could win any battle,
A sacred stone that showed a holder the truth,
A Cauldron of Plenty that never ran empty,
And a harp that could mend broken hearts.'

The sudden memory of Mum and Gran at the piano threatened to unmoor her.

'Pretty good. Bit out of tune, but you were put on

143

the spot,' remarked Fionn. 'Why don't you tell us the story of Dagda's Harp, Mr Apollo? I like hearing a good yarn, helps me mind like the clouds do. And it's been a while since I've had one told to me.'

'But you know the story already!' the pooka protested.

Fionn shushed him. 'Quiet, rat. Mr Apollo, go on.'

Nervously, Apollo began: 'According to the stories, the wise god Dagda had many wonderful treasures but his favourite of all was his harp. Its music could make any creature, magic or mortal, laugh or weep. And only those who were worthy could pluck songs from its strings.'

He looked to Fionn, who gestured for him to carry on.

'Long ago, Dagda's enemies stole his harp,' Apollo continued, getting into his stride now. Orla was impressed by how much he remembered. He was a good storyteller. Conor was also leaning in to listen and even the pooka had gone quiet.

'When Dagda discovered the harp was missing, he tracked it down and found a great mass of enemy warriors sleeping before it. The two soldiers Dagda had with him wondered how they would get past, but Dagda simply called his harp and it flew to him! His enemies woke and drew their swords. Dagda struck the strings and called forth the Music of Mirth. His enemies began to laugh so hard that their weapons slipped out of their hands. But when the song ended, they snatched them up again . . .

'Dagda struck the strings once more. This time, he called forth the Music of Grief. His enemies began to weep and dropped their weapons. But when the music faded, they took them back up . . .

'Dagda struck the harp's strings a third time, so softly that they seemed not to make a sound. He brought forth the Music of Sleep and every last one of his enemies fell down into a slumber. Dagda and his two helpers left with the harp. Word spread and never again was the harp of Dagda stolen,' Apollo finished.

'Very well told!' said Fionn, clapping his hands together with a loud boom.

Orla gave Apollo a small smile. She was impressed by this brave new side of him. She'd always referred to Apollo as her hopeless younger brother – quite often directly to his face. But was that really the case? Apollo had saved their lives tonight and seemed to have won the giant over, at least for the time being.

But their troubles were far from finished. How on earth were they supposed to get this magical harp? Surely, if it were easy, the Wild Hunt's leader Balor would already have it.

Conor, she noticed, was posed against a tree as if he thought he was in a fashion magazine. When he saw Orla looking over at him, he shot her a wink, apparently fully returned to his overconfident, arrogant self.

Orla scowled and rolled her eyes.

'Except you got the ending wrong,' Fionn added. 'That *used* to be it. Until a few thousand years ago when the harp *was* stolen again. That's the trouble with endings, they're always wrong eventually.'

'So where is the harp now?' Orla asked impatiently. Time was ticking by.

'Couldn't Dagda just go and get it like before?' asked Apollo.

'Ach, well, you see, Dagda isn't around any more, is he? The *old* gods disappeared long ago. His harp was supposed to remain hidden for ever, but its power is greatly desired by all magical beings, not just the Wild Hunt . . . Anyway, the goblins got to it, didn't they?'

'So the goblins have it?' Orla asked.

The giant scoffed as if the question Orla had asked was stupid. 'Well, o'course they don't got it any more! They had it for a few hundred years, but then the trolls stole it.'

'So the *trolls* have it?'

'O'course not!'

'Then who's got it?' Orla asked, exasperated.

146

'Why, the merrows, o'course!' Fionn said, as if this were obvious.

'The merrows?' Orla repeated. Those she *did* remember. Vividly. Half-mortal, half-fish, mermaid-like creatures. Only a lot more vicious and murderous. Orla remembered the tales of mortal soldiers who'd patrolled the coast of Ireland. The merrows turned into beautiful maidens and lured these soldiers into the sea, where they tore them apart, limb from limb, and ate every part of them except their feet. Orla's throat was suddenly dry. They'd never even get the chance to *face* the Wild Hunt if they had to go through the merrows first.

Gran used to tell them tales of the merrows when they were tucked up in bed and Dad always told her off for scaring them. But Gran said they were far braver than he gave them credit for. Orla's heart panged. They might not have much chance, but they had to at least try.

'All right,' she said, trying to summon her courage. 'So if the merrows have the harp, I assume it's hidden somewhere underwater?'

'Wow,' the pooka said sarcastically. 'How could you possibly have guessed that? Are you sure you've not been to the Sunken City before?'

Orla glowered. 'But how do *we* get to this Sunken

City? If it's possible to get the harp, why haven't the Wild Hunt gone to get it themselves?'

'Because they can't breathe underwater,' said Conor in a know-it-all tone. 'Not even Balor.'

'Er – newsflash, neither can we!' Orla pointed out. 'Let alone fight an army of merrows who'll want to kill us!'

'Well, I suppose you'll just have to leave your grand-mother to become one of the Wild Hunt,' said Fionn. 'Maybe if you're lucky, she'll come to visit and take you with her. In all honesty, that's likely to be what happens. I can almost smell the sadness coming off of youse. The Wild Hunt are already hunting yer, so maybe you can just wait . . .'

Orla and Apollo exchanged terrified looks.

'Why can't Balor command a spy or something to get the harp for him?' Apollo asked. 'One of his victims who *can* breathe underwater.'

Fionn sounded like he was getting bored. 'Balor commands no creature that can breathe underwater – his victims are mortal, remember – so he cannot send anyone to the Sunken City to claim it. He once tried to lure the merrow Queen Coomara to the surface in order to capture and blackmail her. That did not go well for him.'

'What happened?'

'He lost an eye.'

Orla shook her head. If the leader of the Wild Hunt couldn't even get the harp, how were they meant to?

'Now, if you wouldn't mind, I've enjoyed the story and the distraction of you lot has helped a wee bit with my thoughts. But I'm off to catch those clouds up north—'

'Fionn, you haven't given them enough information,' said the pooka. 'They'll be searching the sea for that harp for ever . . . Unless . . . do you think the merrows will kill them?'

'Stop sounding so hopeful about us getting killed!' Orla snapped.

'Won't be any point them searching after tomorrow night, anyway. Soon as their gran loses her mind, that's it. I reckon you can just wait, Pooka.'

'But I've been in a shed three nights already! I don't want to wait!'

'You always were horribly impatient. It's something you should work on.'

Orla's heart dropped. Was that really all the giant was going to tell them?

'Please, Fionn,' said Apollo softly. 'I know you still care about your brother . . . despite what he did, you must miss him hugely. Well, we miss our gran too. That's why we need to get her back. Please, just tell us how.'

Fionn frowned. He seemed to be thinking deeply about Apollo's words. Finally, he sighed and said, 'The water sprites will be able to make you breathe under-water in exchange for a gift.'

'A gift?' Orla repeated. *Water sprites* now! It was hard to get her head round all the magical creatures they needed to appease or fight before they even had a chance of bargaining with the Wild Hunt and getting Gran back. She couldn't remember Gran ever mentioning water sprites. Judging by the blank look on Apollo's face, he couldn't either, which meant Gran probably hadn't.

The pooka, however, had its ears back again. 'This is the last thing I need!'

Fionn guffawed. 'Quite funny that, you having to go and see the water sprites!'

'I don't find it even remotely amusing,' the pooka growled.

Orla didn't get the joke either. 'What could we possibly have to give a bunch of water sprites – whatever those are? And why couldn't Balor just do that too?'

'Because, like all the Wild Hunt, Balor's heart is blackened and empty. It beats, but it does not love. You have to give the water sprites the gift of something you love; something that means something to you; something from the heart,' said Fionn.

'Let me get this straight . . .' said Orla slowly. 'Our only hope is to go and give the water sprites some presents we care about to get them to help us breathe underwater, then sneak into the Sunken City, fight some barbaric merrows, steal an invaluable magical possession, and use it to go and ask the leader of the Wild Hunt to trade with us for Gran's release?'

'That's about the sum of it.'

Orla's courage ebbed away. She felt completely deflated. It seemed an overwhelming number of obstacles, with plenty of opportunities for them to get killed. 'It's madness,' she muttered.

'Yes,' Apollo agreed. 'So are we doing it?'

CHAPTER 19
The Broken Bridge

Orla nodded. Apollo gave her hand a small squeeze and she felt a tiny bit of her courage return.

'Where do we find the water sprites?' she asked.

'My broken bridge is probably the best place to reach them,' said Fionn. 'You mortals know it as the Giant's Causeway.'

The Giant's Causeway was one of the most famous tourist attractions in Northern Ireland. Orla thought of the two occasions they'd been there with Mum. Once when they'd been very young and once a few years ago. Both times it had been raining heavily. She remembered holding the soggy information pamphlet and looking at the strange, grey volcanic rock formation: *40,000 interlocking basalt columns.*

'I love that place,' said Apollo. 'You can tell it was once an amazing bridge.'

The giant's chest puffed up.

Orla felt a crushing wave of hopelessness at yet another hurdle. 'That's miles away!'

'Better start walking.' The giant grinned.

Even by taxi – a very *expensive* taxi – it would take a long time. Time they could not afford to waste. With every passing second their hope of saving Gran was slipping further away from them. There was only one person who could travel quickly enough, and he wasn't even technically a person. The only way Orla could see them getting across Ireland in time was if Fionn carried them.

'Well, thanks for all your help, Fionn,' Apollo said politely. 'I hope you catch some more clouds so you can sleep again soon. Come on, Orla. We'll figure something out . . .' He turned to go.

What was he playing at? He must know as well as she did that they still needed the giant's help.

Fionn frowned and touched his forehead lightly. 'Actually, you know what,' he called, 'today's your lucky day. I'm heading that way anyway. And seeing as I'll be needing the pooka's assistance with catching those clouds, we might as well all go together. Don't be getting any funny ideas, though. I'm just giving you a ride . . . provided the boy tells me some more stories to calm me mind.'

Orla stared at the giant. Was she hearing right?

'Do you mean it?' Apollo asked excitedly. 'That's so kind!'

Fionn grimaced. 'Easy. Don't be calling me things like that and making me think again.' The ground shook as he stomped into the enormous wooden house behind him, pulled a giant-sized suitcase out from under the bed and, with a great deal of clashing, packed the empty glass bottles into it.

'Right, let's go!' he said eventually, clipping the clasps on the suitcase and shoving a huge woolly hat on his head. He reached down, offering them his palm to step on to. Apollo looked anxious. Orla suddenly remembered how afraid he was of heights. It was her turn to give his hand a squeeze.

Gingerly, they all stepped aboard the giant's palm.

'Watch the fur!' the pooka growled, as Fionn lifted them high into the sky and placed them on his right shoulder. The pooka was nearest Fionn's neck, Conor was beside the pooka, then Apollo, then Orla. They all clung on to Fionn's shirt for dear life.

Orla's stomach swooped as she looked down at the forest floor far below. The ground boomeranged.

Beside her, Apollo seemed extremely queasy. Orla hoped he'd be OK. He'd nearly passed out on the Big Wheel at the fair once and they were a lot higher than that now.

Conor, however, was hardly holding on. 'This is brilliant!' Did he have to look like he was having such a good time?

Fionn extinguished his lantern. It took Orla's eyes a moment to adjust to the darkness again.

'Fasten your seat belts!' the giant called.

'We haven't got any!' Apollo shouted, looking around for one.

'Looks like I forgot to install them,' Fionn guffawed. 'Oh well! You'll just have to hope you don't fall off . . .'

Orla's hand slipped. Before she could get a good grip again, Fionn had started to run.

'Wait!' she shouted, but it was too late.

Orla was flung off the giant's shoulder and tumbled straight towards the hard ground. The weight of her backpack made her fall faster. She reached out, desperately trying to grab on to something. A tree branch slowed her descent as it bent, until it broke. She thumped off several other branches and landed on the forest floor with a thud. Her backpack flew off her shoulders.

Orla lay there coughing, assessing whether she'd broken any bones or damaged any major organs. It didn't seem that she had, which was a good thing. A less good thing was that Fionn and the others were nowhere to be seen.

She was alone.

No need to panic, she told herself as the hairs on the back of her neck prickled, Apollo would persuade Fionn to return for her. Orla climbed to her feet and retrieved her backpack – amazed to see that the zip had stayed secure and nothing had fallen out. She shrugged the straps back on to her shoulders, trying to calm her nerves. She just had to hang tight and—

What was that sound?

Orla froze.

A leathery flapping. Wingbeats.

Was it an owl? A shiver ran down her spine.

'Fionn?' she called fearfully into the darkness. 'Apollo?'

The wingbeats got louder. There were more now and Orla suddenly felt very cold. She looked up.

A large black cloud loomed over her. It was so dark that she shouldn't have been able to see it, but some-how this cloud made the previous darkness appear merely grey.

Panic seared through her as the snatched fragments of the old folk song rang through her head:

The Wild Hunt rides in the dead of night,
Spreading terror, misery and fright . . .
. . . Clouds black as coal . . .

It was here.

The Wild Hunt.

The black shape disintegrated into screeching black birds that pinwheeled towards her.

As they got closer, their screeching changed to screaming and sobbing. The wretched sound of people crying in despair. Orla wanted to press her hands against her ears and block it out but she was too paralysed with fear.

Help me. Help me . . .

Orla started. It was just like in one of her nightmares where Mum called for Orla to save her, but she could do nothing.

Help me. Help me . . .

Orla recognized one of the voices amongst them and her heart missed a beat. It wasn't Mum this time. And it wasn't a dream.

'Gran!' she screamed.

Help me. Help me . . .

'Gran, where are you?'

She squinted upwards but all she could see were the black birds. As they swooped down, they transformed into skeletal, bat-winged horses with empty white eyes. Their pounding hooves created a wind as if a storm was raging above. They cantered towards her. Orla tried to run, but they charged from all angles, blocking her escape.

She was surrounded.

Help me, someone please, help . . .

The voice tugged on Orla's heart.

'Gran, where are you? Please let her go!'

As the horses landed on the ground, they transformed into mortal forms that laughed at her hideously. They were just as haggard as in the drawings in Gran's book, their leathery wings folded on their back like tattered cloaks. Their empty eyes gleamed in the darkness.

Orla felt the sad emptiness inside her expand. There was nothing she could do to protect herself; the Wild Hunt had found her grief and were drawing it up to the surface. Agonizing hopelessness consumed her. She tried to fight it, to be strong for Gran. But it was no good. There were so many of them and she was all alone.

'Please don't hurt her,' she moaned. Her voice was very weak.

A cold voice replied, 'Oh no, you've got it all wrong. I take the pain away. Let me take yours too.'

She turned and saw the speaker. Unlike the other creatures, it was wearing robes instead of rags. It had one white eye, the other scarred closed. Fresh fear ripped through her. Balor.

'Why do you keep struggling when there is no need to?' the creature whispered. 'I offer what you want most: to no longer be plagued by sadness and sorrow. I will take all that pain away. Let me help you.'

It was almost a relief to hear these words and Orla felt herself being drawn in by them. Balor was right. Why did she continue to struggle and fight? When the odds were stacked against them. What was she fighting for, anyway? Even if they didn't lose Gran to the Wild Hunt for ever, Gran would still die eventually, just like Mum had. Why was Orla trying so hard to stop the inevitable? Whatever happened, she'd eventually have to lose more people she loved and feel that deep stabbing ache of loss all over again. Wouldn't it be easier to just give in?

'Let me take the pain away.'

She took a step towards him.

There was a crashing sound, then the ground shook as Fionn came hurtling through the trees.

'Orla!' Apollo yelled.

The creatures of the Wild Hunt screeched and scattered. Balor transformed back into a black horse and galloped away into the air. The screams and cries faded.

Orla snapped out of her stupor. 'Wait,' she cried

after Balor, 'give our gran back!'

An enormous hand closed around her. Fionn scooped her up and threw her on to his shoulder but with too much force and she went sailing right past it. For one sickening moment she was falling through thin air again, then someone caught her hand and gripped on tightly.

Orla looked up to see Conor holding on to her. 'I've got you,' he said, flicking his hair back.

'Thanks,' she breathed gratefully, smiling at him for the first time.

'Oh, thank goodness.' Apollo's face appeared beside Conor's. He was white as a sheet but leant right over and grabbed on to her firmly too. Together they pulled her up.

'I can't believe the Wild Hunt were in fairy territory!' Conor exclaimed incredulously. 'They really must be getting stronger to be that bold.'

'Are you all right?' Apollo asked.

'I—' Orla croaked. She wasn't sure how to answer. Tears streamed down her cheeks and she was trembling uncontrollably. Her fingers flew to her earrings to check they were still in place. Apollo regarded her with grave concern.

'I'm fine,' she tried to reassure him, though she felt anything but fine. Orla had experienced only a tiny glimpse of what Gran must be going through and it had been awful.

They had to save her.

CHAPTER 20
The Giant's Causeway

Orla gripped the giant's shirt so tightly that her knuckles turned white. There was no way she was going to fall off again. The cold night air sent her hair flying back and made her teeth chatter.

It was only once they'd left Balor and the Wild Hunt far behind that her shock faded and her heartbeat returned to a more normal rate. As it did so, her mind finally processed the reality of what was happening: they were riding on a giant! *An actual giant.*

She couldn't believe how high up they were. The stars seemed bigger, brighter and more mystical. Was that because she was so much closer to them up here? Or was it because there was no longer any way Orla could deny that there was magic in the world?

Orla, Apollo, Conor and the pooka kept having to duck under wisps of cloud that were wet and freezing. Each time, the pooka made furious remarks about the state of his fur and shouted insults into Fionn's ear, which the giant seemed at first to ignore. However, after each of the pooka's complaints he deliberately steered them into more and more clouds. Occasionally they'd be swallowed up by one completely and Orla could see nothing but hazy grey, as if they'd travelled into a snowstorm. It struck Orla that the giant must be very particular about which clouds he bottled because there were plenty for him here otherwise.

Beside her, Apollo groaned and mostly kept his eyes shut.

She spotted the twinkling lights of a city below that looked like a toy town. Orla stared down at the tiny houses. Each one had people living inside it. People with their own hopes, dreams, worries and fears.

'Hey, blue-haired one, you're meant to be telling me stories,' boomed Fionn.

'I will . . . just not right now,' Apollo groaned. 'I'd like to but all I can think about is how bad I feel.'

'If you get *any* vomit on my fur, it will be the end of you,' the pooka warned. 'I swear I'll—'

'Yeah, yeah, we get it with the death threats,' Orla replied.

Conor, on the other hand, seemed to be feeling great. 'Wahoo!' he yelled, letting go with both hands and grinning across at Orla. A couple of hours ago, Orla would have found his showing off immensely annoying but now she smiled sheepishly, grateful to him for saving her from falling a second time.

The pooka continued to mutter darkly to itself, 'Bunch of idiot kids! This whole thing is a waste of time.' Orla tried to ignore it.

The next moment, her stomach lurched and even Conor had to cling on as the giant leapt over a large hill. It was like riding an extreme roller coaster. Beside her, Apollo groaned louder.

'Are you all right?' she asked.

'You mean, apart from feeling like my insides are in a washing machine?'

Orla smiled. 'Apart from that . . . anything I can do to help?'

'Distract me? Take my mind off the fact that we're hundreds of metres up, riding on a giant?'

'OK . . . how exactly?'

'Mum used to sing when I got scared.'

Orla stiffened. 'I don't sing any more.'

'I know.' Apollo sighed. 'Talk to me, then?'

'About what?'

'I don't know. Anything . . . What happened just now? What was it like when they attacked you?'

Orla shivered. 'It was horrible. Not just the Wild Hunt themselves but there was this screaming . . . Mortal voices crying and begging for help. It made me feel so sad. It . . . it made me think of Mum.' The words tumbled out before she could stop them. 'Gran too, of course, when I heard her voice.'

'You heard Gran?'

She nodded again. 'That was awful . . . But, before that, it was Mum it made me think of. I often dream about her, she's always asking me to help and I can't . . . I can't save her, though I really really want to.' Orla swallowed hard. She'd never told anyone this before.

Apollo was silent for a moment.

'I dream about Mum too,' he murmured. 'All the time. I miss her so much. Sometimes it's so overwhelming that I doubt if I'll ever feel completely like myself again.'

'I didn't know you felt like that. You always seem so OK.'

'Just because my sadness isn't as visible, doesn't mean it's not there.' There was an edge to his voice that was unfamiliar.

Orla did not know how to reply. She gave his hand a small squeeze. 'What are we doing?' she wondered aloud. 'This is madness.'

Apollo shivered. 'But we have to try to save Gran. Even if there's only the tiniest chance, we've got to take it.'

'Agreed.'

Fionn was now hugging the rugged coast.

'That's Seagull Rock,' Conor called. 'And that beach is Runkerry Strand.'

Apollo let out another groan as the giant turned sharply then slowed.

'We're here!' announced Conor excitedly.

Orla looked ahead and there it was: the Giant's Causeway. The same interlocking, hexagonal basalt columns that Orla remembered from their visit all those years ago. They were an amazing sight – all of them stacked so neatly together, like puzzle pieces. Some were very tall, like turrets – others were small and stubby. Tonight, there were no crowds of tourists or buses. The whole place looked more majestic, more *magical*.

The ocean beyond was wild and full of white horses that raced under the pale moon and smashed against the rocks with loud booms. Orla tasted the salty tang of the sea on her tongue. Memories of the last time she'd been here rose in her mind. It had been one of Mum's bad days. Dad had hardly been able to get her out of the car and when he had, she'd been so weak that she'd not been able to walk far. Orla touched her crescent-moon earrings and pushed the memory away. Thinking of Mum as helpless made her heart ache. It felt like a betrayal somehow too; Mum had always been strong and full of life before she got ill and Orla preferred to remember that version.

When Fionn put them down on top of the causeway, it was like stepping on to land after being in a boat for a long time. Orla stumbled and swayed, before she eventually found her balance. The giant pulled something flat from his pocket and popped it up like origami. It turned into another lantern, which he lit with his box of matches.

They all blinked at each other in the sudden brightness. Apollo, who looked a bit green still, insisted that, after the Wild Hunt's attack, they needed food to get their strength up before confronting the water sprites. He unpacked his supply of jam sandwiches. They'd been badly squashed but were otherwise delicious.

'Yum!' Conor exclaimed. 'Where did you learn to cook, Apollo?'

Orla looked at him sideways. He had to be kidding. 'It's like you've never had a jam sandwich before . . . wait, have you not?'

Conor shook his head.

Orla stared at him. 'Where did you grow up, under a rock?'

Conor gave her a jammy grin. 'Something like that.'

Orla wondered if Conor's family were too posh for jam sandwiches. He certainly carried himself that way.

'Would you like some too?' Apollo offered the sandwiches to Fionn and the pooka, much to Orla's bewilderment. 'I mean, it might not do much for you, Fionn. More like a canapé . . .'

The pooka snatched a sandwich. The giant, however, took his gratefully and seemed touched. He laid out a clean spotty handkerchief on top of some of the flatter rocks for them to use as a picnic blanket. Orla regarded it warily.

'Don't worry,' Fionn said. 'It's fresh. No bogeys.'

It was so windy that they had to sit on the corners to stop the handkerchief flying away. Orla munched on her sandwich, trying not to eat her own hair as it blew into her mouth.

The pooka settled on the side furthest away from the water. It clearly didn't like being here at all, and Orla remembered its reaction when Fionn had first mentioned the water sprites. The pooka's obvious fear did nothing to help the nerves zinging through her body. Fionn also seemed unsettled. He was staring out to sea, a strange mournful expression on his face.

Orla nudged Apollo and pointed up at the giant nervously.

'Are you . . . OK?' Apollo asked Fionn. 'Do you want me to tell you a story?'

'It's this place.' Fionn sighed. 'Makes me feel sad.

Thought it wouldn't any more, that long enough had passed . . .' A large tear rolled down the giant's cheek and splashed on to a rock nearby. Orla had never heard of a giant crying before and the sight was alarming. Her instinct was to stop asking questions at once.

But Apollo didn't skip a beat. 'Are you thinking about your brother?'

The giant nodded and gave a very loud sniff. There was a large plop as something dripped from Fionn's nose.

'Yuck!' exclaimed the pooka, jumping up in alarm.

Orla saw another drip forming under the giant's nostrils. 'Quick! Give him his hankie.'

Hurriedly, Conor, Apollo and the pooka moved off the spotted handkerchief and passed it up to the giant. For them, it was the size of a parachute, but when the giant took it, it looked pocket-sized again.

He blew his nose. 'Don't know why I'm getting so upset. It was a long time ago . . .'

'It's because you still miss him,' Apollo said softly.

The giant sniffed again. 'I do. A lot.'

'But I thought it was you who broke the bridge?' Orla asked, confused. She immediately realized she'd said the wrong thing.

Fionn let out a loud howl of rage. 'It wasn't *my* fault that Benny was being so unreasonable that I got angry and smashed it!' He stamped his foot, making the ground shake so violently that they had to cling on to one another to avoid being thrown off the rock. The pooka jumped on to Orla's back, its claws piercing her.

'Ow!' she cried, shoving it off.

'Believe me, that was more painful for me,' the pooka hissed. 'Anyway, you're the one who's winding him up!'

Orla glanced at the giant fearfully, but once again his mood shifted in a moment. He stopped stamping and his shoulders drooped.

'I wish I'd never done it. I know Ben misses me. I tried to get a message to him to say I missed him too once, but my brother's reputation is much more grisly than mine and the fairies are too afraid of him to take a note for me, ungrateful little flies. And I can't rebuild the bridge without Ben's help – it would take too long. We'd be needing to work together again.'

'Why don't you swim over?' Apollo suggested.

Orla gave him a hard nudge, worried this comment would set Fionn off again. But the giant merely frowned.

'Can't swim. Banjaxing that bridge is the biggest mistake I ever made. I thought I was cutting *him* off, but really it was me I was cutting off. And now I'm all by myself and I wish I weren't.'

Despite herself, Orla empathized. She'd been

cutting herself off from people ever since Mum died – Dad, Apollo, Ellen and her other school friends, even Gran. She'd banjaxed more bridges than she cared to think about. If they made it through this, could hers be rebuilt?

'Oh, thinking about it is making me feel bad!' Fionn moaned. 'And now too many thoughts are comin'. . .'

'Want me to tell you a story?' Apollo offered kindly.

Fionn shook his head. 'Leave the storytelling for now. What I really need is some good clouds, for which I'll require the pooka. C'mere then, stop putting this on the long finger. It's time you gave the water sprites yer gifts.'

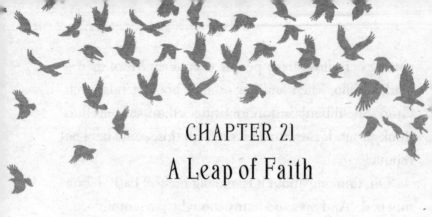

CHAPTER 21
A Leap of Faith

'So, we go to the edge of the rocks,' Orla said, repeating Fionn's instruction. 'And then what? Do the water sprites just appear?'

'*Do they just appear?*' Fionn guffawed as if Orla had told some hilarious joke. 'O'course not. You got to sing to them.'

'Sing?' Orla spluttered, her chest tightening. 'You didn't say anything about that before!'

'Oh, you've gotta sing for sprites to come,' Conor said. When Orla and Apollo both looked at him blankly, he added quickly, 'I thought that was common knowledge . . . is it not?'

'Common knowledge is knowing how to make a jam sandwich,' Orla muttered, shaking her head. 'All right, so we . . . sing, then what do we do after that?'

'Expect me to hold yer hand too, do ya?' Fionn roared, irritable again. 'I already told ya. You give them yer gifts. Remember, they've got to be meaning something important, or else on yer head be it.' He looked directly at Orla.

Orla shifted uncomfortably. She should have thought about what to give on the journey but she'd had too many other things going through her mind, like Gran's screams and being attacked by the Wild Hunt. She rummaged through the contents of her backpack. All she had was the tiffin, which while delicious and a reminder of Gran, probably wasn't valuable enough . . . Otherwise there was just an extra jumper, the torch . . . Wait! She noticed the glint of something silver. It was a bracelet Dad and Penelope had got her for Christmas. She'd shoved it in here and forgotten about it. She was sure it had cost a lot. It would have to do.

'Well . . . don't drown,' Fionn said discouragingly, before walking away towards the cliff, clearing at least half a kilometre with each stride. As he sat down, there was a cracking sound and fresh crevices appeared in the rock face below him. For a brief moment, Orla wondered how much of the erosion of coastlines and mountains was really just from giants sitting on top of them, but she pushed this thought aside. It was time to focus.

'I think I'll go and join him,' said the pooka, turning tail.

'No way, Pooka! You're coming with us,' said Orla firmly. If the pooka wanted to leave, then she wanted it to stay. Besides, she figured it was better to have the creature where they could keep an eye on it and make sure it didn't plot any other ways to get them murdered. Unless, of course, this whole business with the water sprites was another of its schemes? What if Fionn was in on it too?

The pooka regarded the dark sea fearfully. 'Technically this part isn't in my contract . . . The water sprites and I have history, you see. A promise I fulfilled for someone. Long story short, they're not exactly my biggest fans.'

Orla didn't care about the pooka's history. 'You promised to help us with whatever we request until we find Gran. I'm requesting you come.'

'Orla, don't you think that's a bit mean?' Apollo muttered. 'It seems frightened.'

'It's *frightened*?! I was frightened when it tried to get a giant to kill us! The pooka is coming. No more discussion,' she said firmly. 'Now, has everyone got their gifts?'

Apollo and Conor nodded. Apollo looked pale but determined. Conor, as usual, looked like he was about to strut on to a catwalk.

Together, they scrambled over the slippery stones.

The pooka trailed behind, muttering darkly to itself as usual. Orla ignored it and racked her brain for stories or songs about the water sprites but she couldn't think of any. What would they look like? The cold, salty wind coming off the sea whipped their cheeks raw and made their lips sting. They reached the edge of the columns.

Fresh nerves fizzed through Orla's body as she thought about singing. It wasn't that she didn't miss it. Music had been a huge part of her life before . . . But after Mum had died, it had been another thing she'd cut herself off from. She was scared to sing now, afraid of what it might unlock inside her.

'I think we've got to jump on to that rock out there!' said Conor, pointing.

Just off the coast, a flat rock humped out of the water. It looked much too far away to jump to, not to mention perilously slippery. Below, more jagged rocks stuck out of the water, the sort that would crack your head open if you fell on them.

'You've got to be joking . . .' Apollo gasped.

'Oh, it'll be easy, don't worry,' said Conor. 'See!'

Before either of them could stop him, he leapt across to the rock. He landed gracefully, struck a victory pose and waved for them to follow. Orla shook her head in disbelief.

She and Apollo could have done with a bit of

Conor's confidence. Below, the sea churned around the rock, making Orla's stomach churn with it. She knew Apollo must be feeling even worse.

The pooka was also hanging back.

'I can't do this,' Apollo muttered.

'Apollo, in the last twenty-four hours you've faced a pooka and convinced a giant to help us. You can do anything.'

'Can I just point out that neither of you exactly "faced" me,' interjected the pooka. 'I was chained up and you blackmailed me. It was hardly a fair fight—'

'I know you can do this, Apollo,' Orla continued, ignoring it. 'Because – because you're one of the bravest people I know.'

'You really think that? You're not just saying it to make me feel better?'

'Would I ever just say anything just to make you feel better?'

'Fair point.'

'I mean, you act a bit hopeless sometimes,' Orla teased, hoping to cheer him up. Seeing Apollo's shoulders sag, she added, 'But you're not. Quite the opposite, actually. You were braver than me that day when—' She stopped because there was a large lump in her throat.

She knew Apollo knew what she meant.

That morning at their old house, Apollo and Orla had dressed in black. Apollo had gone downstairs, and Orla had climbed back into bed, refusing to come down.

'Are you two coming or what?' Conor shouted.

'Look,' she said. 'I'm going to jump first and you're going to come right after and I'll catch you, all right?'

Apollo whispered something that the wind drowned out.

'What?'

'I can't lose you too, Olo.'

The lump in her throat grew larger. He hadn't called her that in years. She swallowed. 'You won't, Polo.'

'Promise?'

'Tell you what, I *pooka*-promise. How's that?'

'That works.' He sounded like he was smiling.

'Hate to ruin the moment, but why don't I give you two some privacy,' the pooka suggested. 'I'm sure you'd prefer to conduct this little vomit-fest in peace . . .'

'Why don't you jump before us, Pooka?' Orla said.

It squeaked. 'You don't understand. If they recognize me, I'm dead. Then how am I supposed to help you? It's really in your best interests if I sit this one out . . .'

'You'll just have to hope they don't recognize you,' Orla snapped.

The pooka sighed. 'After this is over, I'm going to cut out that tongue of yours and feed it to a troll.'

Orla rolled her eyes. 'Can't wait. Enjoy your jump! Don't mess it up unless you can swim.'

'I never mess up a jump.' The pooka growled. It leapt smoothly through the air and landed almost balletically next to Conor.

Orla squeezed Apollo's hand one more time, let go, steeled herself and jumped. For a moment she was sailing through air, then her feet planted firmly on the rock. Conor reached out to steady her.

'Thanks,' she muttered, before turning back to look over at where Apollo was shivering. 'OK, Polo?'

Apollo hesitated, but only for a moment more. With a tremendous shriek, he launched himself across the gap, limbs flailing, colliding with Orla and knocking her flat.

'Oof!' she exclaimed.

Apollo quickly pulled himself upright, shrugging his backpack back on to his shoulders. 'I did it!' he exclaimed delightedly, before registering her position on the ground. 'Oops, sorry for crushing you.'

'Think you punctured a lung.'

'Just the one? That's pretty good going.' Apollo grinned, helping her up.

'Bravo, both of you! Now what shall we sing?' Conor

asked. He was beaming as if this was all fun and games. Perhaps it was for him. His grandmother's life wasn't at stake. To stop herself wanting to push him off the rock, Orla had to remind herself that he'd saved her earlier.

Apollo glanced at Orla nervously. 'How about something easy like . . . *Happy Birthday*? Everyone knows that one.'

The pooka snorted. '*Happy Birthday*?!'

'What's wrong with *Happy Birthday*? It happens to be my favourite song,' said Apollo defensively.

'That's because there's normally cake at the end of it,' Orla pointed out.

'Exactly!'

'Actually I think that sounds like a great choice,' said the pooka. 'And if it doesn't work, we can always just abandon this whole silly mission . . .'

'I don't think that song will work. It's got to mean something personal,' Conor said. 'Like the gifts we're giving. The water sprites won't come otherwise.'

Orla looked at him sideways. How did Conor know so much about this stuff? Would Orla and Apollo know it all too if they'd grown up in Gran's village? She wondered if Conor had ever crossed paths with magical creatures before. He hadn't said so, but he'd also been unperturbed by the sight of the pooka. She made a mental note to ask him about it if she got the chance to, but now was hardly the right time.

'There is a song we *could* try that feels like it might be right,' Apollo said suddenly. 'The one about the sea that Mum used to sing. Do you remember it, Orla?'

She nodded and bit her lip. 'Think so.' Her stomach twisted and she was tempted to ask Apollo to sing on his own, but she'd let him do enough hard things by himself these past two years. Gran needed her to sing, so she would.

Orla turned to the open water and took a deep breath of the salty sea air. Below, the dark waves lapped the edges of the rock.

'This feels weird,' said Apollo.

'I know,' Orla agreed. 'But weird is our status quo right now . . . Count of three. One, two, three.'

They began to sing.

'Oh, once there lived a lovely maiden,
Who more than anything longed,
To be free as the blowing wind,
And find where she truly belonged.'

At first Orla's voice was rusty, but soon the song filled her lungs and heart, vibrating through her body.

It felt *good* to sing, like coming home to herself. She closed her eyes and let herself get lost in the melody.

> '*Oh, she never felt more free,*
> *Than when she was in the sea,*
> *And one day the sprites said she,*
> *Could be whatever she wanted to be.*'

Orla sang soprano, with Apollo singing the lower part. A tenor voice joined theirs before the third verse, adding a caramel richness. Orla opened one eye. Conor seemed to know all the lyrics to the old folk song.

> '*But she had to give up something,*
> *In exchange for a life that was free,*
> *She tried many things but none were right,*
> *Until one night that girl gave her life . . .*'

Memories of Mum singing in their old kitchen came flooding back. Mum smiling and dancing as dinner burnt on the stove. Orla faltered. This was why she didn't sing. The memories were there, waiting under the surface. Waiting for the music to unlock them.

Apollo gasped, 'Look!'

Orla stopped singing and gripped his arm.

The water in front of the rock was no longer dark and empty, but glittering with lights, as if the stars had fallen out of the sky and into the sea. And now they were forming into glowing outlines walking underwater towards them.

The water sprites!

CHAPTER 22
The Water Sprites

The slow way they approached reminded Orla of wolves in nature documentaries she'd watched – how they closed in on their prey. There were a lot of them – too many to count – and soon they surrounded the rock on all sides.

The pooka growled softly.

The water sprites stopped under the surface. They were fairy-like in appearance, except they had webbed hands and feet and no wings, and their sparkling skin was the colour of the sea.

This must be the moment for the gifts. How did they do this? Fionn hadn't given them any instructions. Maybe Conor knew? But he didn't appear to. Apollo was also completely silent – for once he seemed not to know what to say. It was her turn to be brave.

Orla cleared her throat. 'Er – hello,' she said nervously, unsure how to address the creatures. Should she bow? 'We've come to ask for your help . . . We need to breathe underwater for a short time. We have gifts to exchange in return for this favour . . . if-if that's all right?'

In response, the sprites made strange, otherworldly sounds, like the noises created when someone blows across the mouth of an empty bottle.

'Was that a yes or a no?' she muttered. They held their glittering palms up to the surface, ready to receive. It seemed to be a yes.

Orla swallowed. What happened if the sprites didn't accept their gifts? It had not escaped her attention that some were blocking their route back to land.

'I'll go first,' Conor said. He leant down to the water's edge and dropped in something yellow. Before Orla could see what it was, a sprite snatched it and pressed it to its body. The yellow object disappeared.

The sprite made a clicking sound. It was like the sound you hear when you put your head under the sea and hear pebbles clinking against one another.

'Did it work?' Orla whispered.

'Conor, watch out!' Apollo yelled.

The sprite who'd taken Conor's gift was rising up out of the water, like a seal. It reached towards Conor with a fist. Orla held her breath, but the sprite simply opened its palm and in the middle was a glowing pearl.

Orla's heart lifted. This must be the thing that

would help them breathe underwater! Fionn hadn't explained how that would work either, but Orla hoped it would become clear. At least this part of the plan seemed to be working.

Conor took the pearl. 'Thank you,' he said.

The sprite closed its palm and returned below the water.

The other sprites clicked their tongues and swayed.

Bolstered by Conor's success, Orla reached inside her backpack and fumbled for the bracelet. Before she could pull it out, Apollo stepped shakily towards the edge of the rock and took a toy bunny out of his own backpack.

Rabbit.

Orla gasped. Apollo couldn't throw Rabbit in! He'd loved that toy his whole life. 'Polo, you can't—'

'You were the one who said I was too old for it.'

'I was winding you up! You love that thing.'

'Exactly, that's why I have to give them it. For Gran,' he said firmly. He squeezed Rabbit to his chest, burying his face into the patchy fur and breathing in its comforting scent for one final time, before he forced himself to drop Rabbit into the sea. A sprite snatched the toy bunny up immediately and pressed it to its watery body. The next moment Rabbit was gone.

Apollo suppressed a small sob. Orla's heart broke

for him. He'd miss Rabbit so much. She wanted to go and put her arm around him, but the sprite that had taken Rabbit was already clicking and rising up out of the water. It held out its palm to Apollo and offered him a glowing pearl.

Apollo wiped his eyes, bent down and took the pearl delicately, murmuring, 'Thank you.'

Again, the other water sprites clicked and swayed.

That was two for two.

Just Orla left to go.

She shrugged her backpack on and gripped the bracelet tightly. It had felt like a good-enough gift a few moments ago but now she wasn't feeling confident. After Apollo had given Rabbit, the bracelet felt mean-ingless, but it was all she had with her.

The water sprites stopped swaying and waited.

Biting her lip, she dropped the bracelet. The silver links glinted as it flipped through the air and plopped into the water.

A sprite snatched it.

Holding her breath, Orla waited for it to absorb the bracelet.

But it didn't.

The bracelet was hurled back out of the water. Orla only just managed to get out of the way in time without losing an eye.

The sprites made menacing, wailing sounds.

'Now you've done it!' the pooka cried, looking terrified.

Not just one, but all the sprites drew closer. The waves around the rock started churning. Orla did not like this at all.

'I don't think they're very happy,' cried Conor.

'Really? Get away from the edge!' Orla called to Apollo.

The pooka cowered between their legs. 'I'm going to die . . . I'm going to die! And with a bunch of smelly mortals. It's too much to bear!'

'Orla, watch out!' shouted Apollo.

The sprites started climbing up the sides of the rocks and reaching for Orla's legs. She jumped backwards, dodging their watery grasp. What happened if they grabbed hold of her? Would she disappear like the gifts? Or would they pull her down with them beneath the waves?

The water sprites were only interested in Orla. Apollo and Conor tried to protect her by standing on either side, with their bodies between hers and the sprites, but the sprites kept coming from all angles. What if they grabbed Apollo or Conor by mistake? It didn't help that Orla kept tripping over the pooka who was right under her feet, using them all as shields.

'Please stop,' she gasped, panic surging through her.

The sprite closest to her held out its open palm.

But Orla had nothing else to offer. Out of habit, her fingers touched her earlobes. She felt cold, curved edges and realized that she did have something else, though she didn't want to give it.

But she supposed that was the point.

And what other choice did she have?

'Wait!' Orla cried. 'I have another gift.'

The sprites abruptly stopped wailing and stood motionless. It was suddenly eerily quiet and all she could hear was Apollo and Conor panting beside her.

With an aching heart and trembling fingers, she undid the clasps of the crescent moons and scrunched them inside her fist. The sharp points stabbed her palm. For a moment, she didn't think she could let go.

But Apollo had been brave, and she needed to be too.

She stepped towards the closest sprite and dropped the earrings into its hand. The sprite closed its palm around them and pressed it to its chest, in the place its heart should be. Orla's own heart lurched. She felt Apollo and Conor holding their breath with her. The moment seemed to last for ever.

Then the clicking sound started again. Orla's body sagged with relief as the sprite held out its palm. The earrings had vanished and instead there was a glowing pearl. Releasing a shaky breath, Orla took the pearl carefully. It was smooth and cool. As her fingers closed around it, elation fizzed through her. They'd done it!

But her triumph didn't last long.

The sprites weren't leaving.

Why weren't they going? She'd given them a gift. What more did they want from her? But it wasn't her they were focused on any more. Their attention was on the pooka. And they were starting to wail again. The pooka's orange eyes widened and it pressed its furry body even flatter against the rock, trying to keep under Orla's feet.

'What? Me? I don't need a pearl, thanks. I'm just a poor innocent pooka, helping these sweet mortals out of the goodness of my—'

The sprites continued to draw closer around it. The pooka tried to bolt under Apollo's legs but the sprites cut off its path.

'No! Get away, you slimeballs!' the pooka snarled, its voice rising in panic.

The sprites reached for it, still wailing hideously. The pooka tried to swipe at them, but its claws went right through. The sprites, however, were able to wrap their watery limbs around the pooka. Freezing cold spray came off them and drenched Orla, Apollo and Conor. Snarling and shrieking, the pooka was dragged off the rock and down towards the dark, churning waters.

'No!' cried Apollo, darting forwards. He threw himself down, leant over the rock and grabbed the pooka by one of its legs. 'I've got you! Hold on.'

'Apollo, what are you doing?' Orla yelled, grabbing hold of Apollo before he was pulled down too. Conor rushed over and helped.

'We can't let it die!' shouted Apollo.

'It would happily let *us* die!' Orla pointed out.

'I would gladly, especially after this ordeal,' snarled the pooka, before letting out a strangled cry as the sprites continued to pull him downwards.

Apollo was being pulled over the edge too.

'Maybe you should lay off the chocolate biscuits next time, Pooka,' called Conor, heaving under the strain of all the weight.

'Oh, ha-ha,' snapped the pooka. 'If you let me die, I swear I'll—' But for once words seemed to fail it.

Orla and Conor tugged harder, trying to keep them all on the rock, but they were still slipping forwards.

'You need to let go, Apollo,' called Conor. 'Or else we're all going in.'

There were squeaks of terror below.

'I'm not letting go, don't worry. I've got you,' Apollo called down, straining and pulling with all his might.

The sprites were wailing even louder now and goosebumps rippled across Orla's skin. She wanted to clamp her hands over her ears but she didn't dare let go of Apollo.

'Here, catch!' she heard Conor yell. There was a plop. He'd thrown something into the water. Whatever it was, it distracted the sprites for only a moment. But a moment was all they needed.

She felt the weight on Apollo release as the pooka managed to slip out of the water sprites' grip. Apollo hauled the pooka up and then someone, maybe Orla herself, was shouting, 'Jump! Jump! Get back on to land, quickly!'

Orla, Apollo, Conor and the pooka leapt over the gap between the rock and the shore. Without looking back, the four of them raced across the slippery columns, putting as much distance between them and the water sprites as possible.

CHAPTER 23
The Banshee and The Burren

'What did you throw in?' Orla asked Conor later, when they were back on the giant's shoulder and travelling across land again.

'Oh, I didn't really like the crusts of my sandwich earlier, so I put them in my pocket. Figured they might come in handy.'

Orla shook her head. 'You really are something else, Conor.'

'Thank you!' said Conor with no trace of irony.

'So where exactly are we headed now?' she asked. 'I know we're going to the merrows but where are they?'

'*Tír fo Thuinn*, the land beneath the waves,' Conor said. When Orla looked blank, he added, 'It's south, near County Kerry.'

Orla had been very disheartened when she'd first discovered that they'd have to make another journey to where the merrows dwelt, but to her surprise and relief the giant had offered to give them a lift.

'Yer took so long that the good clouds here blew off down there,' he'd explained. 'So I'm heading that way anyway.'

'How exactly does the pooka help you get the clouds?' Apollo asked curiously.

'Its claws are delicate enough to cut the cloud from the sky for me. There are these wee threads attaching it, you see, too wee and fiddly for me to be able to cut neatly. And if I rip the threads wrongly, I ruin the whole cloud. It's much easier if I get the pooka to do it.'

Orla marvelled. The world kept getting weirder and weirder.

This journey was even less comfortable than the previous one. Their clothes were now damp and the cold wind cut through to their bones.

Still, Orla was feeling hopeful for the first time. They'd managed to get the pearls from the water sprites and were one step closer to saving Gran. Maybe they could do this after all! She touched her earlobes. She felt naked without Mum's earrings and missed them, but she also felt closer to her brother than she had for years, as if some invisible wall between them had come down.

There had been the singing too. Orla's body tingled as she recalled how it had felt. She'd missed that feeling so much.

As they travelled, Apollo told the giant stories. Orla had expected Fionn to want retellings of epic legends, but instead he asked for ordinary mortal tales, just like the fairies had asked Gran for. Apollo told Fionn the story of how Mum and Dad had met.

'They were at a karaoke night and he was so impressed by the way she sang, and how kind and interesting she seemed, that he wanted to ask her out by dedicating a song to her. But when it was his turn to go up on stage, Dad was so nervous that he fell over and accidentally unplugged the speakers so the whole place went completely silent!'

'It didn't?' The giant guffawed.

'Yup. Mum went and helped him up from where he was tangled in the wiring. She always said that was the moment she fell in love with him.'

'Pathetic,' the pooka muttered.

'Romantic,' countered the giant, clearly enjoying the story.

Orla was surprised to find herself smiling. She'd thought hearing tales of Mum would make her uneasy – that she wouldn't want Apollo to share them, but actually it was nice to hear Mum spoken about. It reminded her of how in love Mum and Dad had been. Sometimes seeing him with Penelope these days, she felt like Dad hadn't loved Mum. But he had. Deep down she knew he always would.

Apollo went on to tell Fionn of how, at Christmas each year, Mum would take them down the road to play music and sing at the old people's home. 'She and Orla were the ones with the voices and musical talent but Dad and I did our best . . . I happen to be particularly good on the triangle. Mum would ask the residents for their favourite songs and carols. She always said music was healing; that it could bring people back to themselves. And it was true! The staff were always amazed at how the old people who'd lost their memories could sing along to all the words!'

'Well I never!' said Fionn, sounding impressed.

Orla's smile faded. Whatever Mum had said, music hadn't been able to heal her.

They passed crumbling castles silhouetted on hilltops in the distance, more mountains and forests, streams and lakes. For a long time, they hugged the coast, before moving inland, keeping away from towns. From up here, it was easy to see how beautiful and varied the island of Ireland was. It was a land of contrasts: of water and rock, stillness and movement, harsh and soft, howls and whispers. A herd of wild horses galloped between the giant's feet, like dolphins playing in the spray of a boat. Even Apollo peeked over the edge to see them. Cows mooed grumpily as they passed and sheep scattered.

While animals seemed to sense the giant easily, people didn't seem to at all. The odd person Orla spotted driving by in a car or walking down a dark lane never looked up, as if the giant was simply too big for them to comprehend.

Over the roar of the wind in their ears, there were other sounds: the hum of aeroplane engines, the squeak of bats. At one point, birdsong cut through the night with an impressive range of whistles, trills and gurgles.

'What's that?' Apollo called.

'That sounds like a nightingale,' exclaimed Conor. 'They're really rare here.'

Orla thought it was the most beautiful sound she'd ever heard. She suddenly remembered coming into Mum's room when Mum was ill and had had a particularly bad night. Orla found her sitting up in bed with her eyes closed, smiling and listening with rapt attention. There had been no music playing so Orla had been confused until Mum opened her eyes and commented on how lovely the birdsong was. Orla hadn't noticed it until then, but when she did she wondered why she hadn't before. It was beautiful.

'The world is full of magic,' Mum had said. 'You just have to keep paying attention.'

Orla thought of this as she listened to the bird's lovely song. But then another sound that was anything *but* lovely cut across it.

A terrible high-pitched keening.

Orla tensed, fearing the Wild Hunt again. But there was no flapping of leathery wings or screaming.

'Banshee,' said Conor, pointing.

Illuminated by the moonlight, a ghostly woman floated over the ground below. She had long, streaming silver hair and a tattered grey cloak. Sensing the giant, she stopped and turned to look up. Her eyes were black, her cheeks concave and her mouth open in a wide O.

Orla recoiled. She wanted Fionn to move away before the hideous woman came any closer and was surprised when, instead, the giant took off his woolly hat and nodded respectfully. The woman continued to float on her way, heading towards the lights of the nearest village.

'She's heading for that village!' Orla exclaimed. 'Shouldn't we stop her?' She knew there was some connection between banshees and death but she couldn't remember what it was.

'Oh, you can't stop a banshee,' said Conor. 'They're not evil, they don't cause death. Just announce that it's coming.'

'Often get the blame, though,' sniffed Fionn. 'People always look for someone to blame with death.'

'Terrible occupation,' the pooka agreed. 'No one's ever pleased to see you.'

'I bet you know all about that,' muttered Orla. Her heart dropped as she registered what Conor had said. 'But wait, does that mean someone in that village has died?'

'Ach, it does,' replied Fionn. 'But that's mortals for you. Dying all the time, you lot are! You should hear how many mortal deaths are going through my head right at this very second. Don't know why you're always so dramatic about it really. You seem to live your lives as if you don't see it coming! Anyway, it happens all the time, the world moves on . . . As should we! But before we do . . .'

Fionn bent down beside a patch of bright blue flowers. 'Spring gentian. Highly useful. Pooka, will you do the honours?'

The pooka humphed but it jumped down, landed on its feet gracefully and sliced the stalks of a few blooms.

'You can put them in your pouch for now,' said Fionn.

For some reason Orla couldn't help laughing. 'You have a pouch?' She wasn't sure why but the notion of the pooka with a pouch like a kangaroo's seemed absurd.

'Close your eyes!' the pooka snapped. 'It's rude to look at a pooka's pouch. I mean it. I'm not moving until you do.'

They did as it said, and the next moment, the pooka had jumped back on to Fionn's shoulder, and they were off again.

CHAPTER 24
Swimming Lessons

Orla rubbed her tired eyes and looked down at a beach covered in soft sand that shone silver in the moonlight. Behind the beach, in one direction stretched a woodland; in the other were miles of farm-land criss-crossed with tumbledown stone walls. Far in the distance, the ragged shapes of craggy mountain peaks cut an impressive silhouette against the glow of a sky that was already worryingly red. Dawn was on the way. Orla looked towards the shadowy sea fearfully. Somewhere, deep beneath those black waves, were the merrows and the magical harp that might be their only chance of saving Gran . . .

The giant placed them down on the sand and looked towards the mountains. 'We'd best be going to find some clouds before the sun's up, Pooka.'

'What?' Orla spluttered. 'But you've not even told us how to find the merrows.'

'Won't be any use you going to find them now,' said

Fionn. 'Not enough time before daylight. Merrows sleep in the night and wake in the day. Take it from me, you don't want to visit when they're awake.'

'So what are we supposed to do? Just sit around on the beach all day and wait while our Gran is being tortured by the Wild Hunt?'

Gran had been with the Wild Hunt for nearly two nights now. Would she still be herself by the time they reached her?

'Well, you don't have to just sit,' said Fionn, 'but that's up to you.'

'What about Conor?' asked Apollo.

Everyone turned to Conor, who looked a bit startled. 'Me? What *about* me? I mean, not that I don't love all the attention.'

'Yes, what about Conor?' said the giant. A smile tugged at the corners of his of mouth and his rainbow-coloured eyes glinted, as if this was some hilarious joke.

Orla frowned, unable to see what was funny.

'He's been so kind helping us but he didn't know he'd signed up for *two* nights,' said Apollo. 'His family will be worried about where he is!'

'I don't think his family have even noticed he's gone,' said Fionn, still with that same glimmer of humour in his eye.

'He's right,' said Conor quickly. 'It's all good.' He

shot them one of his dazzling smiles, but his eyes flicked to Fionn and, for a moment, Orla thought she saw a flash of something else in his expression. What was that? Sadness? Fear?

'Can't you just tell us what to do before you go?' she begged

'Nope. Because I know you're likely to try to go before tonight if I do, and that wouldn't be wise.'

Orla glanced down at the pooka, expecting a snide remark about how it would be delighted if the merrows ate them for breakfast, or something similar along those lines. It was long overdue an insult. But the pooka remained quiet. It had been uncharacteristically subdued ever since Apollo had saved it from the water sprites. Maybe it was still in shock. Orla didn't expect this peace to last.

'But what are we meant to do here all day?' she asked, exasperated. 'We don't even have any money for food.'

'You do. Apollo packed some cash in his backpack.'

Orla nearly asked how Fionn knew that but stopped herself. 'What if he doesn't come back, Polo?' she hissed.

Apollo, however, was gazing out to sea thoughtfully. If he'd heard Orla's question, he didn't show any sign of it. 'How come you can't swim, Fionn?'

'I beg your pardon?' the giant roared.

It was Orla's turn to flash Apollo a warning look. The giant was clearly sensitive about the fact that he couldn't swim over to see his brother in Scotland, so what did Apollo think he was doing mentioning it? The pooka's hope for them to be trampled was still very much a possibility.

Apollo seemed undeterred by Fionn's anger. 'But you must *know* how to swim? You know everything.'

Fionn sighed and once again his anger dissipated as swiftly as it had come. 'No use having the book without the learning . . . Meaning: o'course I *know* how to do it, but that's not the same as doing it, is it?'

'I'm good at swimming. Won a bunch of medals at school,' said Apollo. Orla looked at her brother sideways. Maybe Conor was rubbing off on him; Apollo wasn't usually a bragger. 'I could teach you.'

Fionn's expression changed. 'Could you? Right now?'

'I guess so. Unless you've got to go . . .'

'Suppose we've still got a wee bit of time before sunrise. And the pooka and I can catch clouds tomorrow night. Why not!'

'Hang on!' growled the pooka. 'How many times do I have to tell you people that my fur is sensitive to sunlight. You know I don't know this area, Fionn. I need you to show me to a safe cave. Now. Before I burn to death.'

'I will, I will. We've got time,' said Fionn.

Orla glared at Apollo. What was he doing? He should be getting the giant to tell them how to get the harp, not teaching him how to do breaststroke! Was this just Apollo trying to be everyone's best friend like usual? Could he not help himself?

'Provided you give us your word that you'll come back tonight and help us with the merrows,' Apollo added.

Ah – so that was his plan! She instantly felt bad for doubting him. Clever Apollo. But would it work? Orla held her breath.

'Ah, seems someone is becoming attuned to the magical ways of doing things. All right, mortal boy, you have yourself a deal,' Fionn said gruffly. 'Teach me how to swim!'

Fionn waded out to sea and Apollo ran up and down the shoreline, shouting instructions.

'Kick your legs like a frog, yes that's it – wait, not too hard, we don't want a tsunami on our hands . . . Now your arms too. *Gently*. That's it! You're doing it! Excellent.'

The pooka huffed and slunk away to curl up under a rock, muttering darkly and regarding the lightening sky nervously.

Orla sat down on the cold sand, nerves fluttering

inside her chest as she thought of Gran spending another day in the Wild Hunt's clutches. Her fingers kept drifting up unconsciously to brush her naked earlobes and her stomach twisted as she remembered Mum's earrings were now gone for ever. Would Gran soon be too?

Conor sat down beside her.

They watched the giant in the water, creating waves, and the smaller figure of Apollo on the shoreline. Orla was certain that this was one of the strangest things she would ever see: her little brother teaching a giant how to swim. But despite this, she found herself yawning and struggling to keep her eyes open. She shivered as a cold wind blew across the beach.

'Are you chilly?' Conor asked. 'Here, let's get more comfortable.'

He went over to the giant's suitcase and started rummaging around in it. He produced one of Fionn's handkerchiefs and strung it up between two trees that edged the beach, creating a makeshift tent. It worked surprisingly well.

He gestured to Orla and she sidled over to join him.

They used one of Fionn's woolly hats as a blanket and Conor found three of the giant's socks to use as sleeping bags.

'Are you sure he won't mind?' Orla asked, as Conor

dug around in the huge suitcase and pulled more things out.

'Who cares!'

Orla grinned. It was cosy huddled in the makeshift tent protected from the wind.

'What did you throw in the sea?' Conor asked abruptly, as if the question had been waiting to burst out of him for hours.

'My mum's moon earrings,' she said quietly. Maybe it was because she was tired or worried or sad, or maybe it was a bit of everything – but once she'd started talking, she found it hard to stop. 'She used to wear these silver crescent moons on her "bad days", when she was feeling her worst, and gold sunflowers on her "better days" when she had more energy. It was meant to help us know when we should give her space and let her rest, and when we could push her more to come on walks and go for ice cream and stuff if she was feeling better . . .'

'Your mum died,' Conor said.

Orla nodded.

'Why do you wear the "bad day" earrings, not the "good day" ones?'

Orla had wondered about this too sometimes. 'I think they're my way of saying how bad it all is.'

Orla hesitated, but Conor didn't look uncomfortable

or try to change the subject.

He just continued to listen.

And maybe it was this feeling of being listened to and heard that prompted Orla to tell Conor more than she'd told anyone.

'That must have been really, really hard,' Conor said when she'd finished. 'It must still be.'

His kindness brought fresh tears to her eyes. Orla nodded and bit her lip. 'It is . . . Sorry.' She wiped her eyes and burrowed her toes into the sand.

'Why are *you* apologizing?' Conor asked, sounding confused. 'You're sharing your story, and I feel honoured that you've shared it with me. Anyway, isn't sharing and being there for each other what us mortals do?' He nudged her gently with his shoulder.

In spite of everything, Orla smiled. The empty feeling inside her felt a little smaller.

The moment was interrupted by a retching sound behind them.

Orla jolted upright. 'I'd forgotten you were here!'

'Evidently,' the pooka said dryly. 'As much as I'm loving this little therapy session, please could you keep the soppy stuff to a minimum. Some of us are struggling with being here enough as it is.'

Orla's cheeks got hot. 'I see you're back to your usual self,' she muttered.

The world shook. The giant was returning up the beach.

'That was brilliant!' he hollered. 'Did you see me, Pooka?'

'We're all seeing far too much of you right now!' the pooka called in alarm as the giant pulled off his wet underpants to put his trousers back on.

Apollo, who got the back view, let out a cry of dismay. 'My eyes! My eyes!'

Orla and Conor turned away just in time. They caught one another's gaze and giggled. Despite all that lay ahead and all the fears swirling around Orla's mind, it felt good to laugh.

'Oops!' the giant called. 'Thought it was still dark enough not to be seen . . . Uh-oh!' he added, looking at the sky. It had brightened to a soft pink. The pale moon was almost completely gone and, in the distance, the sun was starting to peek up between the mountains. 'We'd best be getting going, Pooka.'

'You don't need to tell me! You're the one who's been wasting the darkness splashing around like a lunatic.'

'Was having so much fun I lost track of the sun. Thank you, Apollo. Reckon I'll make it to Scotland?'

'Definitely,' Apollo said. 'You've just got to build your confidence.'

Fionn grinned. 'Super. Right. Let's go find a cave, Pooka. Maybe, if we're lucky, we can catch a cloud or two on the way.'

'As if I haven't done enough already . . .' the pooka grumbled. 'How many times do I have to tell you people that this fur is sensitive to sunlight!'

'All right, fine, we'll catch clouds tomorrow. See you later, mortals!' Fionn scooped up the disgruntled pooka and began to run. Orla, Apollo and Conor watched him clear whole fields in a couple of strides before he leapt over the mountains and gradually disappeared from sight. The colours of the world honeyed as daylight brought out its paintbox and dissolved away the last of the inky darkness.

How were they meant to just wait here all day when Gran was suffering? But did they have any other choice?

Suddenly there was a loud growling sound. Orla jumped, wondering if the pooka was back, before she realized what it was. 'Apollo, was that your stomach?!'

Apollo nodded. 'I'm starving. Reckon there's anywhere close to buy some supplies?' He pulled out a crumpled note from his backpack.

'I can go and find some,' said Conor at once, taking the money and scampering away across the sand towards the headland.

'Where are you going?' Orla called after him in bewilderment.

'Not sure,' Conor shouted, waving, 'but I'll be back soon!'

Orla shook her head and smiled.

Apollo yawned and it made Orla yawn too. They both climbed into the handkerchief tent. It really was surprisingly cosy. They lay down in the sock sleeping bags as the sun rose.

'I never thought I'd be more tired than hungry, but maybe we should rest our eyes, just for a little bit . . .' Apollo muttered.

'Mm,' Orla replied, snuggling into the giant's sock. She didn't think she'd be able to sleep with all the worries and fears buzzing around her head. But she was so exhausted that she fell into a deep slumber as soon as her eyes closed.

CHAPTER 25
A Day at the Beach

The next thing Orla knew, she could smell bacon. She blinked her eyes open and looked up at the spotty material of the handkerchief tent.

Apollo wasn't beside her any more.

'Polo?' she called groggily, pulling the flap of the handkerchief back and blinking in the brightness. It was a proper sunny summer's day, the first they'd had their whole trip. There were only a few clouds in the bright blue sky and the calm of the shimmering sea pushed Orla's dread of the merrows away. They'd face them soon enough. Untangling herself from the sock sleeping bag, she stepped gratefully out into the cool air.

She spotted Apollo and Conor sitting together a little way along the beach. Conor must have been in the Scouts or something because he'd managed to start a fire and fashion a rudimentary stove from piled driftwood and a large flat stone, on top of which bacon and eggs were sizzling. Orla was impressed.

She hesitated, feeling awkward as usual and a bit embarrassed about how open she'd been with Conor earlier. Conor looked up and gave her one of his dazzling smiles.

'Ach, grand! You're awake!' he called. 'How did you sleep?'

'Apparently very well,' she said, smoothing down her bedhead as she walked over to them.

'Hungry?'

'Starving! Where did you get all this?'

'A gentleman never reveals his secrets,' Conor replied.

Apollo coughed pointedly and cut his eyes towards a Dunnes Stores bag lying on the sand.

They ate directly off the stone, using sticks and doing their best not to burn their fingers. The eggs were rubbery and difficult to eat, the bread wasn't toasted, and the bacon was burnt. Yet it tasted like the best breakfast in the world. Apollo handed her a big bottle of water, which she gulped down. She hadn't realized how hungry and thirsty she was.

'Isn't this fun!' Conor exclaimed. 'Us friends camping on the beach! What a profoundly dull and ordinary thing to do.' He beamed.

Orla exchanged a look with Apollo and shook her head. 'If you say so, Conor.'

Nothing about this felt 'ordinary'. She rolled her shoulders a few times to get rid of their stiffness and noticed Apollo tucking a few bacon sandwiches inside the tent, no doubt for the pooka and the giant when they returned. She marvelled at his capacity to always think of others, even those who were more than capable of hunting their own suppers.

'What time is it?' she asked, looking up at the blazing sun.

'Twelve thirty.'

'You're joking! I thought this was breakfast.'

'No one should ever joke about breakfast,' Apollo said solemnly.

'When did you wake up?' she asked, anxious as she remembered her strange slumber the night before.

'Only a bit before you,' Apollo reassured her.

'You both needed the sleep,' Conor added.

'Didn't *you* need some sleep?' Orla asked.

Conor shrugged.

Orla found her gaze drawn to the sea and her stomach twisted.

Conor read her expression. 'Don't look so worried, Orla. Remember what Fionn said? The merrows will be asleep. That's why we're waiting until nightfall. They won't even notice we've paid the Sunken City a visit until we're long gone.'

'And if they do?' Orla asked. She was certain getting the harp wouldn't be as easy as they hoped.

'They won't,' said Conor firmly.

Orla gave him a small smile and her insides unknotted a little. It was good to have someone around who at least *seemed* confident about their chances, when she felt anything but.

After breakfast, Conor and Apollo raced each other up and down the beach, playing tag until they grew tired and sat back down on either side of her. Together, the three of them watched gulls wheel on the horizon and crabs scuttle in and out of rock pools.

Conor dared them all to go swimming, which they did, abandoning their clothes on the sand, and running in vests and pants into the water, laughing as they splashed into the waves.

A few families arrived on the beach and, to Apollo's delight, an ice cream van appeared. They had just enough change left to buy a 99 Flake each. Conor ate his so fast that he got brain freeze and ran around moaning and clutching his head like it was falling off, which made them all laugh.

'Did they not have ice creams under your rock either, Conor?' Apollo teased, which made everyone laugh again.

It was so nice on the beach that, for the briefest of

moments, Orla could almost make herself believe she was just here to enjoy herself on holiday, rather than to face killer merrows. *Almost.*

Afternoon became evening. The other families left and soon it was just the three of them again. The sky turned pink then red as the sun dropped, throwing long shadows up the beach.

They each fell silent as it grew darker. The heavy weight reappeared in Orla's stomach. The day's magic faded and her sense of time running out returned. As did her nerves.

It had been decided that they would leave their backpacks on the beach. Apollo put his penknife in his pocket. Orla shivered as she looked at it; what kind of weapons would the merrows have?

Just as she was wondering this, the pooka appeared.

'How was your cave?' Apollo asked politely.

'Rat-infested. Dark. Smelly . . . So a thousand times better than being stuck here with you lot.'

Orla rolled her eyes. 'Where's Fionn?' she asked anxiously.

'How should I know?'

'*What?*' Orla baulked. 'Is he not coming back to help us?'

'Don't look so surprised! I've only come because I'm

bound by a death promise. It's not for the riveting conversation, trust me.'

Apollo looked crestfallen. 'But he gave us his word. I thought he was our friend . . .'

'Your *friend*?' The pooka laughed hysterically. 'You thought a giant was your *friend*? Oh, that is too good!'

'Shut up, Pooka!' Orla glowered. No one was allowed to be mean to her brother except her.

'What do we do now?' Apollo asked.

Orla found herself looking to Conor. Right now, they needed someone who at least seemed as if they knew what they were doing.

'Well, we'll just have to find the Sunken City ourselves,' Conor said firmly. 'Shouldn't be too difficult. Fionn must have brought us to this beach because it's the right place to set off from. We'll just have to swim out for a bit until the pearls get activated by the water. After that we'll dive down and go on our little city break. I wonder if the Sunken City does postcards?'

Orla didn't smile. Her stomach felt heavy. *Merrows eat mortals*. They'd better not get caught . . . Dimly, she wondered how Conor knew so much about this stuff. Fionn's cruel words came back to her: *I don't think his family have even noticed he's gone*.

But now wasn't the time for questions. It was time

for action. Tonight would be Gran's third night with the Wild Hunt. If they didn't get that harp tonight, they'd lose her for ever.

'Lead the way, Pooka,' she said. The pooka looked at the water in terror.

Apollo shook his head. 'We can't make it come! That's mean. It doesn't have a pearl to breathe under-water.'

'So?'

'Olo!' Apollo squeaked.

Orla sighed. 'All right, fine. You can wait on the beach. But any more snarky comments from you and I'll change my mind.'

The pooka growled, though it didn't make any further remarks.

'Are you hungry?' Apollo handed over one of the bacon sandwiches he'd saved earlier.

The pooka regarded it suspiciously. 'Is it poisoned?'

'I guess you'll have to find out,' said Orla before Apollo could reply. 'Come on, we've wasted enough time already. Conor's right, we're just going to have to swim out and hope the pearls work and that we can find this city and the harp.'

'That's a lot of hoping,' said Apollo.

Orla sighed. 'I know. But right now hope is all we have.'

They started down the beach towards the black sea. It no longer looked inviting.

'Wait!' the pooka called. 'I wasn't going to give you these – at least not without making you do something humiliating first – but I suppose I sort of owe you for that thing with the water sprites or whatever, even if that whole situation *was* your fault in the first place . . . And, well, don't be getting used to it or anything, but . . .' It turned around and reached into the fur by its belly. When it turned back, it held out its clawed hand to Apollo. Even in the moonlight, the flowers gleamed bright blue.

'The spring gentian!' exclaimed Apollo.

'Put the petals in your ears and don't take them out. Don't worry, you'll still be able to hear each other wittering on just fine.'

'Why do we need to plug our ears with petals?' Orla asked, confused.

'*I guess you'll have to find out*,' mimicked the pooka, before stuffing the bacon sandwich in its mouth and scampering back up the beach.

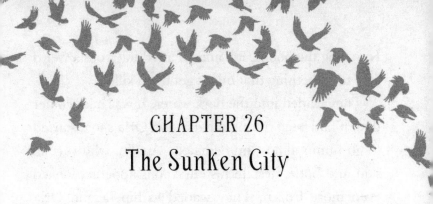

CHAPTER 26
The Sunken City

Orla did not trust the pooka one bit and was reluctant to use the petals or anything else it recommended, but Conor insisted.

'Spring gentian is a special flower,' he said. 'I'm sure Fionn picked it for a reason.'

'Well, if he'd bothered showing up he could have told us, couldn't he?' Orla retorted. They couldn't trust Fionn any more than the pooka.

'Let's try it,' said Apollo. 'What harm could some petals do?'

'If the pooka is involved, I'd say a great deal,' she muttered. But, in the end, she agreed.

'Can you still hear me?' Apollo asked after they'd stuffed the petals in their ears.

Orla nodded. Even though she could feel the petals blocking her ears, she could still hear Apollo perfectly well. The pooka had been telling the truth about that, at least. So what was the point of the petals exactly?

Knowing the pooka, it could be anything from a weird joke to something that might get them killed.

They waded into the dark water. It was a lot colder than it had been during the day and Orla's toes started to go numb almost immediately. Apollo, who was all skin and bone, despite his enormous appetite, looked even more frozen. They waded to hip height. Orla opened her fist under the water and looked down at the pearl. It gleamed faintly in the moonlight.

'It's n-n-not w-w-working,' she said, her teeth chattering.

'M-m-maybe we have to g-g-go further out?' said Apollo.

'Yeah,' agreed Conor.

Orla looked at the dark sea. She couldn't help thinking about the brutal drownings, the merciless torturing, the *eating* . . . Queen Coomara cutting the feet off her mortal victims while they were still alive . . .

It was possible that they might not survive this. *More than possible*. It felt *im*possible that they'd ever make it in or out of a city full of merrows – even sleeping merrows – alive, especially with the harp. All they had to help were pearls, petals and whatever they managed to remember from the folk tales.

Every part of her wanted to run back up the beach, not swim further out.

But if they did that, they'd be giving up on Gran and that wasn't an option.

They swam out until they could no longer touch the bottom. Orla's clothes dragged her down; the water was getting colder and the darkness more absolute. Orla's senses sharpened. She was uneasily aware of every splash of her limbs moving through the water, as well as those of Apollo's and Conor's. Would the merrows be able to sense them from here, if there were any left awake? 'The pearls!' she heard Apollo shout.

Orla opened her fist under the water again. The pearl glowed, white and ethereal. 'They're working! What do we do now?'

'Try to swim down, I guess!' said Conor. 'Everyone ready?'

Orla glanced at Apollo. He gave her a nervous nod. 'All right,' she said. 'Count of three. One . . . two . . . *three* . . .'

They dived underwater. Orla tried to keep her eyes open, but the salt stung badly and she was forced to close them and swim blindly. Her wet clothes were cumbersome and, after a few strokes downwards, her lungs squeezed. Her survival instinct kicked in. Orla burst back up to the surface, gasping.

A few seconds later, both Conor and Apollo re-emerged too.

'How are we meant to reach the Sunken City if we can barely hold our breath for more than a couple of minutes? It must be really deep down.'

'Yes, that's not ideal,' agreed Conor, examining the pearl. 'I was sure it would help us breathe underwater. It should do . . .'

Again, Orla boggled at Conor's blind faith. How could he think anything from this strange, supernatural world 'should' do anything?

'Wait!' said Apollo excitedly. 'Do you remember that song Gran and Mum used to sing about a girl who wanted to be a fish?'

Orla's memory stirred. She *did* remember the song.

There was once a girl
Who longed to be a fish
She gulped a pearl
And got her watery wish . . .

'Swallowing it? Do you really think that will work?' she asked. 'What if it's just a silly song?'

'Have any of the other songs turned out to be silly so far?'

'Fair point.'

'Let's try it,' said Conor. He put the pearl in his mouth. In the darkness, it glowed through his cheeks.

Apollo did the same.

Hesitantly, Orla opened her mouth and placed her pearl on her tongue. At first, it felt solid but then it disintegrated like a sugar meringue, dissolving into nothingness. It didn't taste of anything and didn't seem to do anything either. That was until Orla swallowed. Suddenly, her lungs started to squeeze like she'd run out of air again, but this time it was happening above the water.

She tried to suck in a breath but couldn't. She gasped, panicked, before she noticed Conor gesturing downwards wildly. Orla plunged her head below the water with her eyes squeezed shut. She took a nervous breath, expecting to inhale water, but instead she felt the release of breathing. *What on earth* . . .

Her body was suddenly warm and her clothes felt weightless and easy to move in. Opening her eyes, Orla found she could see underwater clearly too and that the salt no longer stung. A thrill of amazement buzzed through her.

Apollo and Conor floated nearby.

Apollo was looking around in wonder. 'Wow!' he said.

Orla heard him as clearly as if he'd spoken across a room. There was none of the usual bubbly distortion like when they'd used to sing songs to each other underwater in the swimming pool and make the other guess the title. She felt a tiny flutter of hope. If the merrows really were asleep, maybe they *could* do this.

'Look! Seems all roads lead to the Sunken City,' called Conor triumphantly.

Orla looked where he was pointing and saw trails of glowing lights stretching downwards, like catseyes lining a motorway.

Into the deep.

'Ready?' Apollo asked.

Orla tried to hide her fear. She needed to be strong for both of them. She nodded. Conor swam down along the glowing path. Apollo followed. Orla kicked hard and brought up the rear, her heart in her throat.

They glided through the water smoothly. Orla felt fish-like, as if she had flippers on her feet.

The deeper they swam, the darker it became. Orla gazed back up at the glistening surface. It was already very far away, at least a giant's height, maybe two. A new fear rose inside her. What if the pearls' magic stopped while they were down here?

But there was no going back.

Deeper and deeper they swam, following the tiny lights, until these ended abruptly, and they were plunged into the darkest black Orla had ever known. It was like swimming into a void.

Something grabbed her, something that felt like octopus tentacles. Orla nearly screamed. But it was only seaweed.

'Everyone still here?' Conor whispered.

'Yes,' Orla and Apollo replied.

'Good. We must be close now.'

Sudden light blinded them. Orla shielded her eyes and gazed through her fingers in astonishment, unable to believe what she was seeing.

The Sunken City was a jungle of buildings, too many to count, and threaded through with enormous seaweeds that were as tall as trees. The windows were filled with mosaics of coloured stones that gave the impression of stained glass. Suddenly their plan felt like utter madness. There must surely be hundreds of merrows living here, maybe thousands. If even one of them was awake . . .

Orla's heart was beating so loudly she was afraid the merrows would be able to hear. She gazed in wonder and fear at the vast temple-like structures, towering bridges and high walls covered in murals depicting battles between merrows and a host of sea creatures: sharks, whales and giant squid, as well as other hideous monsters with multiple heads and hybrid bodies. Orla gulped. The images of the sharp-toothed merrows themselves were just as frightening, with scenes of the mermaid-like creatures pulling human fishing boats down to the depths and ripping their captives apart.

Was that the fate that awaited them too if things went wrong?

'Ah!' Apollo screamed, making Orla jump.

She whirled around. Ahead was a giant merrow, half as tall as Fionn, with a long fish tail, wild green hair, scaled skin, sharp pointed teeth and a murderous expression. Its spear was raised. Orla careered backwards until she noticed how motionless the merrow was and let out an immense sigh of relief. 'It's just a statue!'

'Oh, yeah. I knew that . . .' Apollo said, still very pale.

'Don't worry, it frightened me too,' Orla said.

She hoped no one had heard Apollo's scream. But all remained quiet and no real merrows appeared.

'Where do you think the harp is?' asked Orla, eager to find it and get away from this strange, ghostly underwater city as quickly as possible. They'd never have time to search every building.

'I bet it's in Queen Coomara's palace,' said Conor firmly. 'According to tales, that's right in the middle of the city.'

'*Of course*. Has to be in the *middle* of the city, doesn't it?'

Apollo was also looking extremely nervous. 'Did you hear the stories, Conor, of how she collects human feet? Sometimes she gets sharks to bite them off, other times she saws them off with jagged shells . . .'

'So let's not wake the merrows,' Conor said. Orla was still trying to work out whether his confidence was inspired or delusional.

Looking down on the city, she was feeling less positive. They'd been lucky so far, but surely their luck would run out at some point . . . Her eyes met Apollo's. This time, he was the one who reached out and gave her hand a squeeze.

'For Gran,' he whispered.

She nodded. 'For Gran.'

Orla saw the bravery in Apollo's face and felt so proud of him. She reached out and hugged her little brother. Her throat felt choked with all the things she wanted to say.

'Apollo, I'm sorry . . . I'm sorry for being such a rubbish sister and taking things out on you.'

'It's OK, Orla.'

'No, it's not. I should have been nicer . . . I should have told you that . . . that I—'

'It *is* OK, I promise,' he soothed. 'And I know. I love you too.'

Orla's throat caught and she hugged him tighter.

Her brave, kind, clever little brother. He'd always been there for her, even when she'd pushed him away.

'And I'm sure everyone loves me, no need to say it! I'm just very loveable, so it's hard not to,' Conor said, winking at her over Apollo's shoulder.

Despite the gravity of their situation, Orla and Apollo laughed. Then they turned to face their fate.

CHAPTER 27
The Merrows

It was only when they swam closer to the buildings and peeked inside the doorways that they got their first glimpse of real merrows. They lay inside enormous shells like they were beds. Their eyes were closed and the only signs that they were alive were the bubbles escaping their mouths and noses, as well as the rise and fall of their muscular chests. While they were much smaller than their statues, they were still *terrifying*. Scaled and hideous with large forked tails. Their mortal-like torsos and faces were unsettling, and their lurid green hair drifted around their heads eerily as they slept.

It was strange – how deeply they all seemed to be sleeping. Not one merrow so much as stirred when Orla, Apollo and Conor swam past. It was as if they were all enchanted . . .

Orla was glad. There were at least two merrows in every building, sometimes up to six. Even if just *one* woke up, there would be no hope of escape. The power in those tails was obvious, and several of the merrows also had sharp-looking spears resting close by. While they might not be expecting visitors, they were clearly a species of war.

Apollo caught Orla's eye and grimaced. Gritting her teeth, Orla followed him and Conor through the city, her nerves jangling.

What did they do once they reached the palace? Just swim in and take the harp? Surely it wouldn't be that easy . . .

Suddenly there it was – a palace made of shells looming up ahead. Two fan-shaped sandstone struc-tures created a grand walkway, or rather, *swim*-way up to its dark entrance, which gaped open like a mouth.

'Why are there no guards awake anywhere?' Apollo whispered.

'The merrows don't expect anyone to be brave enough to come down to their city,' said Conor.

'Brave enough or stupid enough?' Orla muttered.

They swam through into the palace's cavernous entrance hall. The hall was circular and the walls were covered in a display of shells, bones and teeth. Many of the bones and teeth looked horribly human; others were enormous and must have come from monsters Orla never wanted to meet. And – wow, her sense of smell underwater was just as good as above ground – the stench of mouldy seaweed was hideous! But seaweed wasn't the only thing causing the rotting smell . . .

In the centre of the hall was an oddly shaped sculpture. As they got closer, its building material became clear.

'Feet,' said Apollo in a thin voice.

Orla felt sick. The mortal feet were propped at odd angles, tilted rakishly and stacked together. Some were just white bone, while others still had muscle and skin attached. On some, she could even see anklets and tattoos. Tiny sharp-toothed fish nibbled at the ghastly creation, like flies around a carcass, and dried black-red blood stained the sand below.

'Yuck!' squeaked Apollo. 'Let's find the harp and get out of here before our feet get added to the pile!'

Orla looked away from the grotesque sculpture to the three passages that led off the hall. Her ears strained for any sound, but the palace seemed desolate and still, just like the rest of the Sunken City.

Too still.

She tried to ignore her creeping sense of dread. It was because she'd just seen a sculpture made out of human feet, she told herself, but the fact remained that they still didn't know if the harp was even in the palace. There were three passages and who knew how many rooms down each of these. They couldn't afford to spend too much time searching; they had no idea how long the effects of the pearls would last. Anyway, the longer they lingered, the more likely they were to be caught.

'We need to split up. We'll be quicker that way,' she whispered. 'Apollo, you take the passage on the left, I'll try the one in the middle. Conor, you take the one on the right.'

'I think we should stay together,' protested Apollo.

'There's not enough time. Like you just said, we need to find the harp quickly.'

Unwillingly, Apollo agreed. He and Conor swam away. Orla moved into the middle passage. It was still horribly quiet and a pressure was building behind her eyes. There were no doors off this passage. Instead, after swimming down it for some distance, she found it opened into a large room. In the centre of it was a giant shell, big enough for three people to lie down in comfortably, with spongey pink seaweed inside. It looked like the shells the other merrows had been sleeping in, only this one was gilded in gold. Orla's stomach dropped. This must be Queen Coomara's bed.

But it was empty.

The queen wasn't asleep.

She had to warn the others!

Orla swam back to the hall as fast as she could and raced along the passage Apollo had taken. Ahead, she heard a horrible crunching. What was that?

Her body trembled as she peeked around the corner. Apollo crouched underneath a giant dead crab in the middle of a room, his eyes popping, his body rigid with fear. The crab was positioned in such a way that its legs looked like those of a table. A large merrow was hunched over the top of it, devouring something. It had its back to Orla, but she noticed a crown of crab claws tangled in its floating green hair.

Queen Coomara.

There was another passage leading off to the right – Apollo must have hidden under the crab-table when he heard Queen Coomara coming and got trapped there.

There was something blue stuffed in the merrow queen's ears. *Petals.* Orla frowned.

Queen Coomara threw something down to the ground. It skittered across the sand. A human finger! Apollo stared at it, looking sick.

Orla gestured for him to swim towards her. Apollo shook his head in alarm. Orla continued to gesture urgently. If he didn't come out, it would only be a matter of time before the queen found him.

Apollo looked utterly petrified, but started to swim slowly towards her . . .

The queen seemed absorbed in her feast, but when she paused suddenly, they both froze. However, she simply belched loudly before returning to her crunching.

Orla and Apollo swam quickly back towards the entrance hall.

'I told you we shouldn't split up!' Apollo hissed, adding, 'Did you see that the queen has spring gentian petals in her ears too?'

Orla nodded. 'Why does she have them? Why do *we* have them?'

'I don't know but I think we should definitely keep them in for now.'

'Me too,' she agreed. 'And get out of here.'

Thankfully Conor was already in the entrance hall waiting.

'We have to go!' Orla whispered urgently. 'The queen's awake.'

Conor frowned. 'Well, that's inconvenient.'

'To put it mildly!'

'But I've just found her treasury – I'm sure that's where the harp must be. Come on, it's just up here.' Before Orla could say anything else, Conor swam back down the right-hand passage. Orla and Apollo gathered up the remains of their courage and followed. *For Gran*, Orla reminded herself.

At the other end of this passage was an ornate archway covered in gold coins that must have been pillaged from all the shipwrecks the merrows had caused.

The high-ceilinged room beyond was almost as big as the entrance hall and filled with ancient and precious-looking objects displayed on stands. Orla's heart lifted. Conor was right: if the harp was anywhere, this seemed the most likely place for it.

Orla was about to swim through the arch when she spotted two merrow guards slumped against the walls just beyond it. Like the other merrows, they were asleep, but they had spears close to hand. Orla tried not to look at the sharp, blood-stained points too closely. What was the point of sleeping guards? Why did Queen Coomara seem to be the only merrow awake in the entire Sunken City?

Please stay asleep.

As they passed, Apollo accidentally bumped Orla and knocked her into one of the guards.

Orla froze, expecting the worst.

However, the guard remained asleep and didn't even react.

Further unease crept across Orla's skin. Again, she had the strange feeling that the merrows were under some kind of spell. Had Queen Coomara bewitched them? If so, how and when would they wake up? Orla hoped they wouldn't be around to find out.

The gleaming pinkish walls of the treasury were studded with abalone shells arranged in a pretty undulating pattern. Unlike the rest of the palace, the floor of the treasury was made of stone instead of sand.

Orla, Apollo and Conor swam along the rows of displayed objects, keeping their eyes peeled for the harp. But while there were all sorts of amazing treasures – including a pearl the size of a human head, a harpoon encrusted with diamonds, a net that looked like it was spun from pure gold, and a collection of silver swords – there was no sign of a harp anywhere.

Apollo halted by an enormous, rusted black cauldron.

'Wow,' he gasped. 'I think this is the *coire ansic*.'

'The *what*?'

'The Cauldron of Plenty. Another of Dagda's treasures. From the song, remember?'

'Queen Coomara keeps these treasures hidden away where only she gets to enjoy them,' Conor muttered. 'She could use that cauldron to feed her merrow army, but instead she keeps them hungry. She says it makes them better at capturing mortals.'

Orla looked at him, surprised. Why hadn't he said he knew more about the merrows before? It would have been good to know that at least one of them had some understanding of what they'd be swimming into.

'Woah!' exclaimed Apollo, pointing to another exhibit – a small round object the size of a golf ball displayed on a stand. It was white and bloody and had been pierced all the way through.

'What's that?' she asked, moving closer.

'I think that's Balor's missing eye!' gasped Conor.

Orla recoiled. 'Gross!'

'Well, maybe we can trade that instead, if we can't find the harp?' Conor suggested. 'He might like it back. I know "eye" would . . . get it?'

Apollo frowned. 'I don't think Balor will give us Gran back for his missing eye. He seems to be doing fine without it.'

'You're right. Sorry, I was just trying to lighten the mood.'

They continued along the rows of objects. When they reached the far wall and the harp still wasn't anywhere to be seen, Orla's hope faded. What if Queen Coomara kept it close to her at all times?

'I think we have to go back,' she said. 'I don't think it's here and the pearls' magic might run out soon . . .'

'What about behind there?' Apollo said, pointing to a curtained-off section that Orla hadn't noticed.

Sure enough, when they pulled back the velvet

curtain, behind it, displayed inside a glittering case was a harp!

Orla nearly whooped for joy. This had to be the harp they were searching for. It was the size of a small shield and its ornate oak frame was encrusted with thousands of jewels. You could tell just by looking at it that the harp was powerful.

'Thank goodness,' she breathed, hardly able to believe that they'd actually found it! She expected the other two to share her elation but Conor let out a groan.

'What's wrong? Is this not the right one?' Orla asked, though she already believed it was with all her heart.

'Oh, it's the right one,' he replied glumly.

Then she saw why he'd groaned. The harp's strings were moving. At first, Orla thought it was the water causing them to sway, before she realized that there was an intricate pattern to the *way* the strings moved, one at a time, as if invisible fingers were plucking them.

The harp was playing.

But why couldn't they hear its music? She touched her ears and, instead of Mum's earrings, felt – the petals! They must be protecting them from hearing the harp's magical melody . . .

And another realization hit her like a heavy iron cauldron.

The harp was playing the Music of Sleep. *That* was what was keeping the merrows from waking.

CHAPTER 28
It's Never That Easy

They all stared at the harp in despair.

'What do we do?' Orla cried out in frustration.

Would Queen Coomara sense it if they tried to take the harp? Would the music stop playing and the entire merrow army wake up? But after everything they'd done to get here, they were not going to leave Gran with the Wild Hunt, and that meant they were not leaving here without the harp.

She moved closer to get a better look. Was there some way to take it without disturbing the strings? The glittering case around the harp was glassless, really just a frame made of diamond-studded bars. Orla could easily put her hands through and grab the harp if she wanted to . . . But that might bring the whole Sunken City to hunt them. They needed to think this through. They needed to—

'Apollo! What are you doing?' Orla shrieked.

Before anything could be discussed or decided,

Apollo had reached in, grabbed the harp and lifted it out.

'Being brave,' he said.

Orla's heart hammered against her chest, but she was impressed by her brother's boldness and, to her surprise and colossal relief, the harp's strings kept moving.

For one blissful moment it seemed like everything was going to be all right.

Then three things happened at once.

First, the diamond bars of the cage lifted and became spears that shot towards each corner of the room, missing Apollo by centimetres. He let go of the harp as he swam out of the way and Conor caught it.

Second, tiny holes opened along the base of the treasury walls and crabs scuttled out – not small, friendly-looking crabs like the ones they'd watched at the beach, but large terrifying creatures with razor-sharp pincers.

Third, and worst of all, the ground below the display case opened and a whirlpool appeared there. Orla, Apollo and Conor, still clutching the harp, desperately swam away as the whirlpool sucked the display case and velvet curtains down into it. With enormous effort the three of them managed to get free of the whirlpool's pull and out of range of its power.

'It's booby-trapped!' Conor shouted.

'You think?' Orla called back over the churning noise of the whirlpool, which sounded like bathwater being sucked down a giant plughole. Apparently Queen Coomara would rather destroy her treasures than let anyone else steal them. Orla glanced at the harp in Conor's hands. Miraculously, it was still playing. Did that mean the merrows would sleep through this racket? She prayed so. But Queen Coomara wasn't asleep and she must have heard them by now.

'Ah!' Orla shrieked, dodging as one of the crabs flung itself directly at her face, slicing at her. 'Let's get out of here!'

'Good idea!' Conor held the harp to his chest and kicked hard. Orla and Apollo, who were able to swim faster without the harp, led the way towards the treasury's exit. As they got closer to the entranceway, however, Orla looked back and saw Conor lagging behind.

'Come on!' she urged.

But the crabs had blocked his way. Conor kicked desperately backwards to avoid their pincers, still grasping the harp. He was getting dangerously close to the whirlpool. If he swam backwards any further, he'd be caught up in its pull again, but he was also in equal danger of being sliced apart by the crabs.

Orla cast her eyes around the treasury for some way to help Conor and noticed the display of silver swords. She pulled one out. It was surprisingly light.

'Apollo, take one!' she shouted.

'Good idea!' Apollo also grabbed a sword. They swam back to Conor and swung the blades in wide circles, knocking crabs out of the way like they were cricket balls.

'Way to go, Apollo!' Orla called.

Together they rounded the crabs up behind Conor, forcing them backwards to the point where the whirlpool sucked them into it.

Orla, Apollo and Conor swam towards the exit. This time Apollo took the lead and Orla stayed with Conor.

'Thanks,' called Conor. 'Although, for the record, I totally had everything under control.'

'Yeah, it looked like it,' Orla shot back.

'I'm just not a fan of things with pincers, OK?'

Orla was about to reply when she felt her body being sucked backwards. Her sword slipped from her grasp, whipped towards the whirlpool and disappeared inside it. The whirlpool's range of force was expanding. Other objects in the treasury were hurtling towards them, including the harpoon, and they were forced to dodge out of the way to avoid being impaled.

Conor acted quickly. He grabbed the edge of the display stand under the Cauldron of Plenty with one hand, keeping hold of the harp with the other. He hollered at Orla to do the same.

She did, just as the current got even stronger. She hoped Apollo had found something secure to hold too.

'Conor, watch out!' she cried, as the Cauldron of Plenty wobbled dangerously. It started to topple towards them . . .

Suddenly the force stopped. The cauldron fell back on to its stand with a clang. Orla and Conor were jolted forwards and then everything was still and quiet again.

The whirlpool had gone. In its place was a gaping hole. Thick cracks ran along the stone floor and up the treasury walls.

Was it over?

'Apollo!' she called, surveying the wrecked treasury. 'Where are you? Are you OK?'

'I'm here!' Apollo's disgruntled reply came from close by. 'Sort of. I'm stuck!'

He was tangled in the golden net. At least he'd been safe from the whirlpool.

'Stay there. We'll come and help you.'

She started to swim forward but noticed Conor looking down at the harp in dismay. 'Orla, the strings . . . they're slowing.'

He was right – the strings were moving much more slowly. 'You don't think it'll stop playing completely, do you?' she asked fearfully.

Seeing the panic in her face, Conor feigned nonchalance. 'Oh, nah, certainly not. Not completely at least . . . Oh wait, yes . . . yes, it's stopped.'

'*What?*'

And even though none of them had been able to hear the music before, Orla could *feel* the silence.

The next moment, Apollo's scream cut through the water. Orla's head whipped around and she saw the glint of spears. The two merrow guards from the entrance were no longer asleep but racing towards Apollo who was still trapped in the net, helpless and defenceless, his sword nowhere to be seen. The merrows' faces were twisted in fury, their enormous tails pounded the water forcefully and their spears were raised.

'Help!' Apollo screamed.

At first Orla didn't stop to think. All she knew was that she couldn't let the guards get to Apollo, at least not without going through her first.

She started to race towards Apollo, but then slowed, reason catching up with her. She'd never be able to free Apollo before the guards reached him and there was no way she could fight the guards and win. She glanced back at Conor who was swimming more slowly because he still had the harp. She noticed the Cauldron of Plenty and had an idea. It was totally mad but it might just work . . . She swam back towards it.

'Olo, where are you going?' Apollo shouted, panicked.

'Just trust me, Polo . . . Hey, merrows! Over here! We've got your queen's special harp!' she yelled.

The guards looked up and spotted her, Conor and the harp. Their dark eyes flashed and they howled in fury.

'Er – Orla, what exactly are you doing?' called Conor in alarm as the merrow guards changed direction and headed straight for them.

'Get behind the cauldron quickly. I've got an idea.'

'I hope it's a good one,' Conor called, but he did as she said.

Once they were in position behind the cauldron, Orla took the harp and held it up so the merrows could see. 'Come and get it!' she shouted.

The merrows let out more screams of rage and torpedoed towards them.

Orla and Conor ducked as a spear sailed over their heads.

'When I say, you push,' she whispered. Conor nodded, his eyes widening as he understood her plan. *Come on*, Orla willed the merrow guards closer. She could see another spear being aimed at her, but they were almost exactly where she wanted them to be . . .

Orla remembered reading once that, in moments of fear, when the life of someone they loved was on the line, people were capable of impossible acts of strength. Mothers managed to flip over upturned cars to rescue their trapped babies. Pet-owners could bust in and out of burning buildings to save their beloved animals. Orla, who couldn't usually unscrew a jam-jar lid, hoped that now was one of those times. She gripped the cold rim of the heavy cauldron and, for a moment, peered into the great empty abyss of blackness inside.

The guards continued to approach, spears raised, teeth bared, ready to rip them apart.

'Push!' Orla screamed. With a loud battle cry, Orla heaved, straining with all her might against the cauldron. Conor heaved too. It was so heavy that for a moment she thought it wasn't going to budge but then, miraculously, it began to tip just as the merrow guards reached them. They swam right inside! Orla and Conor gave the cauldron one final, desperate push and it overturned entirely, trapping the merrows in the dark, bottomless abyss underneath.

'Wahoo!' called Conor. 'That was genius, Orla! In fact, it was so clever that I'm surprised I didn't think of it myself.'

'I'll take that as a compliment.' Orla grinned, experiencing a moment of elation. But again this didn't last. The harp still wasn't playing and it wouldn't just be the two guards awake.

It would be the whole city . . .

And the mortal-eating merrow queen was still at large.

Not to mention the fact that the cracks running up the walls of the treasury had reached the ceiling, which no longer looked stable at all.

They had to move.

Orla swam with the harp and Conor freed Apollo from the net using the penknife Apollo had brought in his pocket, which he'd been too tangled to reach.

'See? I told you it would come in handy!' Apollo said.

Orla swept him up in a quick hug. 'That was far too close.'

Then the three of them were swimming for their lives.

As they reached the palace's exit, Orla looked around fearfully for Queen Coomara.

There was still no sign of her. But Orla didn't feel relieved. *Where was she?* Queen Coomara must have been alerted by the noise coming from her treasury.

'Even if the merrows *are* all awake now, maybe most

of them didn't hear anything?' Conor said hopefully. 'Maybe, if we just keep really quiet from now on . . .'

There was an enormous boom. The treasury had collapsed.

'On second thoughts, maybe not.'

CHAPTER 29
Queen Coomara

'SWIM!' Conor cried.

Orla's hands were full of the harp so she could only kick her legs furiously. There were three of them against a city of merrows, and they had nothing to defend themselves with. Except the magical harp, she reminded herself. But what use was that now it had stopped playing?

Play! she urged the silent strings.

Orla had a strange prickling sensation: could *she* pluck these strings? No, that was ludicrous. She'd never played a normal harp before, let alone a *magical* one. Though Orla remembered her music teacher telling her that if you could play a scale on the piano, you could do the same on a harp. Even if she could play it, though, there was no saying she'd manage to play the Music of Sleep, which she'd never even heard, thanks to the blue petals . . .

But just supposing it worked . . .

Her stomach fizzed. She'd spent the last two years denying the music within her, but what if she could use it to save them now? She remembered what it had felt like singing for the water sprites. How the music had sent warm vibrations shimmering through her and made her feel alive again. How *free* she had felt, how at home.

But there'd also been the memories of Mum, the pain that was easier to shut out than confront. She wasn't likely to be able to play the harp anyway – it was just desperate, wishful thinking, and they didn't need wishful thinking, they needed to get out of here!

The streets were still eerily empty as Orla, Apollo and Conor swam back the way they'd come.

'Where are all the merrows?' she whispered.

'Maybe they're still asleep . . .' Apollo suggested hopefully.

But when they peeked inside the buildings, fresh fear sliced through them. They were empty.

They carried on, expecting to be attacked at any moment. But no merrows appeared. As they reached the edge of the city, Orla felt a tiny flutter of hope. *Maybe they'd make it. Maybe they'd get out of here alive.* High above, the surface glimmered tantalizingly, still very far away.

And that's when she heard it.

Or rather she *felt* it.

A drumbeat.

So loud that it reverberated through her entire body.

Then another.

And another.

Drums beating all over the Sunken City.

Then the merrows appeared, floating up from the city in their thousands, spears raised, their ugly faces full of fury.

Apollo made a strangled sound and Conor let out a yelp. Orla's hands shook so much that she almost dropped the harp. She kept kicking upwards even though attempting escape already felt futile in the face of all this power. Apollo grabbed hold of her arm and kicked with her, but this only slowed him down too. They'd never be able to outswim the merrows, there were too many. They'd got the harp but it wasn't going to make any difference.

Why did she ever think they could do this?

The merrows had still not attacked. They must also know that their intruders had no chance of getting away.

Queen Coomara rose above her army. She had the most hideously cruel face Orla had ever seen.

The other merrows waited for her signal.

Orla glanced desperately towards the surface. She'd

never see the stars again. Or the sun. Or Dad . . .

Regret filled her heart. She wished she'd not spent so much of the past two years being miserable. She wished she'd been nicer to Apollo, to Dad, to Gran. *Gran.* If they made it out of here, she was going to be better, kinder, more grateful for what she had. *If* they made it out of here.

For a moment the drumming ceased but its pulse still thrummed in Orla's ears as she, Apollo and Conor continued to swim and kick towards the surface, their fatigued muscles aching.

When the drumming started again it was faster and more urgent, like the sound of gunshots or a thousand pummelling fists.

A blood-curdling scream ripped through the water. At Queen Coomara's signal, the other merrows surged upwards, a dark mass of teeth, scales and whip-like tails.

Orla tried to propel herself forward with all her might. But it was no use. The merrows were too fast, too powerful. This time there was no magic cauldron to save them . . .

Again, Orla felt the prickling feeling and her mind being drawn to the harp. She stopped kicking. Even if it didn't work, it was worth a shot.

'Orla, what are you doing?' cried Apollo.

There was no time to explain, and she wasn't even sure she could if she wanted to. She just had a *feeling*. She brushed the strings. She could sense the harp's magic – deep and old – waiting inside it.

Play, she willed urgently.

Like a partner in a dance, she felt the harp respond.

Play me, came the reply.

Orla tried. She felt the music there but when she tried to let it flow through her, the melody wouldn't come. Just a few staccato notes.

She glanced down and saw Queen Coomara's eyes fixed on her. There was so much loathing in the merrow queen's gaze that Orla flinched.

Queen Coomara pulled back her spear and released it. The spear tore through the water at an impossible speed. It scraped Orla's shoulder and she screamed as pain ricocheted through her.

'Orla!' Apollo cried.

Blood – such a bright crimson – spread out through the water. For a moment, Orla couldn't comprehend that this was *her* blood. *There was so much of it*. Her shoulder seared with agony. *Red everywhere*. The dark shapes of the merrows materialized behind, their tails thrashing, moving faster now, as if the taste of blood had energized them. Orla had seen video clips of shark feeding frenzies where, confronted with bleeding prey, they went wild, biting anything that moved, including each other.

This felt like that. The merrows were wild and rabid.

Apollo and Conor needed to leave her behind, take the harp and get out of here!

But Orla could already feel them both grabbing her, trying to pull her – and the harp – with them.

'Leave me!' she called. They had no chance of escape lugging her weight too. 'Take the harp. Save yourselves. Save Gran!'

'Not without you,' Apollo cried fiercely, gripping on even tighter.

The whips of tails slamming into the water and the horrid clash of teeth filled Orla's ears. She could no longer distinguish the sound of the drumming from the beating of her own heart. The pain in her shoulder was making her head spin and stars explode over her vision.

Sorry I let you down, Gran.

Orla felt her lungs squeeze tight. The water was colder now and her clothes dragged her down. The effect of the pearl was wearing off.

'Leave me, please,' she gasped. If they let go, maybe they'd still have a chance of getting out of here alive.

'No! I'm not losing you, Olo. You promised.'

'You have to. Please. You've got to make it . . .' The pain was too much. Her eyes closed.

Something scooped underneath her. She felt her body being propelled upwards, breaking the surface of the sea and being elevated safely into the sky. As she gasped in crisp air, her eyes flew open. Fionn loomed above. He had the three of them clutched in his palm.

'Told ya I'd come back to help,' he boomed.

'Talk about leaving it to the last minute!' Conor called.

Merrows jumped out of the water, snapping furiously, teeth gnashing, tails writhing. Fionn held Orla, Apollo and Conor out of reach. The merrows fell back with heavy splashes and yowls, and were swallowed by the sea. Soon the only signs of them were a few ripples and bubbles on the glassy black surface.

Fionn plucked several spears out of the back of his hand as if they were nothing more than toothpicks and tossed them into the water.

Orla lay on the giant's palm, panting hard, her shoulder throbbing. She pulled the petals from her ears, pocketing them with trembling fingers.

When she tried to sit up, the world tipped. She had a final blurry impression of stars before everything went dark.

CHAPTER 30
A New Plan

When Orla came to, she was lying on the cold sand and there was something heavy and woolly on top of her. Her shoulder was on fire. It had been bandaged so she couldn't see the wound, but it felt like she'd been sliced right through. She recalled how red the water had been and the sight of the merrows darting towards them in their thousands. They'd so nearly not made it . . .

She opened her eyes and gazed up at the sky. It was still dark, thank goodness, but how long had she been unconscious? They couldn't afford to waste time! Especially not now they had the harp and might actually have a chance of saving Gran, before morning came and it was too late.

Wait. Where *was* the harp?

Orla looked around and was relieved to spot it propped beside Apollo and Conor, who were sitting nearby. The jewels on its frame flashed in the moonlight.

The dark shape of the pooka lurked at a distance behind them but there was no sign of Fionn, except for his sock, which was currently on top of her. Orla pushed it off, tried to sit up and groaned as a fresh stab of pain seared through her shoulder.

'Orla!' Apollo gasped with relief, moving closer. 'You're awake! Thank goodness. Are you OK? How's your shoulder?'

Orla expected Conor to rush to her side too, but he stayed where he was, staring into space.

'Not great,' she muttered and immediately wished she'd lied, because even in the dark she could tell that Apollo's face had crumpled with worry. 'I'm fine, really. Can you pass me the harp?'

She didn't like the harp being unprotected after all they'd gone through to get it.

Apollo handed it to her. As she took it and her fingers brushed the strings, she again had that prickling sensation. She felt the magic of the ancient music inside the harp, like a humming deep within it. She thought of how she'd failed to play it in the Sunken City and was filled with shame for ever thinking she was worthy enough to try.

'Where's Fionn?' she asked.

Apollo's shoulders drooped. 'He left after he saved us and put us on the beach. He and the pooka caught some good clouds while we were underwater and he said he was headed back home to use them.'

Orla's heart sank. 'He's gone?'

'What did you expect?' the pooka called out mockingly. 'He kept his word.'

Yes, Fionn had kept his word about coming back to help them escape the merrows. If he hadn't, there was no way they'd be alive. Still, to lose his help now, when they were so close to saving Gran, was a crushing blow.

'Did he say anything about what to do next?' she asked despondently, already anticipating the answer to be no.

Apollo shook his head. 'I didn't ask. I was too worried about you. He told me how to bandage the wound and lent me one of his handkerchiefs for it, but after that, while I was making sure you were OK, he just left. I'm sorry.'

'You don't have to be sorry, Apollo. None of this is your fault.' It was hers. She was the one who'd opened Gran's window and got them into this mess. Could they still get out of it and save Gran? They had the harp. They just had to work out what to do next. Maybe they didn't need Fionn. Conor knew a lot about this stuff. Perhaps he could think of what to do . . .

But instead of giving one of his usual speeches about how easy it would all be, Conor remained silent.

'Is he all right?' Orla whispered.

Apollo shrugged. 'Seems a bit shaken up.'

It was strange to see Conor so subdued. What was he thinking about? His own family? He must have thought about them when it seemed like they were about to die. It hadn't been fair to drag Conor into all this, however willing he'd seemed.

Orla looked down at the glittering harp. 'I can't believe we actually got it,' she muttered.

'I know. You were amazing, Olo.'

Despite everything, a smile tugged at the corners of her lips. She shook her head. 'You were the amazing one, Polo.'

'OK, we were *both* pretty amazing. Can't believe the three of us took on a whole merrow army and lived to tell the tale! It's better than any of Gran's stories. I can't wait to tell her when—' He stopped and swallowed. '*If*,' he added.

'You'll get to tell her everything *very* soon,' Orla said firmly, trying to channel some of Conor's usual confidence. 'We got the harp, didn't we?'

'Yes,' Apollo agreed. 'We can do anything – together.'

'Together,' Orla agreed, her chest warming. 'Maybe all we have to do now is call the Wild Hunt here by saying their name three times, like in the song? Then

use the harp to bargain with Balor for Gran's release?'
She shivered, thinking of her previous encounter with
Balor. Even just saying this plan made her feel terrified.

She felt Apollo hesitating. 'Orla, I've been thinking
. . . You know I want to get Gran back more than
anything, but I don't think she would want us to give
the harp to the Wild Hunt. It's too powerful. You saw
how it kept that entire merrow army sleeping – just
think how the Wild Hunt would use it on poor, innocent people! They've already taken so many. If they
could lure others with the harp's music, they'd take
more grandmas and mums and dads and children –
and it would be our fault.'

Orla bit her lip. She hadn't thought about this
before – she'd been too focused on Gran – but she
knew Apollo was right. Now that they'd seen first-hand
what the harp could do, she agreed that it felt wrong to
just hand over all that power to the Wild Hunt.

'But how else do we get Gran back?' she wondered
aloud. If they didn't exchange the harp for Gran then
they'd lose Gran for ever. Everything they'd done, all
the danger they'd put themselves in, would have been
for nothing.

If only the fairies had listened to Gran in the first
place and agreed to stop the Wild Hunt! If only they
didn't have the stupid peace treaty. The only way the

Wild Hunt would ever attract the Good Folk's attention during their midsummer revels was if they actually *entered* the Fairy Kingdom. And Orla was sure that, no matter how strong and bold they were, they were unlikely to do that. The Wild Hunt had no reason to go there. They hunted sorrowful mortals.

Still lurking some distance away, the pooka cleared its throat pointedly. 'I'm still waiting for my thank you, by the way.'

'Thank you for what?' Orla asked, confused.

The pooka growled. 'The petals, of course. If I hadn't given them to you, you'd all be fish food!'

'You're right,' said Apollo. 'Thanks, Pooka.' He nudged Orla.

'Thanks,' she said begrudgingly. Why *had* the pooka helped them? The terms of the pooka's promise were that it only had to help with things that they asked it to do, and they hadn't asked the pooka for the petals outright. How could they when they hadn't even known they'd needed them? The pooka had helped them voluntarily. And that didn't make any sense.

All the pooka had to do was wait until the night ended – however it ended – and then it would be free to go back to whatever it usually did. Surely that would be its plan? So why had it helped them? It worried Orla.

As if to give her a clue, the harp's jewels flashed and everything clicked into place. The pooka wanted the harp! Of course it did. All magical beings longed for the harp's power, Fionn had said.

Orla's fingers tightened around the frame. They needed the harp to save Gran and they mustn't let the pooka take it or trick them. She sat up straighter. This time she barely noticed her shoulder.

'Maybe we don't have to *give* the harp to the Wild Hunt,' she whispered. 'What if we could use it to trick them?'

Apollo frowned. 'Trick the Wild Hunt? What do you mean?'

Orla took a deep breath and lowered her voice even further, aware of how good the pooka's hearing was. She knew her idea was going to sound like lunacy. 'I mean, what if we lure the Wild Hunt somewhere they shouldn't be . . . somewhere they might break a treaty.'

Apollo's eyes widened. 'You want to lure the Wild Hunt into the Fairy Kingdom?'

'We can summon them there by calling their true name three times. Then we'll offer Balor the harp but insist that he hand Gran over first. Hopefully, before we have to give up the harp, the fairies will appear. The treaty will be broken as soon as the Wild Hunt enter the Fairy Kingdom so they'll fight them. And once the fairies see how strong the Wild Hunt have become, they'll be forced to defeat them. We wouldn't just be saving Gran; we'd be saving countless future victims too.' Orla thought of Liam Armstrong, Mary Hart and all the other poor missing people from the clippings in Gran's folder. It was too late to save them, but maybe Orla and Apollo could prevent more innocent people falling into the Wild Hunt's clutches. 'This is what Gran wanted – to stop the Wild Hunt. We'd not only be saving her, we'd be completing her wish too!'

Maybe then Gran would forgive Orla for causing her to be captured. *Maybe.*

Apollo blinked at her, struggling to take all this in. 'But we don't even know *how* to get to the Fairy Kingdom—' he spluttered.

'We do, remember? Gran always said you can enter through any woods in Ireland. All you have to do is find a fairy ring, close your eyes and you'll travel there . . .' In her mind's eye, Orla saw the clearing with the circle of stones in the Tangled Woods where the fairies had gathered two nights ago. 'There's a wood just up at the end of the beach – I'm sure we could find a fairy ring there. The Good Folk are the *only* ones the Wild Hunt fear—'

'Which means *we* should fear them too,' Apollo

interjected. 'Orla, we barely made it out of the Sunken City alive. Arriving in the Fairy Kingdom uninvited, not to mention during their midsummer celebrations . . . it's a death sentence. You must remember *those* stories too.'

Orla did. Any mortals who found themselves accidentally in the Fairy Kingdom during this sacred time, whether through fault of their own or not, were punished according to the old fairy laws. Some were forced to dance at the celebrations until they were so exhausted that they dropped dead. Others were fed strange potions that made them forget everything, including how to breathe. She remembered how frightening the fairies had been in the Tangled Woods.

But the idea of losing Gran was more terrifying.

And time was running out.

CHAPTER 31
A Truth Comes Out

Apollo shook his head. 'It's too dangerous, Orla. And you're hurt.'

'I'm fine.'

'There's got to be another way.'

'There isn't. We don't have time to sit here arguing. By morning Gran will be beyond saving, just like all those other victims.'

Orla could tell Apollo was torn but he kept looking at Orla's bandaged shoulder.

'I could go by myself,' she suggested.

'Absolutely not!' he said furiously. 'Splitting up did not go well before and we said we'd stick together, didn't we?'

'Yes but—'

'No buts, Orla! It's too dangerous and there are too many things that could go very, very wrong. I want to think this through properly. I didn't think things through in the treasury when I grabbed the harp and it led to you getting badly hurt. I don't want to make that mistake again.'

'Me getting hurt wasn't down to you! You did the only thing we could do. If you hadn't, we wouldn't have the harp now.'

But Apollo shook his head. 'I'll think of something else. Just give me a second.'

Apollo walked away down the beach towards the sea and stared out across the water, thinking hard. Orla sighed. Her brother always wanted to think things through and while that was usually a good thing, right now they couldn't afford the time. Her throat felt like sandpaper. She found the water bottle and took a glug.

'You OK, Conor?' she called.

Conor jerked from his thoughts. 'Yeah, all good.' He tried to give one of his usual smiles, but it slipped. Orla longed for just a glimmer of his light-hearted humour. His arrogance, though irritating, had become a source of comfort, as had his friendship and loyalty. He could have abandoned them at any point, but he hadn't. She realized she'd come to care about him and seeing him like this made her worry.

'What's the plan?' he asked, glancing at the harp.

'That's what we're trying to figure out . . . Any ideas?'

'Have you thought about using it?' Conor said

quietly. At first Orla assumed he must have overheard her proposed plan to use the harp to trick the Wild Hunt and was about to explain further, when he added, 'You could play it, you know. Whoever becomes its master will have the harp's power right at their fingertips. They can do whatever they like . . . How amazing would that be?'

His words caught Orla by surprise. She frowned and shook her head. 'I tried to play it underwater, but I couldn't.'

'That's because you were blocking it.'

'What?' How on earth would Conor know?

'There's music inside you,' Conor continued, looking up at her. 'I can feel it. I felt it when you sang for the water sprites. You have a gift, but you block yourself from enjoying it. That's why you couldn't play the harp. Why do you do that?' he added, sounding genuinely curious.

She almost didn't answer, but his words hit home. 'Because of my mum,' she said quietly. 'Music was something we did together.'

'So now you deny yourself?'

Orla felt as if she'd suddenly lost a layer of skin. 'Yes, because it reminds me of her and it's too painful. Music used to make her feel better – I thought, if I was just good enough, I could use it to save her . . . Only it didn't work. The music couldn't save her, nothing could, no matter how hard I tried or wanted it to. Music let me down, just like everything else did. It didn't feel right to enjoy it after that, it didn't feel right to enjoy anything. That's why I stopped playing and singing.' Her throat caught. 'Now we might lose Gran too . . . And it's all my fault.' Shame washed over her and hot tears sprang from her eyes.

Conor frowned. 'What do you mean? Of course, it isn't!'

'It is,' she wailed, and the secret came spilling out. 'I was the one who unbolted Gran's window that night she went missing. I went out through it when I followed her and forgot that it wouldn't be locked. I didn't even think . . . I was just so determined to find out what Gran was up to and so angry with her for keeping things from me. It's because of me that the Wild Hunt got in, because of me that they took her . . .'

Orla heard a gasp. Her heart dropped. She turned and saw Apollo standing behind her, hurt and betrayal etched into his face.

'*You* unbolted Gran's window?'

'Apollo—'

Apollo shook his head. 'After all her warnings! After how many times she asked us to keep them locked!' His voice rose in fury.

'I know. I'm an idiot, Apollo. You have every right to be angry, I'm angry with myself. But right now we don't have time—'

'And the worst part is that you didn't even *tell* me! You told Conor. Were you ever going to mention it to *your brother*? Or were you just going to continue to lie?' he shouted, his eyes streaming with tears. 'We were meant to be doing this together! But you only ever think of yourself, Orla!'

'Apollo—' she gasped. But there was nothing she could say to fix this. She should have told him the truth immediately. She should never have opened the window in the first place.

She tried to reach for his hand. Apollo recoiled. 'Leave me alone!' he yelled, racing away.

'Apollo! Wait!' she shouted after him.

Apollo kept running until he was a small shadow at the other end of the beach.

Orla moved to go after him, but she was still carrying the harp and felt pulled in the other direction, towards the woods. There wasn't time to fix things with Apollo, even if she could. She had to try to get Gran back. If she could save Gran, maybe Apollo would be able to forgive her. If she couldn't, she'd lose them both anyway, so it didn't matter if she didn't survive . . .

Her mind was made up. She was finally going to be the big sister her brother deserved. She shifted the harp into her good hand, picked up a torch and, wincing, climbed shakily to her feet.

'Go after him,' she instructed the pooka. 'Make sure he's OK and protect him from harm with your life. That's an order.'

The pooka's orange eyes flashed in annoyance at being bossed around, but it could not disregard a direct request while the promise still held. It scampered after Apollo.

When it was out of earshot, she said to Conor, 'Will you go after them too and make sure Apollo's all right? I don't trust the pooka, even with the promise.'

'Where are *you* going?' Conor asked, confused.

'The Fairy Kingdom.' She started walking towards the dark woods that edged the beach.

'What? By yourself?' Conor gasped. 'They'll kill you!'

Orla did not stop walking. 'I've got to try and fix this. I don't want to put either of you in any more danger. You can't change my mind, Conor. Please, just go after Apollo and check he's OK.'

It occurred to her that this could be the last time she ever spoke to Conor; she had so much to thank him for but she couldn't bring herself to say goodbye. All she could do was keep moving towards the woods.

She didn't allow herself to look back, so she didn't notice the pooka's eyes flashing in the darkness as it turned to watch her go, and she didn't hear the footsteps that followed her.

CHAPTER 32
Lost in the Woods (Again)

Orla stumbled through the dark trees, her thin torch beam shining on tangles of ferns and snaking roots underfoot. Overhanging branches leered out of the darkness and she kept having to duck. Unseen cobwebs slipped over her face, making her shiver. The dank smell of rotting leaves clogged her nose. Her injured shoulder throbbed and the harp was cumbersome to carry. Still, she pressed on, heading deeper into the woods, hoping to find the fairy ring at its heart. There had to be one.

Orla listened fearfully for wingbeats. Her own breathing felt too loud. The horror of the last time the Wild Hunt had found her was still fresh in her mind. The screaming. The deep sadness that had welled up inside her . . .

She stopped.

What was that? Distant wingbeats? No, it was her mind playing tricks, she told herself firmly, forcing herself on and trying her best to keep any sad feelings at bay in order to not attract them.

She hoped Apollo was OK and that the pooka and Conor were keeping him safe. She felt terrible for leaving him when she'd promised she wouldn't, especially after he'd just found out she'd lied to him. His betrayed expression burnt in her mind. But she was doing this for him and Gran. She was going to find the fairy ring, save Gran and bring their family back together.

But the deeper she went into the trees, the more her doubts started to creep in. There was no sign of any moss-covered stones like the ones she'd seen in the Tangled Woods, and she had no idea how to find them. What if this fairy ring was more hidden? What if there wasn't a fairy ring in these woods at all?

She heard the noise again, faint but unmistakeable this time.

Footsteps.

Orla froze and jerked around, her heart slamming against her ribs.

There was no one there.

But this time Orla was sure she hadn't imagined it. She ran. The trees were getting closer together and more difficult to move between, especially without damaging the harp.

She tripped over a tree root and came crashing

down. Her torch flew from her hand and rolled down a hidden slope. Orla rolled with it. She threw the harp backwards to avoid falling on it and breaking it, while she tumbled headlong into a ditch. She lay at the bottom, panting. Her shoulder seared with hot pain but everything else seemed to be in one piece and, after a few seconds, she found her torch and shone it towards the top of the ditch, making the jewels on the harp glitter.

Orla rolled on to her knees and picked herself up. When she looked back to the top of the ditch again, she gasped.

The harp was gone.

She looked around wildly and her heart stopped. A shadowy figure stood just out of the torchlight's reach, holding the harp.

It was only when the figure flicked his hair back that she let out a sigh of relief.

'Conor!' she exclaimed. 'What are you doing here? I thought I told you to look after Apollo. Though I have to admit I'm pleased to see you. Did you follow me?'

She was so relieved. Conor would know how to find the fairy ring; she was sure of it. She'd been an idiot for not thinking to ask him in the first place. Conor remained where he was, watching her silently. Poor thing, was he still shaken up?

'Help me, will you?' She held out her hand.

Conor didn't move. A cold shiver ran down her spine. Why was he just standing there?

'Where's Apollo?'

Conor turned away. 'Sorry, Orla.'

Orla shook her head. 'What? Why . . . Hey, where are you going? Stop! Give it back!'

But Conor was already disappearing, taking the harp with him.

'Conor!' Orla screamed. She recalled the strange look in his eyes earlier and his words returned to her. *Whoever becomes its master will have the harp's power right at their fingertips. They can do whatever they like . . .* The realization was like a punch in the stomach: Conor wanted the harp for himself. He'd betrayed them.

Ignoring her aching shoulder, she grabbed her torch, scrambled up the side of the ditch and tore through the trees, but there was no sign of Conor anywhere. Her mind reeled. How long had he been planning to betray them? From the very beginning? Had everything he'd ever said been a lie? She'd *trusted* Conor. She'd come to think of him as their friend. She cursed herself for being so stupid. It was Apollo rubbing off on her. Look where trusting people got you!

Mum was gone. Gran was gone. Dad was far away. Apollo would never forgive her, now he knew it was her fault Gran had been taken and also her fault that they'd lost the harp and their only chance of saving her. And Conor, who they'd trusted, had been the one who'd deceived them and stolen their only hope.

Orla stopped running and sank to her knees. She wanted to curl up into a ball and lie there in that wood for ever. What did anything matter now? What was the point in fighting? She'd never felt so helpless.

Everything had fallen to pieces.

There was an odd scuffling sound in the undergrowth.

A pair of gleaming orange eyes regarded her from the dark bushes. 'Well, you look like you're having a good night.'

Orla gasped in surprise. '*Pooka?*'

'No, you've got multiple orange-eyed acquaintances who are bound by a death contract to continually show up to help you. Yes, it's me! Care to tell me what on earth you're doing? Just fancied a little night-time stroll in the woods by yourself, did you? I see you've managed to lose the harp. Well done.'

'I didn't lose it,' Orla retorted crossly, her anger and frustration bubbling up. 'Conor ran off with it!'

The pooka's eyes widened ever so slightly. 'Conor took the harp? Interesting. I knew there was something . . . off about him. He smelt funny. Well, funnier than the rest of you, which is saying something. *Too sweet*, sort of like—'

Orla closed her eyes. 'Please, spare me the lectures about how stupid or stinky I am, will you? You can't make me feel any worse than I already do.'

'Are you sure? I could give it a good shot . . .'

Orla sighed. As if she needed this right now! Why was the pooka here? Had it just come to gloat or was it looking for the harp? Well, it was too late. It would have to go after Conor if it wanted it. 'Didn't I order you to stay with Apollo?'

'You did.'

'Well, Apollo is clearly not here so why are you? Did you come and find me just to insult me? That hardly seems worth breaking your promise and dying for.'

'No,' replied the pooka, coming closer and sitting cross-legged in front of her. 'I mean, I can't really help insulting you – it's just too easy. But I actually came *because* of my promise. Your brother told me to come so here I am. He wanted me to find you before you did anything stupid. Although it appears to be too late for that.'

'But I told you to stay with him!'

'He overrode you.'

Orla's stomach dropped. That meant Apollo was on his own and vulnerable to the Wild Hunt, especially as his feelings were so hurt by what she'd done.

'Well, I order you to go back to him.'

'Can't I'm afraid. Your brother's smarter than you and ordered me to stay with you despite any of your counter-orders.'

Orla sighed. That sounded like Apollo.

'Do you want to sit here all night discussing details, or do you want to try and get your grandmother back before it's too late?'

'I want to get Gran, of course, but—'

'So what's the plan?' the pooka interrupted.

Orla stared at it. There *was* no plan, that was the point. It was all ruined. Unless . . .

'Can you track Conor? Could we get the harp back?'

The pooka sniffed the air and shook its head. 'All I can smell in these woods is fairy dust. The entire place reeks of the stuff. It's odd, though, as I should be able to catch a trace of him at least, but it's like he's vanished.'

Great. Maybe Conor had already worked out how to use the harp's magic. She wouldn't put it past him. There were probably things about it he'd known all along and kept from them.

So what should she do? Fionn had said the harp was the only way to get Gran back, but he couldn't predict the future . . . What if there *was* another way? With the pooka's help, maybe she could find the Fairy Kingdom and still lure the Wild Hunt there by calling their true name.

It was an even more reckless plan than her previous one. But she had nothing left to lose.

She turned to the pooka, her jaw set in determination. 'Can you take me to the fairy ring in these woods? There's got to be one, right?'

The pooka's eyes flashed. '*Can* I, or *will* I? Of course *I can*. But why would you want to go there? Fancy some dancing tonight along with your walk, do you? You do know it's forbidden for non-fairies to enter the Fairy Kingdom during the midsummer celebrations, don't you? Especially mortals.'

Orla bit her lip. She knew it was extremely risky. But like with the merrows, she doubted the fairies expected anyone to be bold enough to enter their kingdom. Maybe that would buy her some time. She wondered why the pooka was telling her all this. It sounded oddly like it was warning her. It was probably just worried she'd force it to come along.

'Take me there. Please.'

'Why? Oh!' The pooka's rabbit ears stood upright. 'Oh, I see. You're going to try to get the Wild Hunt to break the treaty. Risky, very risky . . .'

Orla sighed. 'What hasn't been risky so far? If my plan works, your promise will be done very soon.'

'And if it doesn't?'

'Your promise will still be done.' She didn't add: *because Gran will be lost for ever and I'll be facing the same fate or dead.*

The pooka seemed to understand. 'What about your blue-haired brother?' Again, for a moment, it sounded like it cared.

Orla swallowed and tried not to think about what Apollo would do if neither she nor Gran came back. 'I've made up my mind,' she muttered. 'And don't worry, I won't make you come with me if that's what you're concerned about.'

The pooka's eyes flashed and it climbed back on to all fours. 'Very well. Follow me. You might want to bring that, though. It could come in handy.' It gestured to the torch before turning tail and disappearing through the trees.

Orla quickly climbed to her feet, scooped up the torch and followed the pooka. Just as before, its shaggy black body was hard to keep track of in the woods and it kept blending with the shadows, but this time it waited for Orla when she lost sight of it.

It felt like they travelled for ages, but it was probably only a matter of minutes before they came to a clearing where several majestic, ancient, moss-covered stones were propped up in a circle.

Just like the fairy ring in the Tangled Woods!

Tentative but resolute, she moved into the centre of the stones, closed her eyes and waited.

There was a long pause.

Nothing happened.

Orla opened one eye and looked at the pooka.

It was staring at her with an expression of disbelief. 'You have no idea what to do, do you?'

'Er, not really . . . no. I mean, I know I'm meant to stand in the middle and close my eyes and then I just sort of thought it would happen.'

'*You just sort of thought it would happen?* Without you having to do anything at all? Like some kind of weird lift into the Fairy Kingdom?'

Orla bit her lip. 'That's how it always went in Gran's stories,' she admitted.

'Those stories have *a lot* to answer for. They always scrimp on the specifics . . . This is filling me with a lot of confidence for the chances of the rest of your plan working, by the way.' The pooka shook its head. 'Why am I even surprised . . . You have to close your eyes and *think* of the Fairy Kingdom. You won't get there otherwise.'

'Think of it? How do I do that when I've never been?'

The pooka rolled its eyes.

'Well, I know some details from Gran's stories . . . I'll think of those!' Orla said hurriedly, hating feeling so pathetic.

She squeezed her eyes shut tightly and tried to think of the Fairy Kingdom but the details she remembered were hazy. Her thoughts kept slipping back to her fear for Gran and the hurt expression on Apollo's face, which might be the last look of his she ever saw.

After another pause, Orla opened her eyes hopefully. But she was still in the same woods, staring across at the pooka, which was still wearing an expression of disbelief at her incompetence.

'It didn't work!' she groaned.

'Evidently,' said the pooka witheringly. 'You're not focusing.'

'I'm trying to . . . I have to do this!' Orla gasped, shaking her head. Her eyes blurred. She wiped the tears away, squeezed her eyes shut and tried again, but nothing happened.

'Oh, for troll-bogey's sake,' she heard the pooka say. 'Stop straining like that, you look like you're having a poo. Here!'

A sharp claw scratched the palm of her torch-free hand, but then she felt a surprisingly warm and soft furry paw. She blinked her eyes open in surprise and saw the pooka grimacing as it stood on its hind legs beside her.

'Yuck,' it muttered. 'You're just as clammy as I suspected . . . Right, looks like I have to do everything, as usual. Close those eyes and whatever you do, don't let go!'

CHAPTER 33
The Fairy Kingdom

O rla closed her eyes and the next moment a whooshing filled her ears. The ground dropped away and she was tumbling through the air, somersaulting over and over. She tried to open her eyes, only to close them again as the dizzying whirl of world flying past made her stomach lurch. She gripped the pooka's paw so tightly that its claws pricked her skin, but she didn't dare let go.

Just as it seemed that the falling would never end, she landed with a heavy thump on mossy ground. Her injured shoulder was knocked painfully and her hand tugged from the pooka's paw as she rolled on to her back.

Groaning, Orla opened her eyes and looked up at the sky. For a moment the world continued to spin and lights danced across her vision. As things steadied, she saw that they'd landed in the middle of another circle of stones in another wood.

It looked both the same *and* entirely different.

Both the stones and the tree were far taller here. Colourful lights had been tangled around the branches. No, not lights, Orla realized with a rush of awe, *fireflies*! Above the high treetops, the stars were brighter than she'd ever seen them and not one but *three* moons hung in the sky. A golden mist glittered in the air and jovial music drifted into the clearing from somewhere close by.

'Ugh, the reek of fairy dust here is unbearable!' the pooka complained.

Orla sniffed the air tentatively. For once the pooka's complaint seemed well founded: there *was* a noxious sweetness on the breeze. 'It smells like burnt marshmallows.'

'Ah, so you *can* smell! Good. I was starting to wonder why you even bothered having nostrils.'

Beyond the stone circle, between the huge tree roots, towered enormous bluebells as large as street lamps, and carved into tree trunks were intricately patterned doors – doors that were only reachable if you could climb or *fly*. *Fairy homes.* A blue butterfly with gold-tipped wings danced in front of her. Then another. And another. They swirled around Orla and the pooka.

The pooka yelped and swatted at the butterflies with its claws. 'Get lost, you tattletales!'

The butterflies did, swooping away through the trees at speed.

'Actually, on second thoughts, come back!' the pooka called after them. 'They'll be off to tell King Oberon we're here,' he said to Orla. 'From the sound of things he's in the middle of a party – surprise, surprise! But it won't be long until he's here to punish us for trespassing, in whatever entertaining way he chooses.'

The pooka's rabbit ears had flattened against its head and its tail was flicking back and forth. It looked as afraid as it had been with the water sprites. Orla knew what Apollo would say if he were here. As terrible as the pooka had been and despite the fact it had tried to get them killed before, it wasn't fair to make it come on this fool's errand with her. Though she hadn't actually done that, had she? She hadn't *told* the pooka to come. It was like with the flower petals; the pooka had helped without being directly ordered to. Why had it done that?

Orla looked at it cowering and knew the right thing to do. Still, was it crazy to let the pooka go now? It had useful knowledge about this place, knowledge that she lacked. And maybe she should send it back to check on Apollo, but she'd be calling the Wild Hunt here soon enough anyway so hopefully he'd be safe from them.

Apollo's words came back to her and made up her mind:

You only ever think of yourself, Orla!

It was selfish for Orla to keep the pooka captive against its will, like the Wild Hunt was keeping Gran against hers. Orla didn't want to be selfish any more. She wanted to do the right thing, even if it *was* a really inconvenient time to start doing it.

'You should go. You don't need to help any more. I-I release you from your promise,' she added awkwardly, not sure if she could actually do this.

The pooka stared at her in astonishment, its rabbit ears springing upright. 'You *release* me?'

'Yes . . . I can do that, right?'

'Yes, but you haven't got your grandmother back yet. The promise I made was to help you with whatever you asked until then.'

'I know. But you've already helped. Without you, I wouldn't even be here. I know it's dangerous and I don't want to put anyone else in danger because of my stupid mistakes ever again. I caused all this, it's up to me to fix it. By myself.'

For a moment, the pooka continued to stare at her.

'What?' she added self-consciously, looking over her shoulder to check for fairies then touching her cheek. 'Is there something on my face?'

The pooka shook its shaggy head. 'You and your brother . . . you're just not what I thought mortals were.'

'What did you *think* mortals were?'

'Stupid. Mean. Greedy. Ghastly—'

'All right, I get the idea.'

'. . . But then your brother saved my life and now here you are telling me to go, when you could easily force me to stay. *Why?*'

Orla shrugged. 'Because it's what Apollo would do, which means it's the right thing to do. Now, we'd both better get moving.'

The pooka nodded slowly, its orange eyes gleaming. 'Electric light,' it said.

'What?' Orla asked, confused.

'Direct electric light. That's the Wild Hunt's big weakness. Other than the call of their true name and their hunger for human sadness.' It gestured towards the torch in her hand and Orla finally understood why it had made sure she brought it. She gripped the torch tighter, grateful for a defence, however small.

'Thank you.'

'Goodbye, Orla. Good luck.'

Orla nodded and stepped outside the ring of stones. 'Bye, Pooka. You too.'

The pooka stood up on its hind legs in the middle of

the stones and closed its eyes. Orla blinked and it vanished. If someone had told her a day ago that she'd be sad to see the pooka leave, she'd have laughed in their face, but she found that she *was* sad. Now she had no way of getting back. Now she was utterly alone. *Again.*

Her stomach tightened. The song about the Wild Hunt rang in her head.

The Wild Hunt rides in the dead of night,
Spreading terror, misery and fright,

They'll feast on your despair and pain,
Whatever you do, don't say their name.

For speak it three times and you will call,
Clouds black as coal, a hideous squall –

Birds, horses, beasts – who'll break your soul apart,
Sorrow hunters who once had mortal hearts.

Orla let all the pain and sadness that she usually tried to keep buried inside her come rushing up to the surface. She thought of all the times she'd really wished Mum had been there these past two years when she wasn't – for parents' evenings, for kisses goodnight, to pick up her up from school and to give her advice.

Pretty much every moment of every day, she wished Mum was there. She thought about how hard it had been watching Mum get more and more ill, knowing there was nothing anyone could do – how sad and drained it had made Dad. She thought of how mean she'd been to Apollo and how many times she'd made him cry. Of Apollo's betrayed expression and how he'd been right about her being selfish. She thought of how she'd been punishing Dad for moving on when she couldn't. How she'd not told him she loved him, when the truth was that she really did and she should have been happy to see him smiling again. She thought of how she'd shut her friends out, despite their kindness and the fact that it wasn't their fault they had mums and she didn't. She thought of poor Gran and how she'd shouted at her and then been the reason why Gran was in such peril now. She thought about her deepest fear, which was that she was broken and could never be fixed.

She let all these sad thoughts fill her up, took a deep breath and opened her mouth ready to utter that dreaded word. The true name that would call the fearsome Wild Hunt.

At first, no sound came out.

Orla steeled herself. 'Sluagh.' It came out as a whisper.

Then louder, 'Sluagh!'

She shouted it a third and final time at the top of her lungs 'SLUAGH!'

Her cry echoed off the trees and a few remaining butterflies fluttered up into the air.

Orla waited, panting hard, her ears straining for the sound of other wings. For a moment, it seemed not to have worked. But then the distant sound of the fairies' song became distorted and receded, as if all music and joy had been stifled.

The hairs on Orla's neck bristled and her nerves jangled. A cold wind whipped the trees into a frenzy, so that their leaves rushed against one another with a thousand whispers. The fireflies flickered, then Orla was plunged into darkness as a black cloud fell over the clearing, blotting out the light of the three moons and stars completely.

She suppressed a silent scream. Her heart was pounding impossibly fast. She heard leathery wing-beats . . .

Loud and close.

With a fresh rush of fear, she looked up at the whirl-wind of undulating shadow above.

Clouds black as coal, a hideous squall . . .

The Wild Hunt was here.

CHAPTER 34
The Wild Hunt

Orla felt chilled to the bone.

The edges of the cloud disintegrated and became a flock of hideous black birds. The sound of their screeching made Orla's jaw clench and her knees almost give way underneath her.

As the birds dived, their screeches became those ear-splitting screams, human cries of pure terror and despair.

'*Help me, help me . . .*'

Orla tried not to listen. She didn't want to pick out Gran's voice. If she did, she was afraid she wouldn't be able to focus on what she had to do next.

Every nerve in her body commanded her to run, but even if she trusted her legs to work, there'd be no point. The Wild Hunt were faster and stronger. They would catch her. And Orla had nowhere to escape to. She couldn't get out of the Fairy Kingdom by herself.

Orla clutched her torch tighter in her shaking

hands. She wanted to turn it on.

But not yet. *Wait until they're closer.*

There was the drumming of hooves.

Mid-air, the birds transformed into skeletal horses with empty white eyes. They charged down on her. There were so many! Orla cowered. Her plan felt more ludicrous than ever. How could she have thought she could face them on her own?

The deep well of sadness within her expanded beyond her control.

Look how alone you are.

Look how miserable and broken you are.

Look how you've messed everything up.

A scream of anguish built inside her, but Orla pressed her lips together tightly and tried to fight the sadness. She mustn't give in. Not without at least trying to save Gran first.

The deathly horses had almost reached her.

Now!

Orla switched on the torch and pointed it upwards. The horses careened backwards out of the way of the beam, whinnying and screeching in alarm. She'd caught them by surprise. This was her chance! The Wild Hunt wouldn't be held at bay for long with one torch. She had to act quickly.

She took a deep breath and shouted at the top of her

lungs, 'Balor, I wish to make a bargain with you!'

Her hands were so sweaty on the torch that she was afraid she would drop it. She peered up into the darkness. It was hard to see anything beyond the bright light.

'Who dares to call us here where we are not meant to be and try to bargain with us?' The cold voice made Orla's skin crawl.

'My n-n-name is Orla. You have my grandmother. I want her back. P-p-please. You can take me instead, just release her. I beg you.'

There was a thump. One of the creatures landed nearby. Its rattling breath gave her fresh chills. She wanted to shine her torch at it but was worried that, if she did, the rest of the Wild Hunt would descend on her. Keeping her torch pointed upwards, Orla risked a glance at its hideous face. It wore robes instead of rags and one empty white eye was missing.

Balor.

The torch shook in her grip, sending shadows spinning everywhere. There was an unpleasant scratching noise, as if someone was playing an out-of-tune violin. The sound made Orla's teeth hurt.

Balor was laughing.

'A mortal thinks it can ask us to do its bidding!' he spat. 'We will take it *and* its grandmother.'

'No! Please, no, just let her go—'

'*Take it!*'

More thumps. Other creatures landed around her, the shadow horses and birds transforming into mortal forms. All of them were haggard, with skin that barely clung to visible bones, just like the ghastly illustrations in Gran's book. Orla couldn't believe that these monsters had once been mortals. There was nothing human about them any more. The Wild Hunt wore dirty rags. Their hands and feet were bare and claw-like. Sparse strings of hair hung from their skulls and their white eyes gleamed, ghostly, pupilless and empty.

Birds, horses, beasts – who'll break your soul apart,
Sorrow hunters who once had mortal hearts.

Terror tore through her. They were creatures from nightmares.

She had no idea where to point her torch any more and spun in a circle trying to keep as many of them at bay as she could. They bared their black teeth and swiped at her with clawed hands, drawing closer. Balor continued to laugh.

She was surrounded and outnumbered by at least a hundred to one. Maybe even a thousand to one.

Come on, she willed, grasping at her only hope. The fairies must surely have been alerted to their intruders by now. How long would it take for them to arrive?

One creature grabbed on to her hair. It wrenched her backwards. Orla screamed and twisted around. 'Get back!' she shouted, lunging at it with the torch. The creature fell back, but others were already slashing at her arms and legs. The hopeless feeling of sadness inside her gaped, threatening to consume her. Orla tried to fight it, but the Wild Hunt were drawing it out of her. She felt their hunger for it.

'Why do you fight, little mortal?' Balor hissed from somewhere in the darkness. 'I smell the sadness inside you. It is strong. It calls to me. Why not let me give you what you want and take all the pain away? Isn't that what you've wished for? I can grant your wish. Don't you see? I'm not a monster really. I hear mortals everywhere crying for their sorrow to end so I help them. Let me help you.'

Orla felt herself being lured in by Balor's offer. How easy it would be to stop fighting, to stop feeling anything, to let it all just be taken away . . . But she shook her head. She couldn't. Gran needed her. If Orla could just buy enough time until the fairies arrived . . .

She continued to spin in giddy circles, brandishing

the torch like a sword. The Wild Hunt kept attacking, but they were like cats playing with a mouse, already knowing that their prey had no hope. How long would the torch's batteries last? After that, she'd have nothing to defend herself with. Her phone had died long ago.

The screaming worsened, becoming louder and more desperate.

'*Help me, help me . . .*'

Orla stopped spinning, no longer able to prevent herself from picking out one of the voices. 'Gran? Where are you?'

Her chest tightened as she searched the faces for Gran's. Was it too late? Had she already lost her mind? Would Gran's eyes be blank and empty like these others? She thought she spotted a small hunched figure in tartan . . .

'Gran!' she cried.

A claw sliced across her back. Orla managed to dodge, but as she did, she twisted her injured shoulder and searing pain shot through it. The torch was knocked from her hand and smashed to pieces under a bony foot. The Wild Hunt let out hisses of triumph.

'Gran!' Orla screamed.

But all Orla could hear was the hideous screaming and Balor cackling as the sadness inside her gaped wider. His ghostly eye gleamed in the darkness between the empty eyes of the other Wild Hunt. They closed in, grabbing her from all sides.

A small defiant shout cut through the air. 'Hey! Leave my sister alone.'

CHAPTER 35
Too Late?

Orla's head whipped around.

Apollo?!

Orla couldn't see him through the throng. *He shouldn't be here . . .*

'Let her go or I'll cut it!'

Cut what? 'Apollo, run!' she shouted, struggling against her captors.

Balor turned and looked in the direction of Apollo's voice.

'No!' she screamed. 'Leave him alone. Just take me!'

To her shock, Balor commanded, 'Release the mortal!'

The Wild Hunt released her and fell back. Orla couldn't believe it. How had Apollo done that? And why, under the obvious rage in his voice, did Balor sound nervous?

'Let her come to me safely or I'll destroy it,' said Apollo.

Balor gave an angry grunt. He stepped aside and gestured for the other Wild Hunt to do the same. They hissed and parted to reveal Apollo standing in a slither of moonlight. His face was pale but determined, and he was carrying something – something covered in glittering jewels. Dagda's Harp!

Orla's mind whirred. It didn't make any sense! How had Apollo managed to get the harp back from Conor? How had he worked out how to come to the Fairy Kingdom? There was no sign of anyone with him. Apollo appeared to be alone.

She saw the glint of a blade in his hand. His penknife! Orla nearly laughed, she was so amazed. He was holding it against one of the harp's strings. It was this that Balor's one eye was fixed on.

Clever, clever Apollo!

She moved towards him nervously, afraid the Wild Hunt would still reach out to grab her. But they seemed bound by Balor's command. She made it to Apollo's side. Her mouth opened and closed. There was so much she wanted to say . . . Apollo's gaze slid over her face, but his expression remained unreadable.

'Now hand it over,' hissed Balor.

Apollo shook his head. 'If you want this harp, you hand over our gran too *and* allow us to leave here.'

How brave he was! His voice barely shook at all.

Was he really planning to give the harp to the Wild Hunt or was he still hoping to trick them? Orla looked around with increasing desperation. *Why weren't the fairies here yet?*

Balor laughed. 'Very well. I give you my word. I'll hand your gran over and you may leave here. But first, you must give me the harp.'

Orla did not like the cruel smile that twisted his lips. She sensed a trick but did not know what it was. Magical creatures were experts in trickery, unlike Orla and Apollo. That was the problem.

'Apollo, I don't like this . . .' she muttered.

'Really? Because I'm having a *fantastic* time,' Apollo hissed through gritted teeth.

'I mean, I don't think we can trust Balor to do what he says.'

'If he gives us his word, he has to.'

He didn't have to. He wouldn't die like the pooka would. They were relying on Balor complying with an honour code he'd already broken by coming here tonight when a treaty told him not to. Besides, if they gave Balor the harp, they'd be condemning countless more innocent people to a terrible fate.

'We can't, Polo.'

'What other choice is there?' Before she could say anything else, Apollo stepped forwards and handed

Balor the harp.

Balor snatched it triumphantly.

'Give us Gran!' Apollo shouted.

'Of course, I gave you my word, did I not?' Balor was still smiling. 'Which is yours?'

Apollo pointed. The small figure in tartan – it was Gran.

Orla's stomach twisted with guilt for all the other victims.

'Very well.' Balor gave the command and his creatures shoved Gran forwards.

'Hey, careful!' Orla shouted.

'Gran!' Apollo's voice cracked.

Gran did not reply. Her head was bowed, her gaze on the ground.

'Gran?' Apollo called louder. 'Gran, it's us! We're here. Are you OK?' He reached forwards and touched her shoulder softly.

Gran screamed and recoiled in panic. 'Kathleen?'

Orla and Apollo both froze.

'Gran, it's not Mum, it's us. Orla and Apollo,' Orla said.

But Gran continued to cower away in distress. 'Kathleen . . . I can't lose my little girl. Please, this isn't how it's supposed to be . . . A parent is not meant to bury their child.'

'Gran . . .' Orla was so choked with emotion she could hardly speak. 'Gran, it's us.'

Gran looked up for the first time and Orla gasped in horror.

For her eyes were white and pupilless.

It was too late. Gran had already lost her mind. The version they'd known was lost for ever.

'No!' cried Apollo.

Orla noticed the creatures drawing closer, licking their cracked lips, feeding off Gran's hysteria and Orla and Apollo's anguish.

'Get away!' Apollo shouted. 'You said you'd let us leave!'

'I did, and you *will* leave here – as our captives!'

More of that awful out-of-tune laughter followed. *This was the trick.* Orla felt like the ground had disappeared from underneath her.

'What?' Apollo cried. 'No, that's not what I meant—'

Balor caressed the harp's frame. 'But it is what you *said.* You should be more careful with your words. Thank you for fetching me the harp and sparing me the bother. With this mighty instrument, we will be able to save many more souls and take away their sorrow and pain . . . *Starting with you.*' Balor's bat-like wings unfurled, then he rose with the harp and roared, 'Seize them!'

There was a chaotic rush of movement and screeching as the Wild Hunt descended on them. Two creatures pulled Gran back. Orla tried to stop them, but more grabbed her. They dug their claws into her forearms and tugged painfully on her bandaged shoulder. One creature leapt on to Apollo's back. Apollo screamed as talons dug into his shoulders. It unfurled its terrible wings, taking off.

Orla lunged to grab Apollo, but her brother was already being lifted into the air. 'No!' she screamed. 'Let him go!'

Creatures surrounded her. She fought, kicked, punched, but it was no use. It was over. Balor had the harp, and worse, the Wild Hunt had Apollo. Her loyal, kind, brave brother.

For a second there she'd really believed they'd had a chance . . .

There was a faint tinkling sound. At first, Orla was sure she'd imagined it. But then something large and glittering bowled through the air, knocking down the Wild Hunt around her as if they were skittles.

She thought she heard a cry of 'Wahoo,' as the glittering thing whizzed towards the creature holding Apollo.

Not a thing . . . a *someone*.

A *someone* with golden skin and magnificent butterfly wings, wielding a bow and arrow.

Orla's heart lifted.

The fairies had come!

CHAPTER 36
The Battle of Wings

There was a *swoosh* and a *thunk*. The creature grasping Apollo howled as the fairy's arrow hit it. It reeled backwards in the air, the arrow embedded in its leg. The fairy shot a second arrow. This one hit the creature square in the chest, piercing the place where its blackened heart would be. Its grip on Apollo released and it plummeted towards the ground, bursting into an explosion of black feathers as its body vanished.

Orla's heart lurched. Apollo was also dropping like a stone. There was no way he'd survive the fall! She tried to reach where he would land but Wild Hunt creatures blocked her way through. They slashed at her with their claws, forcing her back . . .

'Apollo!' she screamed.

Just as it looked like Apollo would smash into the ground, the fairy swooped down and caught him. Together they tumbled beyond the edge of the stones, between the trees.

A tiny gap appeared in the creatures surrounding Orla as they looked up to see if more fairies were coming. She seized her chance and somehow managed to dodge and fight her way through to Apollo. She fell to her knees beside him. The creatures chased her but the fairy stood guard, shooting arrows at any that tried to approach. Those hit in their chests howled before they too burst into black feathers and vanished.

'Polo, are you all right?' Orla gasped. The shoulders of his jumper were slashed and stained with blood, but Apollo's eyes were open and he was breathing steadily. She pulled him into a hug. 'Oh, thank goodness!'

'We have to get it back,' Apollo said weakly. 'The harp . . . What was I thinking? Balor's going to use it for such terrible things.'

'You were thinking of me and Gran,' Orla said firmly. 'And you were being very brave. If this is anyone's fault, it's mine. It was my recklessness that created this situation.'

Apollo shook his head. 'We have to stop him!'

But how were they meant to do that? They were just two mortals. Two mortals and—

Orla turned to the fairy. With its back to them, it was still busy shooting arrows at the Wild Hunt. But it would tire eventually and then the Wild Hunt would rush in, if other fairies did not show up soon. Why was this one on its own? And why was it defending them? As far as the fairies were concerned, Orla and Apollo were intruders too.

'Thank you,' she called to it.

The fairy glanced back at her for a moment. The jolt of recognition made Orla gasp.

It was Conor!

Only it wasn't.

At least, not the version they'd known. He'd always been good-looking, but now he was *painfully* beautiful, so that looking at him directly even for that brief second was almost like looking straight into the sun. His cheekbones were higher, his eyes brighter, his jawline sharper and his skin glittered gold. Not to mention the fact that a huge pair of butterfly wings had sprouted from his back! Gone were his ordinary T-shirt, jacket and jeans. Instead, he wore a tunic made from leaves and moss-coloured trousers that flared at the bottom of each leg.

Orla's mouth hung open; she was unable to understand what she was seeing. The last time she'd seen Conor he'd stolen the harp from her. *What was going on?* How had the harp ended up with Apollo?

'Nice aim, Conor!' Apollo exclaimed. 'And nice *wings*!'

Orla stared at her brother. Did he know already?

'Thanks!' Conor shouted back, giving them a quick grin before shooting another arrow. There was a howl as one more creature exploded into feathers. 'There are more of us coming. The King's Guard is on the way!'

And even as he said this, there was a whizzing and tinkling sound, then a rush of golden-skinned figures zoomed into the clearing, their faces fierce, their magnificent butterfly wings glittering in the darkness. They wielded spears and bows, and strange jagged weapons Orla had no name for. Her body sagged with relief. *The fairies had come to fight!*

'Balor!' King Oberon's furious shout echoed around the stones, so that it seemed to come from all around.

Orla craned her neck and spotted the fairy king high above, his antlered crown resplendent upon his dark curls. The Wild Hunt outnumbered the King's Guard, but the fairies looked formidable and powerful.

'How dare you insult us by entering our kingdom and breaking the pact we made with you, especially during our midsummer revels!' King Oberon continued. 'Our treaty is *over*! Now you will pay the price.'

The fairies let out battle cries and dived. They tore into the Wild Hunt, ferocious and determined, knocking many down. Several creatures exploded into more piles of black feathers, which now littered the ground. Others rose into the air and transformed back into stallions and ravens. The stallions reared up and charged at the fairies. The ravens swooped down and ripped their butterfly wings with their beaks. Conor let out a cry and flew to join the battle.

Orla, Apollo and the ragged group of victims were momentarily forgotten. Like Gran, the victims still looked human and their clothes hadn't yet turned to rags but their eyes were blank and empty. Even over the cacophony of howls, wingbeats and fighting, Orla could hear their sorrowful screams.

'*Help me. Help me.*'

Orla tried not to listen, afraid that the sound of Gran's screams would undo her. She counted: there were fifteen in total, matching the number of missing people from the newspaper clippings in Gran's folder. There was one child, a boy who looked Apollo's age.

'That must be Liam Armstrong,' Apollo gasped.

Orla recognized a woman in a faded pink cardigan from the newspaper photo too. It was Mary Hart. *Mother-of-two* . . .

Just like Mum.

'We have to help them!' Orla cried.

Apollo shook his head. 'I wish we could but we can't . . . It's too late. Even for Gran. You can see their empty eyes; they've already lost their minds.' Tears glistened on his cheeks.

'It might not be,' Orla said desperately, willing her words to be true. 'They're not Wild Hunt yet . . .'

'No, but they'll be Wild Hunt soon and there's nothing we can do to stop that.' Apollo's voice cracked.

Orla gazed at Gran, her heart breaking. It was almost more painful to have come so close to saving her and to still fail. Was there really nothing anyone could do? Was it really all over?

At that moment the ground trembled and the leaves on the trees behind them rustled. Orla and Apollo glanced at each other in panic.

'Did you feel that?' Apollo asked.

Orla nodded, her stomach twisting.

There was more rustling. Branches snapped.

Something was coming.

'Not more Wild Hunt, please . . .' she groaned.

They both looked back in horror, preparing to run.

Then the branches parted and an enormous, bearded face peeked through.

'Looks like you're havin' an exciting evening,' Fionn whispered.

'Fionn!' Apollo exclaimed in delighted astonishment.

Orla was equally amazed. Shouldn't Fionn be back at his home in the Tangled Woods by now, occupied with his clouds? What was he doing in the Fairy Kingdom – tonight of all nights?

She looked around to see if anyone else had noticed, but they were all too preoccupied with their fighting. Balor and King Oberon fought in the middle of the battle, their bodies blurs of black and gold. The harp's jewels flashed. Balor still had it for the time being and would not let it go, but holding it hampered his ability to fight. His creatures rushed in to attack King Oberon but the fairies fought them off. Orla hoped that Balor did not get the chance to play the harp and that Conor was OK.

'What are you doing here?' she gasped, turning to look back up at Fionn.

Fionn sniffed. 'Ach, well . . . Figured youse were in a spot of bother and might need a hand . . . a *large* hand at that! Climb aboard an' I'll take yer back to the mortal realm. There's another fairy ring t'other side of the kingdom we can return through. That's the one I used when I realized this one here was blocked.'

He reached down and offered his palm for them to step into.

Orla couldn't believe it. Was Fionn really here to help them to safety out of the kindness of his heart? It went against everything she knew about magical creatures.

'*Help me. Help me.*'

The cries pierced through her and Orla shook her

head. They couldn't just leave. Gran was still here, as were the other victims, and Balor might get away with the harp and use it to take many more people's loved ones. Some of the Wild Hunt – there were so many of them the fairies could not attack them all – were closing in around the victims now, drawing strength for the battle from their sadness. All the victims screamed louder, but Gran's cry was the one that rang in Orla's ears.

'*Help me. Help me.*'

They couldn't simply abandon them. Gran would never do that.

'Help those poor people first, please.'

'Olo, didn't you hear what I said before?' Apollo said gently. 'We can't save them.'

Emotion rose in Orla's chest. 'Even so, we can't just leave them. Those are people's children, mums, dads, friends, *grandparents*. Even if it's impossible, we have to *try* to save them because it's the right thing to do. I learnt that from you.'

Apollo was quiet for a minute. Then he reached out and gave her hand a small squeeze. 'You heard her, Fionn!'

'Right yer are. You twose sit tight now and stay outta sight. I'll be back for youse in a moment.' The ground shook as Fionn stepped over them and into the clearing. He walked right through the middle of the battle. The creatures of the Wild Hunt howled and flew into the giant's eyes, scratching and clawing, but Fionn knocked them out of the sky as if they were nothing more than annoying flies. More black feathers carpeted the mossy ground. The fairies also tried to attack this intruder, but he batted them away too and they were soon forced to return to fighting off the Wild Hunt.

Orla didn't understand why Fionn had come to help but it was good to have a giant on their side!

Fionn reached down, scooping up Gran and the other victims.

Apollo let out a triumphant whoop and hope bloomed inside Orla. Incredibly, and against all odds, the tide seemed to be turning in their favour. The fairies were fighting the Wild Hunt and the giant had come to rescue them. King Oberon might be able to get the harp back from Balor, and Fionn could take them all far away from here. Maybe he could even help them find a way to heal the victims.

Maybe, just maybe, everything would be OK.

But they weren't out of the woods yet. Fifteen mortals meant a lot of awkward bodies for Fionn to keep safe – the victims were confused and afraid, so getting them to hold on to his shoulder would have been impossible. Instead, Fionn put some in his top pocket and held the rest. This meant he did not have his hands free to fight the Wild Hunt creatures on his way back to Orla and Apollo. They flew into his face and slashed at him.

But it wasn't the creatures that brought Fionn to a halt. It was the glittery golden dust in the air. His nose wrinkled and his eyes squeezed tight. '*AH-AH*—'

'Oh no, his allergies!' Orla gasped.

'—*CHOO!*' Fionn's sneeze sprayed the Wild Hunt with globs of green snot so big that many of the creatures were knocked off course.

'Unusual battle technique,' remarked Apollo.

But it wasn't working.

'*AH-CHOO!*' Fionn continued to sneeze violently. His eyes were streaming so much now that he could hardly see where he was going. The Wild Hunt seized their advantage and the creatures swarmed up into his face and around the victims, trying to pull them out of his pocket and hands. The victims didn't even try to defend themselves. If any fell from that height, they would die.

There was no way Fionn would make it back over to Orla and Apollo without losing some of them.

'*Help me. Help me.*'

Orla made her decision.

'Fionn!' she shouted at the top of her lungs. 'Get out of here! Take them to safety!'

'What about youse two?' Fionn called back.

'We'll be fine.' Orla glanced at Apollo for reassurance.

'Yeah,' he agreed. 'So long as we stick together!'

Orla's chest warmed. The past two years she'd thought that by isolating herself from people she loved, she'd been protecting herself and them, but really it hadn't protected anyone. It felt good to no longer be alone. 'We will.'

'All right, don't go getting killed!' Fionn called.

Apollo grinned bravely. 'Wasn't planning on it.'

Fionn nodded, turned and tore through the trees with great booming strides that shook the earth. The creatures fell off him with screeches and howls. The victims' cries faded away into the distance. Soon the giant was out of sight.

Orla breathed a tiny sigh, but her relief didn't last. They hadn't asked Fionn how to find the other fairy ring or how far away it was. Even if they made it there, would they be able to get back through to the mortal realm without help? And there was still the matter of Balor having the harp . . . Not to mention the fact that her shouts had drawn the attention of several Wild Hunt, which were racing over towards her and Apollo's hiding place.

'Run, Polo!' she hissed, but they were both halted by the sound of an anguished cry from high above. A cry they recognized. The creature that Conor had been fighting had Conor's wings pinned behind him. There was a terrible tearing sound and Conor's scream ripped through the air, an animal sound of pure agony.

His torn wing floated to the ground. Conor was tumbling through the air too. There was no one there to catch him.

He hit the ground with a heavy thump and lay very still.

'Conor,' Apollo gasped, desperate to go to him. Orla held her brother back – there were too many creatures nearby and, from the look of things, there would be nothing they could do. Conor wasn't moving and was twisted in a strange position.

Apollo's eyes brimmed with tears. Orla felt like crying too. Despite all her unanswered questions, despite the hurt, anger and betrayal she felt at Conor for taking the harp and lying to them, despite whatever else had been going on with him, there was one thing she was sure of: he *had* been their friend. He'd saved their lives just now, and not for the first time.

And in doing so he'd sacrificed his own.

Orla did not want to just leave Conor, but the Wild Hunt were closing in on their hiding spot. In a few moments, they'd be upon them. 'We have to go, Polo.' She tugged at his arm, but Apollo was too distraught to move. 'Come on. Please!' she urged.

Then things got even worse.

There were more cries from fairies above. Many others had ripped wings. They were injured and retreating.

Wild Hunt creatures swarmed up around King Oberon and his guards, who were also forced to fall back. There were just too many. For every one the fairies slayed, two more appeared in its place.

The fairies were losing.

Orla's insides twisted with guilt. It was her fault the fairies were hurt. She was the one who'd called the Wild Hunt to the Fairy Kingdom when they'd been unprepared for a fight.

No longer hampered by King Oberon's attacks, Balor held the harp up in front of him, moving it into position. A few fairies flew at him, forcing Balor to release one hand to swipe out at them.

'He mustn't play it!' Apollo gasped. 'If Queen Coomara could put a whole merrow city to sleep with its music, think what Balor will do to the fairies? Then he'll be free to use the harp to turn as many innocent people into Wild Hunt as he likes!'

Apollo was right. If Balor won this battle and

escaped with the harp, he'd turn every mortal he could find into one of his creatures. He'd turn the world they knew to misery.

But there was nothing they could do to stop him.

Or was there?

'Call it!' someone shouted feebly.

Orla looked around for the speaker and her heart leapt.

'Conor!' Apollo cried.

Conor raised himself weakly and shot an arrow into the back of one of the creatures closing in on them. It exploded into black feathers. He drew another arrow.

'Call its name,' he wheezed urgently.

Swoosh, thunk. Another creature exploded.

'What?' Orla was puzzled. 'Call whose name?'

'Not *who*! The harp.'

Orla stared at Conor blankly. He wasn't making any sense. Maybe he'd hit his head too hard.

But beside her Apollo gasped. 'Of course, like in the story! Remember how Dagda got the harp back from his enemies, Olo? He called it!'

Orla still wasn't following. 'So?'

'So you have to call it too!'

'What? Me?' she spluttered. 'But I don't know how—'

'You do. Just don't hide the music inside you,'

Conor called weakly. 'The harp will hear you if you let it.' He shot a final arrow and another creature vanished. This act cost him the last of his strength. He slumped back, motionless again.

'Conor!' cried Apollo. 'You've got to do what he said, Olo!'

She shook her head. She'd tried to play the harp before and it hadn't worked, so how would she be able to call it now? 'I can't.'

'You can, Olo. You're the most gifted musician I know, you always have been! Everyone's always said so. You got Mum's talent. Conor thinks you can do this. And so do I . . . You have to try.'

Orla nodded. He was right. After all the mess she'd got them in, she owed it to him to at least give it a go. 'OK.' But how did she do this? The story hadn't given clear instructions. Did she just shout for the harp like she'd shouted for the Wild Hunt? How did she let it hear the music inside her?

There was no time to think. Balor had flown free of the fairies and was raising the harp into position again. His clawed fingers brushed the strings.

Orla didn't hesitate any longer. She took the deepest breath she could and yelled at the top of her lungs, 'Harp of Dagda, come to me!'

CHAPTER 37
The Harp's Music

T he harp remained firmly in Balor's grasp.

Balor looked down and laughed his hideous laugh. 'Stupid mortal! Why do you still try to fight me when you are so weak and I am so strong? Give in and let me help you.'

At his words, Orla felt her sadness come rushing up inside and she let out a small wail, but Apollo immediately squeezed her hand and the warmth of his presence chased the dark feelings away. With him beside her, she felt strong, not weak.

'Maybe that just wasn't the right name,' Apollo muttered.

'Of course!' Orla gasped. She hadn't called the Wild Hunt here by using the name which they were known by. She'd summoned them with their true name. Their ancient name. And the harp must have one too.

A magical, musical name.

The harp will only hear you if you let it.

All of a sudden she knew what she had to do.

She concentrated on the harp and felt the music inside it call out to her. The music inside Orla stirred in response. Instead of burying it, Orla opened her mouth and let it come bursting out.

A pure note rang through her. High and choral, like a nightingale. Orla knew, without anyone having to tell her, that she was calling the harp's *true* name. One it had had long before it even became Dagda's possession.

The harp flew from Balor's hands and down into Orla's. She caught the glittering frame and gazed at it in amazement. It had worked!

Balor howled with rage. 'Get it!' he screeched at his creatures, who stopped fighting the fairies and plummeted after the falling harp.

Orla lifted the instrument into position against her right shoulder and placed her trembling fingers on the strings. Again, she had that prickling sensation. It was stronger this time. The harp's music felt closer now that she'd already sung some of its notes. Still, the thought of opening herself up further to the music made her tremble even more. She hesitated, doubts swirling inside her. Part of her wanted to keep blocking the music and the feelings that would come with it. Maybe she *was* just a weak mortal . . .

'You can do this, Olo,' Apollo shouted and Orla felt stronger. He was right. She *could* do this. She *had* to.

Her skin tingled. She stopped resisting.

Orla began to play, plucking the harp's strings delicately. A melody bloomed out, and suddenly Orla was playing the harp as if she had done so her whole life! Her fingers were being guided by an invisible force. She just seemed to *know* where they needed to go.

But something was wrong. With the music, painful emotions rushed up inside her. Grief, loneliness, hopelessness . . . This time, she did not have the blue petals to protect her and as the music filled the woods, she heard it clearly. It was heartbreakingly sad. Balor's grating laugh sounded from somewhere above her. With a jolt of panic, she realized which song she must be playing: the Music of Grief. The song was making the Wild Hunt stronger. She was doing Balor's work for him.

Stop! she willed her fingers furiously. But the dark sadness inside her was made even worse by the music.

Mum's voice echoed in her head. Just like in her nightmares.

Orla? Apollo? Why won't you help me?

Through blurry eyes, Orla saw the anguish in Apollo's face. She could tell he must be fighting his own silent battle.

'Isn't the sadness too much to bear? Let me take it from you. Let me save you,' Balor hissed.

It was tempting to give in, *so tempting*. But Orla shook her head. What Balor offered wasn't happiness, it was emptiness, which meant being free of sadness, but also of all the good feelings too. Feelings like joy, love, hope, friendship and wonder. Sadness was part of being mortal, as Gran had told King Oberon that night in the Tangled Woods. It was a sign of how much you had loved and not something to wish away, Orla finally saw that. She would rather love people with all her heart and face the sadness of knowing she would lose them than never feel love at all.

Orla was going to choose life and love instead of numbness.

She concentrated on all the things she loved: like sunshine and ice cream, and swimming in the sea, and shooting stars, and little brothers with blue hair who squeezed your hand when you were scared, and a grandma in tartan trousers who baked apple pies and laughed with glittering eyes. And dads who bear-hugged you, tight and warm.

She focused on the *good* memories of Mum. The way she'd lit up when she'd sung, her head thrown right back. The feel of her hair softly tickling Orla's shoulder as they sat together by the piano. The deep, infinite, inextinguishable warmth of the love she'd had for Orla and Apollo. A love that was stronger than any magical army and would never fade, no matter how much time passed.

And, slowly, Orla felt the tone and tempo of the music at her fingertips change. All trace of sadness melted away from this new melody, which cascaded out of the harp, glittering and flowing. It felt like a warm summer's day, uplifting and exuberant.

Somewhere above Balor howled in fury, but Orla barely heard. Her eyes were closed and she was lost in the joyful movement of her fingers along the strings. It felt *good* to play music again. How could she have denied this part of herself for so long? The tune enveloped her, filling her up.

Love, that was what it felt like.

'Olo, you're doing it!' Apollo exclaimed delightedly. 'Look!'

She opened her eyes.

The creatures of the Wild Hunt were cowering, covering their ears and wailing in agony at the uplifting music. King Oberon and the fairies seized their advantage. Arrows shot through the air and black feathers rained down from the sky as many more of the Wild Hunt vanished. Balor let out another howl of rage as

King Oberon charged on him, a sword in his hand. This time it was Balor who was forced back.

'Retreat!' he hissed to his creatures as he fled, turning into a black stallion, then a huge raven that flapped away into the darkness.

The remaining Wild Hunt transformed into ravens too, and wheeled off into the darkness after Balor, hurtling away across the three moons.

Orla did not stop playing the harp until the last Wild Hunt was completely out of sight. Only then did she let her fingers fall away from the strings and breathe a grateful sigh of pure relief.

The mossy ground was covered in black feathers.

'You did it, Olo!' Apollo cried, hugging her tightly.

'*We* did it,' she said firmly, putting down the harp to hug him back and closing her eyes. She couldn't believe it! They'd defeated the Wild Hunt. They had the harp. They'd saved Gran and the other victims with Fionn's help and, if anyone would know a way to get those people's minds back, it was him. Elation fizzed through her.

That was until she heard arrows slide into position on bows.

She let go of Apollo.

A circle of fairies surrounded them. Some had torn wings, others had slashes across their beautiful faces.

Every single one of their sharp arrowheads was aimed directly at Orla or Apollo.

King Oberon stepped forwards, his golden armour gleaming. 'Kill the mortal trespassers!'

CHAPTER 38
When the Fairy Dust Has Settled

Orla's heart sank. Of course a part of her had antici-
pated this: that if the Wild Hunt didn't kill them,
the fairies would. But she'd been so swept up in the
triumph of their victory that she'd momentarily forgotten there would be consequences for bringing the Wild
Hunt to the Fairy Kingdom. Consequences they now
had to face.

The harp lay by her feet. Could she reach for it
in time?

The King's Guard drew their arrows back.

'Wait!' came a yell.

Blue butterflies rose into the air as Conor stumbled
through the crowd. He was weak and unbalanced with
only one wing, but somehow still managed a hint of his
arrogant swagger. Orla felt a rush of relief. He was
alive!

Conor bowed deeply to King Oberon. 'Your Grace,
I beg of you, please spare these mortals. They just

saved us all. If they hadn't played the harp, the Wild Hunt would have defeated us!'

King Oberon's eyes flashed like cold steel. 'If they hadn't entered our kingdom and called the Wild Hunt here in the first place, we wouldn't have had to fight them!'

Orla hung her head. The fairy king was right. She was glad to see that the fairies did not seem to have lost any lives, but many were injured and it could have easily been a lot worse. It was kind and courageous of Conor to try to save them, but his words wouldn't change anything. However, maybe Orla could explain to King Oberon that this was her fault and get him to spare Apollo. It was worth a try.

'I'm so sorry,' she whispered, looking around at the fairies and speaking to them all. 'I should never have come and called the Wild Hunt here to your home. I'm sorry for the injuries you have sustained. This is all my fault. My brother came because of me. Please, just let him go and—'

'You *both* trespassed, so you will *both* be punished,' King Oberon replied, and Orla's heart sank further.

'Please—' she gasped, tears springing to her eyes as she thought of how Dad would feel when neither of them returned home.

'Olo, it's OK,' Apollo muttered, squeezing her hand.

'Forgive me for speaking out of turn, Your Grace,' said Conor urgently, 'but if they *hadn't* called the Wild Hunt here, we never would have seen how strong they'd become. You saw how hard they were to beat. Balor needed to be stopped!'

King Oberon regarded Conor with fury. 'Who is this insolent fairy who thinks he can speak to his king like this?'

'The butterflies say that he's the one who brought the blue-haired mortal and the harp here!' piped one of the King's Guard who had a butterfly hanging off their ear.

'*You* brought the harp here?' King Oberon roared.

Conor's cheeks flushed. 'Yes, Your Grace.'

'Never mind the fact that you brought a mortal here when it is forbidden to . . . Why did you not bring such a valuable magical item directly to your king when it is your duty to? You could easily have taken it. You too shall be punished.'

'You can't punish Conor. He was doing the right thing!' Apollo protested. 'And he's lost a wing for it.'

King Oberon's angry gaze flicked over them. 'It would grow back in time. However, he will not have time. He will be vanished. Seize him!'

Vanished. That sounded bad. Two fairy guards grabbed Conor and pinned his arms behind his back.

Conor didn't struggle. 'King Oberon, I know my actions are unforgivable and I must be punished for that. However, I beg you again, please let these mortals go back to their world.'

'They summoned our enemy here and they will pay the price.'

'They will do no such thing!' shouted a voice that made Orla's heart swell to twice its size.

She whirled around, astonished. 'Gran?'

For a moment, she thought she'd imagined it, but Apollo and the fairies were looking around too.

A small, dishevelled figure in tattered tartan pyjamas strode through the trees towards them. Gran looked pale and tired, but her expression was fierce and, best of all, her eyes were bright and green again! Orla felt like she'd been struck with a bolt of pure joy. Gran was OK! Fionn must have found a way to fix her. Maybe he'd fixed the others too.

Orla wanted to run over and hug Gran at once, but the fairies' arrows were still aimed at her and Apollo.

'Stop pointing those horrible things at my grandchildren!'

Whispers rippled around the fairies. A few lowered their bows and looked towards the king uncertainly. They didn't seem to know what to do. Gran wasn't just any mortal; she was their friend.

King Oberon seemed thrown by Gran's arrival too. 'Ms Elizabeth, my friend! It is good to see you safe.'

'Your *friend* – is that what I am?' Gran scoffed, pushing through the fairies to stand between him and Orla and Apollo. 'You knew the Wild Hunt had taken me, yet you did nothing! What kind of *friend* does that?'

'We couldn't . . . the treaty,' King Oberon stammered. It was odd to see such a formidable figure who had been so terrifyingly furious a moment ago suddenly on the back foot. 'You know we are not meant to get involved in the Wild Hunt's affairs. You have to understand – we were sad to lose you, of course we were, but we knew we would lose you soon anyway, in fairy terms at least. Mortals die quickly by our measures. That is just the way it is.'

Gran folded her arms across her chest. 'So my short life wasn't important enough for youse to even try to save? Well, it's clearly important enough to *some* people. Two rather brave and brilliant people,' she added, turning to look at Orla and Apollo, her green eyes shining.

Orla and Apollo beamed back.

'I don't know *how* they managed it,' Gran continued, turning back to the king and shaking her head, 'but they didn't just save me, they saved all of us – including you, King Oberon.'

'But, Ms Elizabeth, they were the ones who—'

'Yes, I know they brought the Wild Hunt here. Fionn's told me everything. But they've done youse a favour and if you can't see that you're an eejit and I don't mind telling you so any more.'

Orla's eyes widened at the way Gran was speaking to the fairy king. She half expected King Oberon to order for them to all be shot on the spot, but he didn't. Instead, he cowered like a naughty child getting a telling-off.

'Had they not,' Gran continued, 'then, even without the harp, Balor would have continued to collect more mortal victims, built a bigger army and become so strong he'd have been impossible for anyone to beat! He was already too strong. Youse were losing the battle and would have done so, were it not for my amazing grandchildren. Balor wanted the harp's power but he did not need it. He was already becoming unstoppable. After tonight, however, his army is greatly reduced.' Gran gestured to the carpet of black feathers from the slain creatures. 'My grandchildren not only helped you do that, but they managed to keep a powerful weapon from his claws.'

King Oberon's gaze slid greedily down to the harp. Orla snatched it up from the ground and gripped it tightly. There was a moment of silence as the fairy king hesitated, but finally he nodded. 'You know we fairies cannot lie, Ms Elizabeth. I see the truth of your words.'

That was right, fairies couldn't lie, Orla remembered suddenly and glanced at Conor. Had he lied about being mortal? Or had he simply withheld the truth?

'Good. Then you will stop threatening my grandchildren and let us go home.'

King Oberon's jaw clenched, but he sighed and said, '*Very well*. Hand over the harp and you are free to go. Fairies, lower your weapons.'

The fairies sheathed their arrows. Gran turned and swept Orla and Apollo into an enormous hug. She seemed so weak that Orla was worried about hurting her, but Gran clung on tightly. 'Oh, thank goodness youse two are all right!'

'We were more worried about *you* and the fact that you'd been captured by a bunch of monsters!' Apollo replied.

'Ach, nothing I couldn't handle!' Gran smiled, but her eyes gave her away. Underneath their brightness, there was a haunted look. Orla remembered the screaming and how it had felt when Balor and the Wild Hunt had drawn out her sadness. She hugged Gran tighter.

Before she could ask about the other victims, she

heard shouts and turned to see Conor had broken free of the fairies holding him.

'I just need a moment,' he insisted, looking at Orla. 'I know you'll never forgive me and I'm not asking for that. But before I'm vanished, I need you to understand.' He closed his eyes and touched her arm.

At once, a series of memories flashed in front of Orla's eyes.

Conor's memories.

She saw Conor watching Gran when she visited the fairies in the Tangled Woods. She felt Conor listening as Gran told stories of mortals, with the same rapt attention that Apollo had when Gran told magical folk tales. She experienced Conor's longing to know what being mortal was like, to feel all the feelings mortals felt.

The memories skipped ahead. Orla saw herself in the Tangled Woods the night she'd followed Gran. She saw how Conor had spotted her, how he'd blown fairy dust into her eyes to send her to sleep and take her home safely. How he decided that night to use his fairy glamour to make himself look like a mortal boy. How he'd planned to ask Gran for help with being mortal. That was why he'd been so eager to help Orla and Apollo find her. But it wasn't just that – Conor wanted to spend time with mortals, learning how they behaved.

But he then began to feel more and more mortal himself. He felt a tugging, tethering feeling towards Orla and Apollo. Orla watched through Conor's eyes as he tossed her yellow scrunchie into the sea, meaningful enough for him to be a gift for the water sprites.

He had started to care about them.

But he was still a fairy, irresistibly drawn to magical objects and bound to bring these to his king. She saw how conflicted he'd been around the harp. How he had been unable to resist following Orla into the woods to steal the powerful instrument from her. How, soon after he'd taken it, he'd realized his mistake and gone to fetch Apollo, given him the harp and brought him here to find Orla. How he'd protected them when they'd needed him.

Orla felt the pressure of Conor's hand release from her arm.

With a jolt she came back to her body and the present moment.

The fairies pulled Conor back, pinning his hands behind him again, but more forcefully this time so Conor yelped in pain.

'Stop hurting him!' Apollo cried.

'Vanish him,' commanded King Oberon.

Conor cowered, closing his eyes.

'No!' The shout came out louder than she'd planned

337

it to. 'I mean, please don't, Your Grace,' she added, remembering that, even though Gran had got away with it, King Oberon did not usually take kindly to being told what to do. Still, she had to try to stop this. Conor had stood up for them; now it was their turn to help him.

In her hands, the harp's jewels glittered. Orla suddenly knew what to do. 'Still got that penknife, Apollo?' she muttered.

Apollo frowned. 'Yeah, why . . . Oh!' He grinned, pulled out the penknife and put it against the strings just like he'd done before. This time, Orla felt a deep pang. Part of her wanted to shove his hand away and protect the harp now that she'd felt its beautiful music and power. But the magic of the harp did not run in her blood. For the fairy king, the thought of losing this rare magical possession when it was so close to being his, would be unbearable.

'Let Conor go or say goodbye to the harp,' she said fiercely.

King Oberon's eyes bulged. It was a dangerous game to play. They risked upsetting him so much that he changed his mind about letting *any* of them go. King Oberon could still order the fairies to shoot them all at any moment, and he might be able to do that before they could cut the harp strings anyway. Orla knew it would have been a lot wiser to just get out of here while they were safe, but they couldn't leave Conor behind. Not after all the help he'd given them. He was their friend.

Gran and Apollo stood shoulder to shoulder with her.

Orla glanced at Conor. He smiled weakly. An echo of the friend she knew.

They all held their breath.

'Fine,' King Oberon snapped, sounding simultaneously annoyed and bored. 'He is free to go, if it means that much to you. Now give me the harp.'

Apollo lowered his penknife, but the fairy king's hungry expression still made Orla hesitate . . .

'You must give us your word that you will never use the harp's magic on mortals,' she said. She was pushing her luck and she knew it, but the harp was too powerful to just hand over.

King Oberon glowered. 'You're spoiling all the fun . . . Oh fine, you have my word.'

Orla offered him the harp. The fairy king snatched it and gazed at the jewels on its frame admiringly. 'It is as beautiful as I have heard . . . The deal is done. Conor is no longer welcome here so you might as well take him back with you to the mortal world. But be warned, none of you must ever return to the Fairy

Kingdom. I will not be so forgiving next time . . . And when Conor has stayed in mortal form for forty days and nights, he'll remain mortal for the rest of his shortened life. After which he will die, just like the rest of you.'

'Sounds brilliant!' said Conor, grinning.

Apollo snorted.

'Except for you, of course, my dear friend,' King Oberon said to Gran. 'You should come back again to visit us once the midsummer period is over.'

Gran shook her head and gripped Orla and Apollo's hands tightly. 'Thank you, Your Grace, but I'm afraid I won't be coming back. Since my Kathleen died, I've been spending more time here than I ought to. From now on I'm going to be staying firmly in the mortal world – with my family. Especially as it seems we now have one more member . . .' She turned to wink at Conor.

Conor beamed, his dazzling smile returning to full voltage as his chest puffed out with pride. 'Do you mean me? Really? Oh, thank you. That's amazing!'

'Then I suppose this is goodbye, Ms Elizabeth,' said King Oberon loudly.

'I suppose it is. Goodbye, King Oberon. I wish you well.'

'And I you.' King Oberon looked a little sad.

Despite not saving Gran from the Wild Hunt, it was clear he was fond of her – as much as any fairy could be fond of a mortal. But then he looked down at his harp and smiled. 'Fairies, let's away! We have a victory to celebrate! My new harp will play us songs that will make us merry all night long.'

The air filled with whoops and cheers.

'But first, let's send our guests back where they belong.'

'Guests?' Apollo muttered. 'We were about to be shot a moment ago.'

Gran, Apollo, Orla and Conor were ushered into the middle of the fairy ring. Orla suddenly remembered the pooka and looked around for it, but it was nowhere to be seen. King Oberon and his guards stepped outside the perimeter of the stones.

'Everyone hold hands,' Gran instructed. 'Close your eyes and think of the Tangled Woods. Think of home.'

Orla looked across at Apollo and gave him a final grin before closing her eyes. She felt Conor's warm, strong hand in her left hand and Gran's delicate, papery-skinned hand in her right. She thought of the Tangled Woods. Of Gran's cottage. A whooshing sound filled her ears and then the earth dropped away from under them as they were catapulted back to the world they knew.

CHAPTER 39
Profoundly Dull and Ordinary

Orla landed with a thump and opened her eyes. They were back in the Tangled Woods. There were no black feathers on the ground, no golden fairy glitter in the air. No King Oberon and King's Guard. Just the ordinary-sized trees and the much smaller moss-covered stones standing like sentinels around them.

'Made it!' Gran let go of their hands, her eyes widening as she took in their injuries. 'What happened to yer shoulder, pet? And you're bleeding, Apollo! We'd best be getting home at once and I'll check youse both over and see if we'll be needing a doctor—'

Listening to Gran being *Gran* and fussing over them, Orla found herself overwhelmed with emotion.

'We thought we'd lost you,' she choked.

'Did Fionn work out how to save you?' Apollo asked, his eyes glittering with happy tears.

Gran shook her head. 'It was Orla's music. That

song you played was so powerful, so full of joy and love. It brought me back to myself. And not just me, the other victims too!'

'What? All of them?' gasped Orla in delighted amazement.

Gran nodded. 'All of them.'

'*A harp that could mend broken hearts.*' Apollo sang the line from the folk song and Orla realized the clue had been there all along. 'Of course!' he exclaimed.

'*Music can bring people back to themselves,*' Orla murmured. 'That was what Mum always said.'

'Well, as per usual, yer mum was right. Music *can* bring people back to themselves. Especially music from a very powerful, very ancient, very *magical* harp. I never would have believed it possible to reverse the Wild Hunt's harm. But then, I'd never have believed that we'd have the Harp of Dagda on our side either!' She winked at Orla, whose heart swelled. After seeing Gran, she'd thought she couldn't feel happier, but knowing that all the other victims were OK too made her beam from ear to ear.

'How *did* you figure out how to play the harp's music, Olo?' Apollo asked excitedly. 'And which note to sing to call it?'

Orla shook her head. 'I didn't really. It just sort of happened.'

'It was the music inside you,' said Conor. 'You stopped fighting it. You were amazing . . . Speaking of amazing, how do I look?' He did a twirl.

His skin had stopped glittering. His clothes had changed back to his T-shirt, jacket and jeans. He was still good-looking but, in contrast to how he'd looked a moment ago, he looked very plain under the bruises and scratches that criss-crossed his face.

'Profoundly dull and ordinary,' said Apollo.

Conor grinned. 'Grand! That's exactly what I was going for.'

Apollo and Orla both fell about laughing.

'What?' Conor frowned, which just made them laugh even more.

'Thanks, Conor, I needed that . . . He's right though, Olo,' Apollo added, wiping his eyes. 'You *were* amazing.'

'We *all* were,' she said firmly. 'I played the harp, but the only reason we had it was thanks to all of us working together. Even if one of us *did* try to steal it at one point . . .'

Conor grimaced. 'Ach, don't remind me. I'm truly sorry about that. It was the fairy in me but in forty days that will be gone.'

'And then you'll have no excuse,' Orla teased. 'Will the arrogance go as well?'

'What arrogance?' Conor asked, looking genuinely perplexed.

'He brought the harp back, which is what counts,' said Apollo. 'If it wasn't for Conor's idea for you to call it, Balor would have won!'

'Yes,' Orla agreed. 'Although now I'm wondering why he didn't suggest we just call the harp when we were in the Sunken City and save us bothering with Queen Coomara and her army!'

'You were in the Sunken City?' Gran squeaked in alarm.

Orla and Apollo exchanged looks.

'So Fionn didn't tell you that part . . .' Apollo muttered.

'He most certainly did not!'

Conor shook his head. 'Calling the harp wouldn't have worked down there, even if Orla had been ready to do it, which I don't think she was at that point – no offence,' he added.

'None taken.' She knew he was right. She would never have believed she could call the harp until tonight.

Apollo yawned. 'I never thought I'd say it, but I've had quite enough of merrow queens and fairy kings to last me a lifetime. I'm actually excited for things to feel a bit profoundly dull and ordinary too! Well, almost ordinary . . .' he added as the ground shook and Fionn emerged through the trees.

'Glad youse finally showed up!' the giant huffed. 'This lot have been a right pain in the backside.' He knelt to show them the people poking out of his hands and top pocket.

'Oh, thank goodness,' cried Mary Hart, who was one of the ones clinging on to the edge of Fionn's pocket. 'Help us! Call the Guards. I don't know how I got here but this . . . *thing* is keeping us hostage!'

'I was only keeping you safe until these lot got back!' Fionn grumbled. 'You could at least act a wee bit grateful and stop complaining, Mary Hart.'

Mary Hart looked gobsmacked. 'How – how d-d-do you kn-kn-know who I am?' she stammered.

'They're not zombies any more!' cried Apollo happily.

'Zombies? Where?' shrieked a bearded man in Fionn's hand. 'This is a dream, right? I mean, I've *got to* be dreaming!'

'Yes,' drawled a familiar, sarcastic voice. 'This is all just a dream. You really are that imaginative.'

'Oh, thank goodness,' muttered the man, experiencing a short-lived moment of relief before letting out another shriek of fear as a small, shaggy black shape separated itself from the undergrowth.

'Pooka!' Apollo exclaimed happily.

'What are *you* doing here?' Gran snapped, glaring at it.

Orla suddenly remembered that the pooka had been Gran's prisoner and that, when Gran had last met it, the pooka had been helping the Wild Hunt. She couldn't believe how long ago that felt. 'Gran, it's OK. The pooka's . . . Well, it's not *totally* awful.'

The pooka blinked at her. 'I think that's the nicest thing you've ever said to me.'

'Thanks for your help,' Orla said earnestly.

'No need to thank me, it was part of my contract. I had to—'

Orla shook her head. 'No. It wasn't. Not everything. You didn't have to give us the blue petals. You didn't have to take me to the Fairy Kingdom, or tell me the information about using the torch, which probably saved my life. We wouldn't be here if it wasn't for you.'

'Don't mention it,' the pooka said stiffly. 'I mean that, *really* don't mention it. I'll never live down helping a bunch of smelly mortals.'

'Why did you help us then? And why are you here now? I already released you from your promise and, anyway, it would be over now we have Gran back.'

'You ended the promise?' Apollo gasped.

The pooka looked extremely uncomfortable. 'Stop looking at me like that! Don't read into it. Maybe I wanted to help you because I was angry with Balor. He held me captive too, remember? I told you, I make everyone who makes me promise things regret it! You watch your backs!'

'Yeah, yeah. We know you'll murder us in our sleep . . . But I also think you love us a bit, Pooka!' Apollo crooned triumphantly, meeting Orla's eye and winking.

The pooka looked like it had just swallowed its own vomit. 'No, that's not—'

'It's OK, we love you too.' Apollo gave the pooka a hug.

'Yuck.' The pooka gagged. 'Get your greasy hands off me!' But it did not move away. There was a sound like an engine humming.

'Pooka . . . are you purring?' Orla exclaimed in astonishment.

'Absolutely not! It's a defence mechanism.'

'Cute!' she said. Of all the things she'd experienced tonight, this was up there with the most unexpected.

'It's *not* cute. It's a specialized tactic for avoiding attack.'

Apollo shook his head. 'I don't know why you can't just admit that you helped us out of the kindness of your heart, Pooka? Surely it would be good for pookas everywhere if people knew that some of you had a conscience?'

'Are you kidding?' The pooka baulked. 'In the magical world that would be seen as a total weakness. Especially with the added promise issue. You must never tell anyone or I'll—'

'Claw out our eyeballs?' Orla suggested.

'Feed us to a troll?' said Apollo.

'Set us on fire?' joined in Conor.

'All of the above and worse!' growled the pooka.

Orla smiled. 'Your secret's safe with us.'

'Naww!' said Fionn. 'Well, isn't that just adorable? Warms the cockles, it does.'

'Er – hello! Look, I don't know what's going on here,' squealed Mary Hart, leaning further out of the giant's pocket. 'Or who any of you are, or why that creature is talking and this man is . . . well, gigantic! But I really think you should—'

'Brace yourself, Fionn!' Conor shouted over her.

'For what?' Fionn asked.

But Conor was already holding his palm up in front of his mouth and blowing across it. Golden fairy dust floated off his skin and into the faces of Mary and the other rescued victims. They blinked confusedly, then closed their eyes and began to snore.

'*AH-CHOO,*' Fionn sneezed. 'Blooming heck, I hate that stuff!'

'Last time I use it, I promise,' Conor said, noticing Orla's reproachful stare. 'I only did it to help. When they wake up, they really will think the whole thing was some weird dream.'

'How will we get them all home?' Orla wondered aloud.

'I'll take 'em. Happen to know their addresses.' Fionn winked.

'Would you really? That would be so kind!' said Apollo gratefully.

Orla marvelled. The pooka wasn't the only magical creature who had helped them without having to. The giant must have a secret conscience too. 'Thank you . . . But, if you don't mind me asking, why would you do that? And why did *you* come to help us in the Fairy Kingdom?'

Fionn shrugged. 'I got to thinking of you and yer gran, an' of all these mortals separated from their families – just like me and Benny have been separated all these years. It made me sad. I wanted to put that right.' He sighed. 'I'm putting something else right too. I'm heading over to Scotland to see Benny tomorrow night. Thanks to your swimming lessons, Apollo, I can make it over there. If he forgives me for smashing the bridge, then maybe we can rebuild it together and go back to spending time with one another.'

'*Swimming lessons?*' Gran mouthed, her eyes popping.

Orla grinned. 'We've got *a lot* to tell you, Gran,' she muttered.

'Clearly!'

'That's great news!' said Apollo.

'Yes,' Orla agreed. 'And I'm sure your brother will forgive you. Mine did, and I was really terrible to him.'

'You weren't *that* bad.'

Orla raised her eyebrows.

'OK, you were pretty awful . . . She's right, Fionn. If I can find it in my heart to forgive her after all she's put me through—'

'Don't overdo it, Polo.'

'Just say sorry and really mean it. If you do, I'm sure Ben will forgive you. Because that's what families do.'

'Will we see you again?' Orla asked, feeling strangely sad that the giant was leaving.

'Perhaps,' Fionn winked. 'I'm not a future-predictor, so I couldn't say for certain but if Apollo's happy to tell me more stories, I'd be happy to listen. Seems like yer Gran's a good storyteller too . . .'

Gran smiled. 'Well, I said no more fairies, but I suppose I could tell stories to a giant from time to time. Especially after hearing that he was so good to my grandchildren.'

The pooka was looking wistful.

'And a pooka?' Apollo added.

'Pah! As if I'd want to listen to a bunch of—'

'And a pooka,' Gran nodded. 'Provided it stops the death threats.'

The pooka's rabbit ears stood up and it started to make the purring sound again. 'Gosh, this is embarrassing,' it muttered.

Apollo gave it another hug.

The bearded man in the giant's hand gave an extra-loud snore.

'Right,' said Fionn. 'Better get moving if we want to get these folks home before morning. Pooka, you can help me unlock the doors and windows, and we'll return them safely to their beds.'

'Do I have to?' the pooka groaned. 'I have a life of my own, y'know. But *fine*. I suppose this is my penance for trying to unlock doors and windows for the Wild Hunt in the first place.' It leapt high into the air and landed on Fionn's shoulder. The giant climbed off his knees and back on to his feet.

'You'll make sure they all get home safe?' Gran checked.

The giant nodded solemnly. 'You have my word, Ms Elizabeth.'

'Oh, what the heck, I'll even promise it,' the pooka called.

Gran's eyebrows rose. 'A pooka making a voluntary promise. Well, now I've seen everything. Thank you, both of you. For everything you've done to help us.'

Orla expected the pooka to protest that it hadn't helped again, but instead it was looking down on Orla and Apollo with its eyes glistening oddly. If Orla didn't know better, she'd have said the pooka was sad to say goodbye to them.

'Well, so long, stinkers!' it called. 'Good riddance to the lot of you.'

'Good riddance!' Orla and Apollo called back fondly.

'So long!' shouted Conor and Gran.

'Until we meet again,' added Fionn with a wink.

Then the ground shook as the giant turned and stomped away through the trees. To Orla's surprise, a lump formed in her throat as they disappeared. But Apollo gave her hand a squeeze and she felt instantly better. She wasn't alone. Far from it. She turned and smiled at Gran and Conor.

Gran smiled back. 'Right, I want the whole story, blow-by-blow, with all the juicy details.'

As they walked up the path to Gran's door, Orla felt lighter, as if a great weight had been lifted from her shoulders. The yawning empty feeling inside her had dissolved away, and instead, she felt full of gratitude that they'd all made it back in one piece.

'I sure am glad to be home!' Apollo said. 'I'm starving.'

'Me too!' agreed Conor.

'Well, I'm sure we can rustle something up,' Gran said. 'After I've seen to your injuries that is!'

Apollo groaned. 'They're fine, Gran, really. I'd quite like a few scars, anyway. They're cool!'

'What will yer dad think when you get home? A week with me and you come back looking like you've been mauled by a tiger!'

'Pah! Just a tiger? This is one of those rare occasions where the real story is actually way better! Although no one's ever going to believe it—'

The three of them bustled into the house.

Orla hung back, gazing up at the vanishing stars. The darkness was dissolving away and the sky was starting to glow pink as the sun rose. Orla looked up at the pale moon and thought of the three moons in the Fairy Kingdom. She was looking forward to going back to normal life again. There was plenty of magic in normal life too; the magic that came from living in a world filled with music and chocolate biscuits and younger brothers. Yes, and a dad with a new person by his side, and two sort-of new brothers too – maybe three counting Conor. Orla had no idea how they'd explain Conor to Dad but Gran would find a way.

There was magic in everything, so long as you didn't stop looking for it.

The sadness was still there inside her, but she no longer feared it, because around it there was also joy and love and wonder.

Orla made a silent promise. From now on, she'd never stop keeping her eyes, ears and heart open to the magic of the world.

She stepped inside the house, closing the front door softly behind her. The morning light glowed through the frosted glass and pooled on to the floor around her.

Orla looked up at Mum's photograph. Her tummy twisted faintly but she no longer felt the need to look away. The pain of losing Mum would never fade completely, Orla understood that now. It wasn't about forgetting Mum; it was about making room for happiness too.

She could hear Apollo, Conor and Gran in the kitchen together, laughing, banging cupboard doors and clattering tins. For a moment, she continued to linger in the hallway, feeling like the Orla of a few days ago as she stood outside alone, as she'd done so often since Mum died.

'Olo, get in here!' Apollo called. 'You won't believe it; Gran's found more tiffin!'

Orla smiled. And suddenly, she couldn't wait to be in that warm kitchen laughing with them.

Acknowledgements

My heartfelt thanks to the wonderful Caroline Walsh and Christabel McKinley at David Higham for their support and wisdom. Also to my editor Jenny Glencross for her excellent suggestions and company on walks. Thanks to Rachel Leyshon for her astute edits and to Kesia Lupo and the whole team at Chicken House Books.

My gratitude also goes to David Dean and Studio Helen for this incredible fold-out cover, which I am thoroughly enamoured with. Thanks, as always, to my beautiful family and friends for their support. Especially to Sue, Matt and Chris.

The biggest thanks of all to the many amazing book-sellers, bloggers, teachers and young readers who've supported my first book, *The Mask of Aribella*. Your kind words and championing of my story have meant the world to me. I hope you have enjoyed this one too.

As I wrote at the beginning of this book, to create the narrative I borrowed my favourite creatures from Irish mythology – such as the pooka (also púca or phouka), banshee, merrows and the Wild Hunt, and mixed these in with other myths and legends I enjoyed growing up – such as those of King Oberon, trolls, goblins and water sprites.

I've included many artistic interpretations, such as reimagining the reason behind the giants' feud. Fionn and Benandonner (Ben in my story) aren't considered to be brothers or to have fallen out over the Salmon of Knowledge. This was another story about Fionn that I adapted. Equally, I've slightly altered Dagda's four treasures and dreamt up the pooka's curse.

Perhaps the most important detail to mention, however, is the tiffin, which, as was flagged by an early reader of this story, isn't particularly Irish. However, tiffin *was* very particular to my wonderful, kind, funny Granny Ireland. It was her favourite thing to make for us when we visited. For this reason, to me, tiffin will always taste like Ireland, which is why it stayed in this story.